THE COMPLETE CASES
OF BILL BRENT, VOLUME 1

Frederick C. Davis

FREDERICK C. DAVIS

THE COMPLETE CASES OF

BILL BRENT

VOLUME 1

FREDERICK C. DAVIS

ILLUSTRATIONS BY
JOHN FLEMING GOULD

BOSTON • 2016

EDITED AND DESIGNED BY
Matthew Moring

PUBLISHING HISTORY

"Please Pass the Poison" originally appeared in the February, 1941 issue of *Dime Detective* magazine. Copyright 1941 by Popular Publications, Inc. Copyright renewed 1968 and assigned to Steeger Properties, LLC. All rights reserved.

"Let the Skeletons Rattle" originally appeared in the May, 1941 issue of *Dime Detective* magazine. Copyright 1941 by Popular Publications, Inc. Copyright renewed 1968 and assigned to Steeger Properties, LLC. All rights reserved.

"Killer, Stay Away From My Door!" originally appeared in the September, 1941 issue of *Dime Detective* magazine. Copyright 1941 by Popular Publications, Inc. Copyright renewed 1968 and assigned to Steeger Properties, LLC. All rights reserved.

"You Slay Me, Baby" originally appeared in the July, 1942 issue of *Dime Detective* magazine. Copyright 1941 by Popular Publications, Inc. Copyright renewed 1969 and assigned to Steeger Properties, LLC. All rights reserved.

THANKS TO
Joel Frieman & Rick Ollerman

TABLE OF CONTENTS

PLEASE PASS THE POISON

TAKE A BRIEFCASE CRAMMED
WITH UNDERDONE PORKCHOPS,
COLD BUTTERED ASPARAGUS
AND HALF A DOZEN BUCKWHEAT
CAKES—A BOTTLE OF LUXURIO
SCALP ELIXIR—THREE HUNKS OF
SALTWATER TAFFY CLUTCHED
IN A DEAD MAN'S HAND WHILE
A HORDE OF GUINEA PIGS
FROLICKED OVER THE CORPSE—
AND STIR THOROUGHLY. GIVE
SAME TO A VETERINARY SURGEON
AND AN ADVICE-TO-THE-
LOVELORN COLUMNIST TO HAGGLE
OVER—AND WATCH THE MURDER
WHEELS BEGIN TO SPIN AS THEY
SALT THE UNSAVORY STEW
WITH CYANIDE AND ATTEMPT TO
DIGEST IT BETWEEN KILLS.

CHAPTER ONE
GRANDMA WAS A QUACK

THE GIRL was breathless from having run up six flights of stairs and as her high heels tick-ticked to a standstill just inside the city-room, Brent squinted at her from the amber shadow of his eye-shade.

He peered at her warily over a scented lavender letter, got up and closed the door because he sensed that she was one hundred pounds of trouble looking for him.

In this stuffy cubicle which served as his office he hid himself as best he could. Partitioned off the remotest corner of the big littered room, it was not much more commodious than a telephone booth. The rest of the *Reporter's* staff worked in the open, moving about like reasonably free citizens with reasonably clear consciences—but not William Coleridge Brent. They exchanged gossip, wise-cracked, grinned and even laughed occasionally while Brent labored in his crowded cell and sweated in solitude. Like a haunted man he shrank behind his typewriter, watching, through the glass panel, the girl who had just hurried in, and hoping, with all his heart, that she would go away.

She didn't, but gazed about, confused by the clatter and hustle, her eyes coffee-colored and big. She was well worth noticing—her hair had the tint of fine sherry, she was over twenty-one and still cute as a kitten—but nobody except

Brent paid her the slightest attention. Garrett, the city editor, ensconced behind a rolltop desk in the corner, kept scowling and slashing his blue pencil across a sheaf of copy. Valerie Randall, whom Brent considered the most lusciously vine-ripened brunette ever to grace a newspaper

staff, was pounding the keys as rapidly as the eight other reporters who were steaming into the day's assignments. Unlike them, Brent had never convinced himself that a deadline was more important than a live woman, and this one's bewilderment was so painful to see that he simply couldn't ignore her.

He trudged to her, shaggy head lowered, blunt chin down, and her intelligent eyes flashed him her gratitude.

"Lora Lorne," she said quickly. "I want to see Miss Lorne."

In her hands she had one of Lora Lorne's columns, clipped from a recent *Reporter*. Lora Lorne was the paper's love oracle, its own Dorothy Dix or Beatrice Fairfax, who sagely advised her harassed readers concerning their philandering husbands, their faithless wives, their nagging mothers-in-law, their broken troths, their unrequited passions, their illegitimate children. Above Lora Lorne's intimately sympathetic letters her portrait was printed—a picture of a sweet old soul, combs in her white hair, wise eyes in a kindly crinkled face, eyeglasses dangling from a reel pinned to her grandmotherly shoulder. Obviously, however, no one resembling Lora Lorne was present in the city-room.

"Afraid you can't," Brent said. "She never comes in here."

"But—but there's no one else I can turn to, no one else who would really understand." The girl's appeal was earnest, heartfelt. "I must see Miss Lorne, really I must!"

"Sorry, too busy," Brent insisted. "Wrapped up in hundreds of problems, you know—can't see anyone personally. Her advice is given out exclusively in her column." He screwed up his face as he said it. "Just write her a letter, and she'll print her answer in a few days—"

The girl murmured in a sick voice: "A few days!" as if he'd said several decades. "But I can't wait, can't possibly. This is so terribly serious, and horrible things might happen before then." Her tearful eyes pleaded with Brent. "Please ask her to make an exception just this once. She's so wonderfully sympathetic, I'm sure—she'll— I'm so desperate for her help— If I can't see her, I—I'll just give up."

The girl choked off a sob and Brent wagged his head, wondering how he could make her realize that she'd never see Miss Lorne. Not today or tomorrow or ever, no matter how plaintively she might implore it. He couldn't tell her the real reason for that. He'd sooner shoot himself than reveal that it was he—a husky, rugged guy whose fullback's shoulders sagged under the weight of his own woes—he who daily wrote the agony column. He, God help him, was Lora Lorne.

BRENT GENTLY took the girl's arm and led her to a chair near his door. She perched on the edge of it, all tense, her chin puckered and quivering, still pathetically believing that only Lora Lorne's homely counsel could rescue her from misfortune.

"I've already written her so many letters. Dozens! I began when I was just a little girl and she's been like an aunt to me. But lately—things haven't turned out the way she thought they would. In fact they're worse—so much worse—that's why I know she'll want to talk to me. If you'll remind her that it's about my mother, and another man, and my step-father, and the awful things my grandfather whispers to me— You *will* ask her, won't you?"

"Can't, damn it," Brent muttered. "Don't know where she lives. Don't even know what her phone number is. Neither does anybody else on the paper, except Mr. Palmer, the publisher. He lives in California, and won't tell. It's been tried hundreds of times. No go. The only way of reaching her is by letter. That's all. No other. Absolutely. An old Negro manservant with a game leg comes in here every day—name's Mose—picks up her mail and that's the closest any of us ever get to her. Sorry. Now please pull yourself together, and if you'd like to borrow somebody's typewriter—"

"No." The girl distraitly shook her head. "Tomorrow it will be too late. Even a few hours—" She stared out the window, stared widely across a checkerboard of roofs, and there was fear in her eyes. "I've always depended on Lora Lorne. Everything's gone wrong now, everything, and it's so terribly hopeless without Lora Lorne's advice." She lowered her head, bit her lips and silently cried.

"Suppose you tell me about it," Brent said miserably. "Maybe I can help somehow."

"You?" And her tone was scornful. "A man! Why, you couldn't understand. But Miss Lorne is so sweet—and wonderful—"

She blinked at the engagement solitaire she wore and again she burst into silent, anguished sobs.

"Now look, I'm far from being hard-hearted," Brent assured her, "but there's only one suggestion I can make. Go home, and figure it out your own way. Whatever the difficulty may be, and whether you can get anywhere with it or not, go home!"

She blubbered again: "Hopeless, hopeless," and a tear fell on her clipping, on the picture of the lady which topped it, on the saccharine face supposed to be that of Lora Lorne.

Brent didn't know who the hell the old dame really was. Nobody did. Probably it wasn't a photograph, but a drawing, and she'd never actually existed. The picture had been run every day, month after month, never changing since the column was begun twenty-two years ago. A long succession of female busybodies had hidden behind the copyrighted nom-de-hooey. The last of them was Mrs. Smithers, the art editor's wife, who had abandoned her amatory expostulations to run away with a mortician named Quackenbush, who was married to Hannah Heckhimer, the editor of the Saturday children's page, who had no children and thereafter, likewise, no husband. So much for the damned column's moral value.

Bill Brent was the first man ever to suffer the indignity of being Lora Lorne, and remembering this didn't help to get his mind off the girl who was still sitting outside his door, utterly bewildered by her tribulations.

He wished to God she'd go away, and Garrett was waiting for today's love feast, so he re-read the last item he'd written: "You must realize, dear Worried Wife, that the romance of courtship cannot last forever, and that it is only when love settles down into glorified friendship after marriage that there is any peace or comfort in it." That was no help, either. He poked into the mound of varicolored correspondence on his desk, and grimaced. "It happened when Phil and I were deeply in love, and it didn't seem so wrong. Now Herbert wants to marry me. Shall I tell him about the sin in my past?" "Would it be terribly bad if I went to Atlantic City for the weekend with my boy-friend?" In various forms those two questions cropped up in practically every mail, but here was something special. A man signing himself B.D. wrote: "I suspect my wife is trying to kill me. I don't want to tell the police. She's too clever for them. I want to catch her at it and show her I'm not so dumb. I know all about her and the man she wants to take my place. She's watching her chance, planning to murder me—"

It was something to get jittery about, all right, but B.D. had nothing to fear half so deadly as this stuff that descended on Brent by the ton, day after day—this stuff that was polluting his mind and sickening his soul.

ABRUPTLY BRENT marched past the girl who was still sitting morosely near his door, marched across the city-room to the desk in the opposite corner, stared down at his city editor.

"If you've got the time, Garrett," he said, "I'd like to murder you and separate you into small, bloody parts, you jackal."

Without glancing up, Barrett said: "Go back to work, Lora."

Brent set his teeth. "Isn't there a drop of mercy in you? Isn't there a spark of kindness? For God's sake, man, you know it's months now since I've been blotto. Months since I've been stinko, or sozzled, or even mildly squiffed. Months since I've so much as smelled a cork or pinched a lady's hinie. I've done my penance. You've punished me more than enough. I'm licked. I'm crying uncle."

"Lora, go back to work, now," Garrett said, going on with his own work, "like a good girl."

Brent closed both fists. "On my word of honor, I'll never get drunk again, I'll never make a pass at another woman, I'll never miss another day's work, not another hour's. Suffering cats, Garrett, put me back on the police shift where I belong!"

Garrett sat back and looked bored. A muscular, ruddy, dynamic man, with granite-gray eyes and a jaw which a bulldog would envy, he'd come out of the first World War a major at twenty-three. He was still a military martinet, an inflexible disciplinarian.

"Do I have to go into that again?" he complained. "There's a contract, remember? You agreed to accept assignments and execute orders as required. Remember? A smart New York reporter should know better than to sign legal documents without first carefully reading same, don't you think? Yes. Well, your orders are to keep the love column going, and it's damn near press time right now, Lora."

Brent said levelly: "Garrett, that column's driving me crazy. I can't stand it any longer. I tell you, Garrett, it's driving me nuts and *I can't stand it!*"

"Any contract can be broken, including yours." Garrett shrugged. "Is that the way you want it?"

That was the way Brent didn't dare have it. He'd get the pants sued off him, and besides he'd be blacklisted. Another reason well worth considering was that Garrett had lured him out of New York with an upholstered salary, payable regularly and unfailingly until the contract expired or was fractured. And furthermore— Brent sent a yearning glance at Valerie Randall, the most delectable brunette he had ever seen inside a city-room. In any department other than Miss Lorne's he would be most happy to remain. But he was stuck with the love column, until such time as Garrett might relent, and his only hope of escape was to persist in appealing to the reason of a thoroughly unreasonable sadist.

"Look, Garrett," he said, controlling his tone. "Our column of medical advice is written by a doctor, not by a blacksmith. Our financial stuff is written by an economist, not a grocer. But me! I'm a fake, even down to my pen-name and my sex. Well, a quack cure for rheumatism may be bad, but a quack cure for an unfaithful husband is plenty worse."

"You're doing fine," Garrett said, his blue pencil streaking across a page of copy. "The column has improved since you took it over, Grandma."

"But it's too damned dangerous! I'm not qualified to play God. Look at that girl sitting over there, for example. She just told me that the advice I gave her has made her troubles tougher than they were in the first place. Look at her! Isn't she a pathetic picture?"

"What girl? Oh, that girl. *That—that girl—*"

Garrett was staring across the city-room, straining up, his face blanched. Brent spun about and swallowed his breath. He'd left the girl sitting in the chair, head bent, sobbing silently because she had failed to see Miss Lorne. Because she hadn't seen Miss Lorne she was now hopelessly leaving. But she wasn't going out the way she'd come in.

She was going out the window.

"Hey!" Brent yelled.

He startled everyone in the city-room except the girl. Every head swiveled toward him except the girl's. She was intent on her purpose and her knees were on the sill and she was crawling out. She was gripping the awning brace, bringing herself to her trim little feet, poising to jump. Brent scrambled to the window as she tottered forward. He dove for her, wrapped his arm around her legs, dragged back.

"Let me go, let me go!"

She pulled at the awning, struggling to free herself, to fling herself into the chasm of the street.

"Stop that!" Brent howled.

She didn't stop.

He tried to brace himself and couldn't. He had nothing to hang onto except the girl. She was dragging him across the sill, slapping his face, and he couldn't see, didn't dare loosen a finger. He was off balance, his head and shoulders out, and the floor was slippery. She was going down in another second and very possibly Bill Brent, alias Lora Lorne, would take the trip with her.

"Don't!" he gasped. "Lora Lorne would advise against it!"

Maybe it was those crazy words that got to her and changed her mind about dying. Maybe it was just a lucky fluke that she fainted then. Brent didn't know which and didn't care. He was too deliriously glad to find himself backing away from the window, clutching the girl's limp body against his, her sherry hair spraying over his shoulder, her dreamy face peacefully upturned, her lips close. She was dead to the world, but not nearly so dead as she might have been when picked off the pavement six stories down.

CHAPTER TWO
THE PRICELESS
PORK CHOP

SINCE THE city-room provided no accommodations for unconscious girls, Brent headed for the women's lavatory, where there was a wicker chaise-longue. He had to plow his way through the entire staff and he put her down in reverse, feet on the tilted head. He was splashing water in her wan face when Valerie Randall tugged him aside.

"You're Lora Lorne professionally," she reminded him, smiling in her sweetly taunting way, "but not anatomically. Let me take care of her."

"You'll take care of her like a tigress takes care of a rabbit," Brent answered grimly. "Even if she were your own sister, you'd take care of her so well she'd find herself splashed all over the front page."

With a nod, Val calmly agreed this was true. "After all, *I'm* a reporter," she said, "so go away and let me get to work on her."

"I feel sorry for the kid—feel responsible. Besides—well, this is a hell of a place and a hell of a time for it—but I'm working myself up to the point of asking you to marry me in the good old-fashioned way."

Val's smile became a bit superior and disdainful. "This isn't at all sudden," she remarked.

"I know. I've got troubles. My job's turning me into a walking mass of inhibitions. I have nightmares. Not just now and then, but every time I try to sleep. Double-feature nightmares. In the worst one, you and I get married and then everything horrible happens to us. I wake up screaming."

"Perhaps," Val said, turning back to the girl, "you'd better ask Lora Lorne's advice."

He moaned and was still chilled by the nearness of death, and when he sidled out Val was shaking the limp girl and asking: "What's your name? What's your address? Why did you try to kill, yourself?"

Again he elbowed through the curious staff, while Garrett snarled everybody back to work. On the floor beneath that yawning window he saw the girl's purse. He retreated into his office and found, among the usual feminine impedimenta, a driver's license. The would-be suicide's name was Jean Chester and she lived at 1180 Willow Street, in the suburb of Greengrove.

The clipping was also there, wadded up, still tear-stained. Yesterday's, Brent saw. Which one of the printed letters was hers? She'd mentioned her mother, another man, a step-father, a whispering grandfather and she'd burst into sobs over her engagement ring.

Dear Miss Lorne:

My employer is a charming, wonderful man and even though he's married and has two grown children he keeps asking me—

That wasn't it, but the last letter in the column fit part of the set-up.

Dear Lora Lorne:

I'm to be married in less than a week, but lately my happiness has turned to misery. I love my fiancé with all my heart and I'm sure he loves me too, but recently he has been saying that I must give up my work. Dear Miss Lorne, I love my work too, but he insists I can't go on with it, just because he is jealous of the fine, older man who has guided me so unselfishly for years. He's so wrong about that, but last night we had a terrible quarrel and he told me I'd have to choose once and for all between them. I don't want to lose my fiancé, because I love him, really I do, but I know I'll be unhappy all my life if I have to give up my other dreams too. Oh, Miss Lorne, how can I decide?

It was signed "So Bewildered," and Brent had answered to the effect that she should make her sweetheart understand that with his unreasonable, selfish attitude he was smothering the beautiful flame of their love for each other. "If he really loves you, and realizes this, you will reach a new understanding with him. He will see that he must take you as the modern and very intelligent young woman you are, dear."

OBVIOUSLY THE thing wasn't as simple as that. The pat make-him-understand prescription not only hadn't worked but had aggravated the predicament. Grimly Brent dug into his file and came up with another of Lora Lorne's attempts to set the world right for "So Bewildered." The second letter, dated ten days earlier, presented a knottier problem:

> Dear Lora Lorne:
>
> It is a shocking, disillusioning thing to discover that your own mother is not playing fair with your father. He's really my step-father, and I don't want to think that Mother has actually done anything terribly wrong, but I know she has met another man many times, secretly, and I think she's in love with this man.
>
> My step-father doesn't dream what's going on behind his back and I'm so terribly afraid he'll find out that Mother is cheating on him and he'll do something awful. Last night when Mother came home, very late, I couldn't keep quiet any longer. I told her I knew, and she denied it—lied to me—and told me to mind my own business. Oh, Miss Lorne, if it goes on I'm sure it will turn into a ghastly tragedy. What can I do?

Publicly commiserating with "So Bewildered," Miss Lorne had urged her to go forthrightly to the other man and call upon his better nature. Lora Lorne had faith that he would be so shamed and remorseful, that Mother too would mend her ways and thereafter devote herself to the sanctity of "So Bewildered's" home.

Effective advice, that. Brilliantly successful. It had improved the situation so wonderfully that so-bewildered Jean Chester had tried to leap outward over sagacious Miss Lorne's own windowsill!

"God save the *Reporter's* subscribers from my well-intended bungling!" said Bill Brent to himself, very sourly.

He stuffed the purse into a drawer, marched again out of his office, marched again across the city-room, and arrived at the desk in the opposite corner, a second behind Valerie Randall.

"She won't talk," Val reported to Garrett. "Not who she is or where she lives. It would disgrace the family name and all that. But Bill knows about her."

Brent shook his head. "Don't know from nothing. She didn't tell me a thing. Anyway, I'm not a news man any more. My specialty is *l'amour*—remember? I am exclusively devoted to guiding our readers' mad passions."

They eyed him suspiciously and Val said: "I'm giving her the absent treatment and don't worry, boss, once she's had a chance to calm down I'll coax a whizbang of a story out of her."

"Let her alone!" Brent protested. "Haven't we hurt her enough already?"

Garrett signaled Val to her desk to write the story. "Don't bother me," he answered. "I've got a paper to get out today and where the hell, Lora, is your part of it?"

White-lipped, Brent leaned over him. "Lay off the poor kid! Suppose she'd gone down into the street. It wouldn't have been suicide. That, Garrett, would have been murder. With my little column I almost killed that girl."

"You grabbed her in time, so what're you worrying about?" Garrett stuffed copy into the pneumatic tube. "When somebody tries to dive out of one of my own windows, I consider it's news, but the story's not yours. It's Val's. She'll make the most of it. What I want from you is a column. Fast. And no arguments—except in court."

"You—" Brent leveled his finger and his face was slightly green. "You'll get your goddam column!"

He strode back to his desk, plucked a new letter off the heap, read with a nauseated expression: "Will a gentleman make an improper proposal to a girl he really loves?" And, Heaven help him, he had to answer in the negative, making himself, he felt, a traitor to his sex.

He pounded out the last line, which mentioned "the bleached remnants of painful past mistakes," and was disgustedly carrying the stuff to Garrett when Val Randall popped out of the ladies' room with a breathless bulletin.

"She's gone!"

"That's swell!" Brent blurted, grinning.

With a scowl, Garrett snarled: "Go after her!"

"Must've slipped down the stairs when nobody was looking," Val gasped.

"That's swell!" Brent repeated, smiling happily.

"Grab her!" Garrett snapped.

Val tossed copy to his desk. "There it is, unknown girl angle. Add later, I hope. She can't be far."

"Bring her back here!" Garrett ordered.

VAL FLEW out the door. Brent delivered his column to Garrett, and Garrett glowered at him, and Brent kept grinning. He went back, put his head out the same window and shuddered. There was a girl on the pavement who looked exactly like Jean Chester. It *was* Jean Chester, and she was on her feet, which were in rapid motion. She ran across the street and, just as Val appeared on the steps directly below Brent, disappeared into Smitty's Dairy Bar.

Brent saw Val scanning the busy sidewalk, and as she guessed herself off in the wrong direction his grin became even broader.

He sauntered to the swinging doors, gave Garrett a lackadaisical salute, leaned through them—and sped. He made the six flights in fifteen jumps, slowed on the sidewalk, made sure Val was well started on her goose chase, dodged across the street, and found Jean Chester in Smitty's—with a man.

The man was shorter than the girl, round-bellied, jerky-eyed. His clothes might have come out of a Sears Roebuck catalogue, issue of 1920, and he wore a dusty derby. He was drinking a glass of milk. His puckered expression testified that he hated milk, but there were three empty glasses lined up on the bar in front of him, beside his briefcase, and this was his fourth. While he applied himself to it, the girl spoke to him rapidly, in a whisper of pleading. He shook his head and turned away, reaching for his briefcase and looking terrified. The girl's hand reached for it first. The result was a tug-of-war. The man and Jean Chester struggled over the case.

"... Kill me!" Brent heard him blurt, hoarsely. "Trying to kill me. This proves it! Wants to kill me!"

The girl won the tussle, and abruptly she spun about, slapped the swinging doors apart and was gone with the case. The man, still appearing to be scared out of his wits, scampered after her. Brent had seen her slip into a coupe parked at the curb, but the man hadn't. In pursuit of her, he disappeared around the corner at a run.

The car spurted away. Brent broke into a lope, chasing it. At the corner, it encountered a red light. He caught up with it, opened the door and crawled in while the frightened girl shrank from him. The briefcase was on the seat beside her. He grabbed it and she gasped.

"The light's green now," he pointed out. "Better get going—and I think I know how to reach Lora Lorne, after all."

Again the name had a magical effect on Jean Chester. Still frightened she sent the car forward. He opened the case, and noticed that two initials were stamped on the flap: *B.D.*

In one compartment it contained four bottles of a scarlet, excessively fragrant liquid which the labels identified as Luxurio Scalp Elixir.

In the other was a piece of oil-silk, wadded up. Brent discovered as he unwound it that it contained a fried pork chop, two boiled potatoes and approximately a dozen stalks of buttered asparagus—all cold and most unappetizing.

THE GIRL, still shaky, kept the car rolling and turned a distressed glance on Brent.

"Will you really take me to Lora Lorne?" she asked plaintively. "Really?"

Sooner than confess that she was already in proximity to the *Reporter's* love oracle, Brent would lay himself down under a ten-ton truck. Let the truth leak out and he would be a laughingstock, but his fear, strangely enough, wasn't his real reason for guarding the secret.

Being deeply sympathetic by nature, he shrank from the thought of destroying the girl's blind trust. He couldn't bring himself to tell her that Lora Lorne actually smoked a pipe, wore size eleven brogans, had once shattered a nose against a Princeton goalpost, and vastly enjoyed the art of Gypsy Rose Lee.

Evading her question, he asked while she drove: "Who was that man? The one who belongs to this case?"

"My step-father. Bernard Dunbar. Can you really take me—"

"Does he carry this cargo of hair-tonic for drinking purposes?"

"He sells it. He's a barber's supply salesman and," she added irrelevantly, "he works very hard—always on the road, scarcely home at all. He's really a nice man, but his stomach bothers him and he's a little queer. Can you really—"

"Does he usually go about equipped with a cold blue-plate dinner, lacking only a cold cup of coffee?"

She grew a little paler and said: "It will be so wonderful to see Miss Lorne! If you'll—"

"Why were you so anxious to take this tasty little snack away from him?"

"He's wrong about it, I know he's wrong!" Being too distracted to explain further, she added: "If you'll only take me to Miss Lorne right now—"

"Just a minute," he countered. "Sooner or later I'd like to find out what the hell you're talking about. But I didn't say I could bring you and Miss Lorne together. I think I know how she can be reached, but I'll have to feel her out first. I found those letters of yours she printed. Suppose you tell me what's gone wrong and I'll do my best to get her to straighten everything out for you."

"Oh, please!" Hope fired Jean Chester and made her radiant. "You see, about my mother— Well, a few nights ago my mother was out, and my step-father was away too, and I was terrified, thinking he might come back unexpectedly and discover what—what Mother was doing behind his back. At last, long after midnight, a car drew up and stopped and its lights went out, and Mother was in it—with that man."

Brent clucked.

"I didn't know who he was. Mother's been so—so secretive, and this was the first time I'd ever seen him. I—I ran out to the car. I made him listen to me, begged him not to see Mother again. He just laughed and Mother got out and told me not to be a little fool and she wouldn't have me snooping. The man drove away and I still don't know who he is or what he really looks like, and I'm so afraid that something—something horrible will happen."

"For instance," Brent inquired, "a quiet little murder, perhaps?"

"Oh!" The girl's eyes were like frightened saucers of coffee, and she rushed off on another tangent. "My step-father is a sort of hypochondriac, and he thinks he has all sorts of pains inside him, but he only imagines them— Mother was furious with me and ordered me out of the house. Now I'm staying at the Wilburn Hotel and my bill is overdue and I can't pay it because I'm not getting any more of my money. Mother's keeping it and won't give me a cent."

"Let's get this straight," Brent suggested. "About the money."

"It was left me by my real father, who died years ago— just suddenly died, and four months later Mother married Mr. Dunbar. Insurance money, it was twenty thousand dollars at the beginning—supposed to be held in trust for me by Mother. I've come of age, and I've used some of it for my researches, and now I need the rest of it, but Mother won't give me a penny of it."

"Sue her," Brent recommended.

"But I couldn't! Don't you see? If I go to court, the whole awful story will come out, about why Mother turned against me, and all about that other man, and it would be a horrible scandal. I couldn't do such a thing, I just couldn't! It's what I'm trying to prevent. And yet I've got to get my money, I need it so desperately. I'm sure Miss Lorne can tell me just how I can bring Mother back to her senses— aren't you?"

BRENT SWALLOWED a protest. Following the main highway eastward, they had reached Greengrove. The girl braked, watching an approaching car that swung into the driveway of a rambling house surrounded by gardened grounds. "It's Doctor Veach," she murmured. She turned the coupe after Dr. Veach's and both veered into a parking space opposite the porch, where two sedans were sitting. Gazing uneasily at them, Jean Chester said: "This is—was my home, and that's my step-father's Chevvy. He must be inside with Mother, he must've come for a late lunch."

"After four glasses of milk?" Brent wondered. "Since you were ordered to clear out, why have you come back?"

"Because I've got to get some of my money from Mother and I've got to explain to Doctor Veach too, because I'm so anxious to go on with our parasitology, and now I'll have to give it up unless— He's probably come looking for me."

Jean Chester hurried to him. Following her with the briefcase, Brent found that Dr. Veach was a man of impressive presence, brisk, ruggedly handsome, gray-templed, with poise and self-possession that came of long professional experience.

"Jean!" he said in a firm, strong tone. "I've been trying everywhere to find you. I need you at the lab, and your cultures are about to spoil. What's wrong, Jean?"

"I'll—I'll come, Doctor," she said obediently. "This is Mr.—Brent?" Her chin lifted with pride. "I'm Doctor Veach's research assistant, and he's the director of the Veach College of—"

Brent was clasping the strong hand of Dr. Veach when the scream rang out. It came, shrilly, from behind the house. A woman cried: "Father, father, *father!*" The sharp note of terror in her voice startled the girl, turned Brent and Dr. Veach. Suddenly the girl was running. Brent and the doctor followed and saw a man sprawled on the ground.

A lean, snowy-headed man was lying on his back inside an enclosure, one of a series of four large cages formed by steel mesh stretched between steel uprights. The ground around him was alive with small, brown-and-white, nose-wriggling animals—guinea-pigs, Brent guessed. He lay just inside the gate, and Jean Chester was the first to reach him.

"Granddad!" she cried.

She dropped to her knees beside Granddad, caught up one of his blue-veined, inert hands and frantically rubbed it. The guinea-pigs scampered up their runways and into their hutches as Dr. Veach quickly tested the old man's pulse. Veach stiffened up at once, looking startled, taking a wary step backward. He grasped Jean's arm, pulled her to her feet, peered at Brent.

"Take her away!" he said.

He hurried to his car and returned with a black medical case and bent over the old man.

Brent steered the girl through the gate and saw the woman standing at the rear of the house. Jean's mother was smartly dressed and looked almost as young as her daughter. She was wearing an apron and in one hand she was gripping a large wooden spoon from which batter dripped.

"I saw him fall!" she said hoarsely. "I saw him go inside and fall!"

In the door behind her, a napkin tucked into his collar, was Bernard Dunbar, Jean's step-father, the hair-tonic salesman with the jerky, scared eyes.

Brent led the girl into the house. Mrs. Dunbar came, her eyes fearfully wide. Her queer husband retreated into the dining-room and stood near the table, staring in terror at a pile of wheatcakes on a plate. His derby sat nearby, and his hair was a shaggy, curly mass, almost like a French poodle's—a testimonial, Brent supposed, to Luxurio Elixir. Nothing was said for several moments. Jean Chester tightening with apprehension, watched as Dr. Veach strode in, paused, glanced soberly at them all, then quickly took up the telephone directory and dialed a number.

"Doctor Taylor, please!" he urged.

Bernard Dunbar spied the briefcase which Brent was still carrying. He advanced abruptly, snatched it from Brent's hand. "It's mine!" he blurted. Clutching it, he retreated toward a door.

"Doctor Taylor, this is Chenery Veach, calling from the Dunbar home. Samuel Elias—Mrs. Dunbar's father—is dead. Yes, very suddenly. Very!" Veach squared his shoulders and said: "I have reason—excellent reason—to believe that Mr. Elias was poisoned."

Brent, all intent, moved toward him.

"I said poisoned," Dr. Veach repeated quietly over the line. "There's a strong odor of cyanide in his mouth."

THE STATEMENT produced a series of effects which startled Brent.

First Bernard Dunbar uttered a frightened squeal. He jerked the napkin from his collar, spun about, rushed from the house, sprang into one of the cars in the parking space. He backed it around, brought it to a bucking stop, jumped out, ran back in.

"Wait a minute," Brent said. "You'd better stick around."

Ignoring him, Dunbar pounced on the plate of wheat-cakes. He dumped them into his hands and again headed for the door.

"You did it!" he squeaked as he moved, pointing a finger toward Mrs. Dunbar. "Your own father—you poisoned him! But you can't poison me! Not me! You—you Borgia!"

Shaking Brent's hand off his arm, he trotted outside again, dove in the Chevvy, sent it spurting down the driveway and vanished, wheatcakes and all.

Next Mrs. Dunbar whimpered. She ran into the kitchen and a door slammed. Brent went after her, and saw another car backing hastily out of the parking space. Mrs. Dunbar sent it slithering toward the highway at a reckless speed. As it disappeared, close behind Bernard Dunbar's Chevvy, Brent turned back with an amazed wag of his head—and found that Jean Chester was continuing the exodus.

The girl had hurried out another door and was climbing into her coupe. Brent ran, shouting. She heard him but didn't wait. He jumped for the running-board, missed his grip, and the jerking acceleration of the car threw him back. Tottering, he watched the girl turn after the other two cars and swiftly pass from sight.

Reflecting that all this was screwy as hell, Brent estimated that within two minutes by the clock, following Dr. Veach's grim announcement, three relatives of the stricken man had made their precipitous departure. He returned to the dining-room and gazed in bewilderment at Dr. Veach.

"Sure you can't do anything for the old guy?" he inquired.

"Nothing," Dr. Veach answered, again taking up the phone. "He's dead. And besides, I'm a veterinarian."

Brent's temperature was soaring. This, he told himself hopefully, was a heaven-sent opportunity for redemption.

This was his chance to divorce himself once and for all from his detestable *alter ego,* Lora Lorne. He was a news man again and he had a murder story by the tail.

CHAPTER THREE

ASSETS TO BURY

IT WAS cyanide, all right. Crouching over Granddad, Brent smelled the acridity of it.

"He wouldn't have lived much longer, anyway," he remarked. "Was he insured, Doctor?"

"I'm sure I couldn't say. Except for Jean, I'm not well-acquainted with the family. The first time in months that I've come here, and"—the veterinarian wagged his head—"I walk right into a murder."

"A dead man with insurance is always an asset to somebody," Brent remarked, and he frowned over the corpse.

Its right hand was gripping the handle of a pail from which cracked corn had spilled. The left was also clenched, and a tuft of cellophane protruded from the fist. Brent pried the bony fingers open and found half a dozen pieces of candy. Two were brown, two white, one was pink, one pale green. The wrappers were trademarked: *Bond's Salt Water Taffy.* Brent let the tidbits remain in the lifeless palm and eased from the yard while Dr. Veach guarded the remains of Samuel Elias from the curious guinea-pigs.

Upstairs in the deserted house, he prowled into three bedrooms. In the one from which Jean Chester had been peremptorily banished he found nothing of interest until he opened a large closet. There was a built-in bench and the air was thick with chemical smells. It had once served as a small laboratory, though now the apparatus and reagents had been removed. Continuing to prowl, Brent straightened the family tree in his mind.

Jean's father had died several years ago, leaving her considerable money in trust, and considerably more, evidently, to the then Mrs. Chester. Jean's mother had presently married the jittery hair-tonic salesman, thereby changing her name to Dunbar. If the death of her father, Samuel Elias, meant another inheritance, it would normally pass, of course, to Mrs. Dunbar and Jean Chester—unless it should be proved that one of them had dosed him with cyanide. The law would not permit the guilty woman to profit and the bequest would then rebound to the other. At the moment, Jean's chances of collecting seemed none too auspicious.

Brent had found another bedroom on the ground floor—the old man's—and was inspecting a box of Bond's Salt Water Taffy which sat on the bedside table. It was three-quarters full of assorted flavors, including almond. A piece of almond-flavored taffy would serve excellently as a vehicle for a lethal potion of almond-smelling poison. There was a card lying beside the box, a card inscribed: *Happy Birthday to Granddad from Jean.*

Presumably Granddad had stepped outside to amuse himself by feeding the guinea-pigs and meanwhile had munched upon a deadly confection.

Happy birthday, corpse!

Making for the telephone, Brent heard tires crunching on the driveway gravel, and saw a car marked by the green cross of a physician. Dr. Taylor, paunchy and bearded, immediately called toward the pen by Dr. Veach, responded in haste. Brent dialed the *Reporter's* number and asked for the city desk. The voice that answered was not Garrett's.

"Burrows?"

"Yuh," said Burrows, who on occasion pinch-hit for the city editor.

"Where's the Number One Scavenger?"

"Off."

Not disappointed—because a delay would give him an even firmer foot-hold on the yarn, Brent said: "When he gets back, tell him a first-class news man, named Brent, has a choice murder for him."

He disconnected and turned away grinning, and his grin at once became a frozen grimace. Two more cars had just arrived. From the first emerged half the Homicide Squad, led by Captain Russo, with Bernard Dunbar in tow, who now lacked his briefcase. From the second climbed Garrett accompanied by Valerie Randall.

Brent marched out and, jaw set, planted himself in Garrett's path.

"Why, hello, Bill!" Valerie said. "Of all people, what're you doing here?"

"Covering a story!" Brent declared grimly.

Garrett grinned. "You don't write news any more. Your specialty is troubled love. Remember, Lora? Hop to it, Val."

Val hopped to it, smiling in her tauntingly sweet way, and Brent remained straddled in front of Garrett, chin tucked low.

"It's a cute little system you're working," he said bitterly. "Giving Val the toughest trick on the staff so you can squire her around, hold her hand, protect her. Teaching her to admire you and sneer at me! You're not editing a paper, you're promoting yourself a woman. It won't work, Garrett. Whoever heard of a female police-reporter!"

"I've heard of a male love expert. If you've got anything on this murder,"—Garrett's hand lifted in a military command—"go right now and tell her what you know."

STEPPING BACK, Brent gave him a full-length once-over. "It's impossible," he said incredulously. "You can't be that low-down."

"Tell her!" and Garrett's voice cracked like a whiplash.

Tight all over, Brent said: "Why sure, sure. I've got to follow orders. The contract says so. But all the dope I've got happens to add up to exactly nothing. I'm a stranger here myself."

With Garrett's eyes stabbing him in the back he returned to the pen. The squad photographer, having shot the scene, was dismembering his tripod, Lieutenant Goode was dictating a list of his findings as he pawed the corpse and Sergeant Tierney was making shorthand curlicues in a notebook. Val Randall, her news instincts aroused, was also scribbling while Captain Russo questioned Bernard Dunbar.

Russo began: "If you'd—"

Dunbar pointed and blurted: "I don't trust *him!*"

Everyone looked at Dr. Taylor. Nobody, including Dr. Taylor, paid more than a second's attention to the accusation.

"If you'd had the courage to come to us sooner," Captain Russo said, "that poor old man would still be alive."

Dunbar shrank inside his skin.

Russo demanded: "Was *he* afraid your wife—his own daughter—would poison him?"

Nodding fearfully, Dunbar answered: "He—he's the one who warned me—told me over and over again how Bella's first husband died—suddenly. He had his meals alone in his room. Before he ate anything Bella cooked for him, he'd bolt the door, sneak out the window and feed a little of it to a guinea-pig first. Then he'd wait and watch the pig—"

"Your wife's going to inherit a sockful of money from him, isn't she?" Russo cut in. "Big insurance policy, isn't it?"

Brent listened to Dunbar gulp and mumble: "I was afraid of her, but wasn't sure, couldn't accuse her. I've been going to restaurants for months, for every meal, only pretending to eat the food Bella cooked here. When she wasn't looking, I'd dump the plate into my briefcase. I needed proof, and three or four times I took it to a chemist. He never found any poison. But she was waiting—waiting to kill me—and she still is!"

"Where's she gone?" Russo asked sharply.

"She—she must be with that man. The man she's been planning to go to as soon as she killed me and collected my insurance. I can't drop the policy, because she pays the premiums." Dunbar rolled his eyes and quaked. "She'll— she'll kill me yet, somehow. I know she will!"

"Not if we get her first," Russo said. His spooky black eyes snapped at Brent because Val Randall, at that moment, observed: "Open-and-shut," which remark Brent answered with a scornful snort.

The meat-wagon arrived and two men brought the wicker basket for the remains of Samuel Elias. Dr. Veach, walking beside Lieutenant Goode, followed Brent into the house. Dr. Taylor, carrying his medical case, was just leaving the dead man's room, and he immediately engaged the veterinarian in conversation. Curiously moving toward Samuel Elias's bed, Brent came to a wary pause, noticing that the box of candy was gone from the table.

The taffy had vanished, along with the card scribbled to her late grandfather by Jean Chester.

CHAPTER FOUR

HELL'S PAVEMENT

BRENT PEERED at Dr. Taylor as suspiciously as Bernard Dunbar had peered at him, and Garrett got in the way.

"You're neglecting your responsibilities to our rapturous readers," he said. "A teletype from publisher Palmer came in. He doesn't like the way Lora Lorne barely manages to scrape a column together at the last minute every day. We've got to have a six weeks' supply ahead, beginning now. That's orders, direct from the big chief himself."

Brent said evenly: "You suggested it to him, you hyena, and he simply gave it a routine O.K. Anything to keep me off the police beat! Anything to kill my chances with Val while you strut your stuff before her! You've been saving this to spring on me in case I got the jump on a hot story. As, for example, this one."

Valerie chimed in: "But this one, Bill, is Val's, and a pretty simple piece of murder it is, too. I've got a bang-up lead, boss. Let's beat it back and write it."

Garrett smugly took her arm and shot a reminder to Brent over his shoulder: "Six weeks ahead is what Palmer said, and get 'em together in short order, what's more. It oughtn't to be so tough, Lora. Just work on it day and night for a month or so, that's all."

Glumly Brent also watched the law function. Coroner Middleton arrived, gave the corpse a perfunctory inspection, and left. The body of Samuel Elias was loaded into the meat-wagon and the Homicide Squad prepared to depart. They still had Bernard Dunbar in tow. Drs. Veach and Taylor, after talking tersely with Captain Russo, had received his permission to go their professional ways. The cars paraded down the driveway, led by the corpse's, and with a suspicious glint still in his eyes, Brent approached the family physician.

"I'm stranded," he said. "If you're going back to the city I'll appreciate a lift."

"Certainly," Dr. Taylor mumbled, thoughtfully caressing his beard. "Get right in."

Brent got right in and grabbed his hat. Dr. Taylor launched off like a hell-bent demon. Clutching himself to the seat, Brent remarked: "Apparently somebody couldn't wait for the old guy to die decently in his nightshirt."

"It's a rather strange case. Mr. Elias was afflicted with angina pectoris." Dr. Taylor drawled—kept the car whizzing madly and spoke with such reflective deliberation that Brent estimated about twenty words to the mile. "Constantly in danger of a fatal attack which might come at any moment. Amazing the way he held on for years, but when Dr. Veach phoned me I immediately thought it had hit him at last. As for his dread of being poisoned—frankly, I considered it groundless."

"Elias doesn't," Brent pointed out. "Not now."

"I was Mr. Chester's physician and I'm quite satisfied he died a natural death," the doctor continued slowly while the car continued like wheeled lightning. "Mr. Elias imagined things. A mild case of senile dementia."

"Maybe so," and Brent wagged his head, "but as it turned out he was dead right—very dead right. And what about Mrs. Dunbar's husband? He isn't a screwball too, is he?"

Dr. Taylor's beard fluttered in the wind. "Bernard Dunbar is in good physical health but a typical hypochondriac. If he catches cold, he's sure it's double pneumonia. A head-ache, to him, is a malignant brain fever. Every normal person has occasional aches in the stomach, you know, and Dunbar simply mistakes his gas pains for symptoms of poisoning. His fears were really induced by suggestion—the old man's. His wife's a fine woman. Wouldn't feed cyanide to an ailing cat, let alone her own father and her own husband. Where can I drop you off?"

"Anywhere near the Wilburn," Brent said, sitting up.

The car lurched to a stop in front of the Wilburn Hotel and Brent said "thanks" to the cloud of exhaust fumes which Dr. Taylor's car instantly whooshed out. He drew a breath, and his eyes sharpened. He walked halfway down the block, paused beside a parked coupe and said: "Hello."

Captain Russo had probably flashed an alarm, and scores of detectives were probably searching for her, and there was Jean Chester sitting in her car on the city's busiest street.

SHE GAVE Brent a quick, teary glance as he folded into the seat, and continued to gaze intently at the neon-garnished entrance of the Wilburn.

"Miss Lorne wouldn't approve," he remarked. "I mean the way you abandoned Granddad to the guinea-pigs. It does not show a proper reverence for one's deceased relative."

Jean Chester's teeth nipped at her lower lip. "I know. But I had to do it."

"Your step-father made haste to carry those suspicious wheatcakes to headquarters. The police believe your mother scrammed the hell out of there because she was about to get collared for an inept job of patricide. You say you also had to take it on the lam. Lora Lorne will have to know why."

"If I could only see Miss Lorne!" The girl's limpid brown eyes searched Brent's, then quickly returned to the Wilburn entrance. "I had to follow Mother—find out where she was going. She came here and went into that hotel—the same one I moved into last week. But she didn't go up to my room, and she hasn't one of her own. I inquired. That man probably lives there—the man she's seen so many times, secretly—and I'm waiting for her to come out. I—I've got to know the truth!"

"A safer way would be to let the police find out and tell you. They're rather interested, you know."

The girl again bit her lip and kept watching the Wilburn.

"Interested particularly in your birthday gift to Grand-dad," Brent added. "Tell me about it."

Again her brown eyes widened into his. "Salt water taffy was his favorite candy, and I just had the store send him a box. Why—why do you ask?"

"The store sent it? Not you?"

"I just told the clerk what to send and paid for it."

"Were you home at any time after it was delivered, prior to this afternoon?"

"Not since Mother told me to get out, more than a week ago." And she blurted: "The poison was in the candy!"

"Speaking of sweets, Mother is going to be in a sweet spot once the police rope her," Brent observed. "If she's still in the hotel, maybe we can smoke her out."

He slid from the car and found it unnecessary to urge Jean Chester to accompany him. She came at his side, pale but determined. Brent was changing his mind about her. She seemed to be a dizzy little thing, but actually, for all her apparent skittishness, she was a purposeful young woman.

"What about Doctor Taylor?" Brent inquired abruptly.

"Oh, he's been the family doctor for years and years and years," Jean Chester said. "He's a wonderful man."

"How often has he been coming to the house?"

"Once a week or so, to check up on Granddad's heart."

"And how about Veach, the veterinarian?" Brent went on. "You seem to think he's also a man of rare stature. You work for him, apparently, so why didn't you ask him for advice instead of writing to Lora Lorne?"

She flicked Brent with an impatient glance. "A sergeant in the Army doesn't take his personal problems to his major," she explained.

"Then your relations with Doctor Veach are purely professional?"

"Purely," Jean Chester said with an indignant lift of her chin, "even though Martin doubts it."

They were approaching the desk and Brent surmised that Martin must be her restive fiancé. "Well, nevertheless, if you see a lot of Veach—"

She stopped short and bristled: "I do. A great deal. Day and night, sometimes. But only in his office or the lab, where we both work hard. It's work, and nothing but work. Between Doctor Veach and me there has never been a suggestion of anything of a—a social nature. Don't you dare—think things!"

"O.K.," Brent said placatingly. "O.K."

THEY WERE proceeding toward the desk when a man emerged from a nearby door marked: *Manager.* Tall, debonair, he spoke briskly to the desk clerk and, about to return, came to a rigid halt. He stared at Jean Chester, and she grew even paler. He broke from her flashing gaze, strode, disappeared into the office. The girl's lashes lowered, ominously darkening her eyes.

"When you get around to it," Brent said, "I'll be glad to hear what's eating you."

Breathing fast but moving slowly, she was approaching the door. "That's that man."

"The man who comes around?"

"Yes."

"Your Mother's doing all right for herself," Brent said quietly. "The gentleman's name is Roger Jordan. You'll find it printed in gold on every book of matches in this hotel and half a dozen others. The society column calls him one of the most eligible bachelors available."

Which left Brent puzzled as to half of Mother's motives. Question: Why was it her father, rather than her husband, who had eaten the cyanide? Had Samuel Elias committed the fatal error of swallowing a bit of poisoned candy intended for Bernard Dunbar?

Jean Chester opened the door marked *Manager* and again paused. This was a reception-room. Roger Jordan was not present, but a lone young man was waiting. He was natty, looked collegiate and surprised. Gazing at the girl, he rose.

"What—what are you doing here?" she asked him faintly.

"Brought the lay-outs to Mr. Jordan," he answered. "He's looking them over now—or was, until he was interrupted. God, I hope he likes them! If I don't close this deal, I don't know how I'll ever make out—I'll have to shut up shop."

"Oh, darling, I hope he likes them, darling," Jean Chester murmured.

This, Brent surmised, was Martin. He remembered an item in the *Reporter* announcing that Martin Rumsey, a young member of the city's founding family, socially the tops but financially average, had opened an advertising agency. Evidently the account with the Jordan Hotels was crucially important to him.

"I had an appointment, but there's a woman in there now," Rumsey said.

He was startled by the girl's change of expression. Not wistful now, it was again one of teeth-gritting determination. She quickly opened the door of the inner office, not heeding her fiancé's blurted protest. Before he could stop her she was beyond it, closing it tightly behind her, and Brent had a hand on Rumsey's arm.

"Easy, chum," Brent suggested. "Mr. Jordan's caller is Mrs. Dunbar."

"Jean's mother!"

"And there's going to be trouble."

There was trouble almost at once. Voices lifted inside the next office—the man's, the woman's, the girl's. Their tones were strained and their words became audible to Rumsey and Brent, in the reception-room.

Mrs. Dunbar: "Don't interfere! I've done nothing wrong, but can I expect any help from Bernard? Of course not. Far from it! He's turned against me, and it's bad enough now, Jean, without your making it even worse."

Roger Jordan, smoothly: "I want to help your mother, Jean. It's only natural that she should come to me—"

Miss Chester, with biting scorn: "Help her! Look what you've done! What if the police find her here with you! It's shameful, and before long the whole world will know—"

Swiftly, Mrs. Dunbar: "Listen to me, Jean! You're my daughter, and I love you, but I won't let you live my life for me. You don't understand. My marriage to your step-father is a horrible bust. Roger and I didn't fall in love deliberately. It happened, and we can't help it—and we don't want to. We've been as decent about it as anyone could be. Somehow we'll work it out—and not by using poison. It was like Bernard to accuse me of that. He's forced me to turn to Roger. Don't look at me like that, Jean! I'm in trouble, and I need your sympathy."

The girl: "It's your own fault, your own doing—yours and this man's."

Jordan: "Please, Jean, try to make it easier—"

"I loathe you!"

BRENT WAS staring in amazement at the door and it swiftly opened. Jean Chester, her eyes flashing, flew out of it. She grasped Martin Rumsey's arm, pulled him into the adjoining office. The door remained open, and Brent witnessed the scene, the four of them confronting one another—Mrs. Dunbar pale with dismay, Roger Jordan suffering under nervous strain, Rumsey reluctant and bewildered, Jean fiery.

"Help me make them see how wrong they are, Martin!" the girl pleaded. "You've told me this man is your friend. He'll listen to you. Make him understand that this terrible thing is all his fault, and he's got to leave my mother alone!"

The color went from Rumsey's face and he blurted: "I'll do nothing of the sort!"

Recoiling, the girl mumbled: "But—but Martin—"

"You look here!" Rumsey said. "What do you want me to do? Tell Roger Jordan he's a rat? If so, you're expecting too damned much. You're right, he's my friend, and I'm all for him. I think your mother is a swell, courageous woman. I wish them all the happiness in the world!"

Of course, Brent reflected, the fact that Martin Rumsey hoped to sign a lucrative contract with Jordan Hotels, Inc.—a contract that would save his business from an early crash—had nothing to do with his attitude.

"What right have you got, Jean," he sped on indignantly, "to tell your mother how to behave? To blame Roger Jordan when he's trying his best to help her? You're not so hot when it comes to running your own life. You waste your time in a stinking laboratory, throw your money into a no-good college for sick cows, go around worshiping a horse doctor! I won't stand for any more of this cockeyed nonsense. It's time you came back to your senses!"

"Oh-h-h-h!" and Jean Chester stamped her feet. "Oh-h-h!" and she tugged her engagement ring off her finger. "I'll never marry you now, never!" and she threw it into Martin Rumsey's face. She spun about, bolted from the office, slammed the door violently behind her. She was still running when Brent caught up with her in the lobby, and she was sobbing.

He steered her into the tap-room. He selected a secluded corner where she could cry her heart out in comparative privacy. She was doing so without stint when a waiter inquired as to Brent's needs.

"A Scotch for the lady," Brent answered. "A double Scotch for me."

Leaving her to her woes, he sidled into a telephone booth and dialed police headquarters.

"Captain Russo," he said, "Brent calling. For her own good, Jean Chester has decided to surrender for questioning. You'll find her in the Hunt Club Bar at the Wilburn."

He spun the dial again, and connections clicked through to the city-desk.

"Garrett," he announced, "within ten minutes Captain Russo will take the murdered man's granddaughter into custody. This front-page bulletin comes to you through the courtesy of Bill Brent, ace reporter, who found her and turned her in while your pet sob-sister was off somewhere powdering her nose. Isn't it high time you put a real news man back on the police trick, you dope?"

When his glass was empty, which wasn't long afterward, and Jean Chester was able to talk, he said miserably: "Well, you've gotten yourself kicked out of your home, you've alienated yourself from your mother, and your wedding plans are wrecked. All as a result of Lora Lorne's advice. What do you think of her now?"

"I don't—don't know what I'll do if I can't see her!" the girl said brokenly. "I'll be lost—terribly lost without her help. She's such a wonderful woman—so understanding and wise and sweet."

"Waiter," Brent muttered, "another double Scotch. No, make it a double-double Scotch, and never mind the soda."

CHAPTER FIVE

DEAD IN HIS TRACKS

THE CITY-ROOM was dark except for the cubbyhole in the far corner, deserted except for Brent, silent except for the dogged clacking of his typewriter. Having delivered Jean Chester into the hands of the law, he was now laboring to deliver a six weeks' reserve supply of domestic heartaches.

Captain Russo, when taking the girl into custody, had been satisfied—had, at least, *appeared* satisfied—with

Brent's explanation to the effect that he had come upon her through pure chance. Garrett had fudged the news of her arrest into the *Reporter's* seven-star final, but hadn't mentioned her real captor, hadn't congratulated Brent, hadn't urged him please to come back on the news end and to hell with the love column.

Bitterly resenting this ingratitude, Brent hadn't volunteered the additional information that Mrs. Dunbar might also be found as close at hand as Roger Jordan's office. Neither had Jordan. Nor, for business reasons, had Martin Rumsey. Jean Chester also wished to protect her mother. Mrs. Dunbar's whereabouts were, accordingly, still unknown to the police, and in this fact Brent found pleasure.

He alone held a lead to her. He wanted the girl to prove her innocence, which would leave the case hanging in mid-air. Once the police became convinced that the missing Mrs. Dunbar was the real Borgia of the family, he would tip them off, even produce her himself. This would demonstrate conclusively to Garrett that Bill Brent had no superior as a news man and that Val Randall's proper place was at the lovelorn desk, if anyone's was.

He was praying for this break, and striving miserably to prescribe for a case of wife-abandonment, when Garrett strode in with Val at his heels. Val was excited. They ignored Brent and at Garrett's desk they compared notes. Keeping up a pretense of being conscientiously busy, and listening through his open door, Brent learned that Val had just come from headquarters and Garrett from the morgue.

"The old man's insurance amounts to fifty thousand, and Mrs. Dunbar is the sole beneficiary," Val began. "There's talk of disinterring the late George Chester, to see whether or not the lady makes a practice of poisoning off her relatives."

"Coroner just finished the post," Garrett said, scrawling tomorrow's lead while he talked. "Nothing in the old guy's stomach but a couple pieces of candy and the poison. On the whole the symptoms don't agree with the book, but Doc Middleton found enough cyanide to murder forty grandfathers."

"The wheatcakes and other food brought to headquarters by Bernard Dunbar have been analyzed," Val reported. "No poison of any kind found. None in the batter left in the kitchen by Mrs. Dunbar. None in the medicine prescribed by Doctor Taylor. Lieutenant Goode went back, searched the house and didn't find a speck of cyanide anywhere—nothing suspicious except the smells in Jean Chester's closet laboratory. Jean's saying very little, but Russo feels she's in the clear. The box of candy was delivered only this morning—it's still missing, by the way—and her story about it checks on every point. She couldn't have touched it before it was sent, wasn't at the house between the time it arrived and the time her grandfather dropped dead."

"Who says so?"

Brent listened to Val explain: "A neighbor. One of these snoopy neighbors who watches everything that goes on across the street. She's a woman appropriately named Mrs. Spye, who's an invalid. She sits in a wheelchair on her sun-porch all day long, and anybody going into the Dunbar place must pass in full sight of her. She states that nobody called today, so nobody was there prior to Grandfather's demise except Mrs. Dunbar, husband, and father."

"That's a break for Russo, but is Mrs. Spye's word reliable?"

"They asked her test questions, then checked up. How long, for example, since Doctor Taylor called? 'Three o'clock last Wednesday afternoon,' says Mrs. Spye. 'Right,' says Doctor Taylor. 'How long since Doctor Veach's last visit?' 'Oh,' says Mrs. Spye, 'at least a week.' Absolutely true, because Doctor Veach attended the meeting of a veterinarian association in Chicago and didn't get back until noon today. Mrs. Spye's testimony is going to convict Mrs. Dunbar of murder. Next big question: Where is Mrs. Dunbar?" Val glanced warily at Brent and dropped her voice. "I think I know how to find her."

Garrett peered admiringly at her and asked: "How?"

Startled, Brent strained to catch her whisper.

"Several weeks ago... Roger Jordan... country club with a woman. Dark corner of the bar... kept to themselves. Nobody knew who she was but... I passed them on my way to the girl's room... heard him call her Bella. Bella Dunbar, of course. Jordan... hotels... thousands of rooms. The woman... hiding in one of them... false name."

Beaming, Garrett chortled: "And I've heard it said a beautiful girl would never make a good police-reporter!"

"Now," Val went on whispering, "we've got to plan a way... surprise her... draw her out... crack the case."

THEY WENT on whispering and Brent began muttering blasphemy. He dug into a pile of letters and found the telephone directory. The instrument was night-connected. He asked for the number of the Wilburn Hotel, then for the office of Roger Jordan.

"Bill Brent calling," he said quietly when Jordan's troubled voice answered. "I want you to know that in case you find a bloodthirsty city editor and female news-hound closing in on you soon, it's none of my doing."

Jordan said: "W-what?"

"I spotted Mrs. Dunbar this afternoon and kept it under my hat. Garrett just found out about her, independently. Trouble's heading your way."

"No charges have been filed," Jordan protested. "Technically she's not a fugitive. She's been talking to my lawyer. Of course, as soon as any action is brought, she'll surrender and—"

"Do it now," Brent recommended. "And fast. The sooner the better. The best way to protect her from the Garrett-Randall team is to put her behind bars. That's a hot tip. Make the most of it."

"I see!" Jordan said huskily. "I—I will!"

Disconnecting, Brent found that Val and Garrett were still sibilantly conspiring. He focused his hearing on them, heard only meaningless snatches, and the city-desk phone jangled. Garrett scooped it up, listened, put it down and relayed to Val: "They've released Bernard Dunbar, and also the girl."

Brent strolled to the desk in the corner, his manner profusely casual.

"I would find all this very amusing," he remarked with disdainful sarcasm, "if it were not so damned dumb. I mean your misguided efforts to make a police-reporter out of this incompetent child while letting a highly trained news man go to seed at your very elbow. In a few minutes you'll learn that Mrs. Dunbar has appeared at headquarters and given herself up. It's all so simple, Miss Randall, when you really know the ropes." He strolled away, wagging his head.

Garrett and Val were staring, and he heard another brief, sharp whisper pass between them.

"In her ignorance Miss Randall persists in deluding herself," Brent urbanely informed Garrett, pausing at the door. "She believes this case is open-and-shut. She actually accepts Mrs. Dunbar's guilt as a foregone conclusion. Mrs. Dunbar is clearly innocent, as I could prove in print if given an opportunity. Well, that's all, for the moment. Good-night."

DISGUSTED AND morose, Brent drove to the Wilburn Hotel. His defense of Mrs. Dunbar, he hoped, might successfully switch Val off in a totally wrong direction. But he didn't believe it himself. He felt hopelessly confused.

Trudging into the Wilburn, he met Jean Chester. She was hurried and tired, but at sight of him her face lighted.

"Oh," she said expectantly, "have you gotten in touch with Lora Lorne? May I see her?"

Soberly he answered: "First I've got to get this thing straight. Where are you going?"

"To the Veach College."

"So am I," said Brent.

She didn't object, but hurriedly led him to her car. As she drove toward Greengrove, he studied her. She was purposeful, tense, and presently she hinted her chief concern of the moment.

"I've lost such a lot of time lately. I'll have to work extra hard to catch up. I'll feel terrible if I've inconvenienced Doctor Veach."

"Just what is this career that's so almighty important to you?" Brent asked. "Are you filled with humanitarian impulses toward invalid dogs and cats?"

"You needn't try to be funny," she said, her chin up. "I've got my veterinarian degree last year, and I'm very fortunate to be associated with Doctor Veach. He's the finest veterinary surgeon in the Middle West, and it's just terrible that he's had so much bad luck, because otherwise he'd now be directing the best veterinary college in the country. He's really a great man, doing a tremendously important work, and I'm proud to be able to help him in my small way."

"Are the guinea-pigs part of it?"

"I breed them and use them in the lab for various tests. My researches are mostly in parasitology," she continued, "and Doctor Veach's work is of priceless value to farmers and breeders of all fine animals. We're studying the nutritive requirements for fecundity in cattle, the relation of hormones to lactation—so many vital subjects! Why, one-third of the nation's milk cows don't produce enough to pay for their own keep, and another third just about breaks even, and even the rest fall short of maximum volume. Did you know that?"

"It's news to me," Brent admitted, "but not quite an eight-column streamer."

"Well, it's true, and the United States would never be able to feed a world at war without fine, public-spirited men like Doctor Veach."

She turned her car past her home in Greengrove, and Brent saw that two cops were patrolling the grounds. Across the street, ensconced in her wheelchair on the sun-porch of her bungalow, was the observant Mrs. Spye. Beyond the corner, on a side road, sat a modern diner, and a little farther on, the skeleton of a partially completed building loomed. Beside it Jean Chester braked.

In its present condition Dr. Veach's college consisted mostly of gaunt steel framework. Its upper stories remained unfinished. Construction had halted months ago, evidently, for weeds were growing rank over stacks of bricks. Only the front half of the ground floor had been made usable. The girl led Brent into an office where they found

Dr. Veach, clad in a white smock, speaking impatiently over the telephone.

"Yes, of course I have a stomach pump, but it's not intended for use on humans— See here! I'm a very busy man. Your step-daughter has just come in. If you'd like to talk with her—"

HE PUT the phone into the girl's hands and disappeared through a door. Brent curiously followed him into an operating-room. It was brilliantly lighted, the floor was red tile, the walls gleamed white, and it was crowded with strange devices. Dr. Veach and a rustic man in overalls were ministering to a bay mare.

The horse was chloroformed, and lay on a huge metal operating-table. Ropes and straps bound it down. Dr. Veach took up a hypodermic syringe scarcely smaller than a bicycle pump and slipped the needle, thick and long as a soda straw, into an artery of the patient. Next he grasped up a two-handled forceps as big as a tree-pruner and went to work on the mare's jaw. He snipped, probed, snipped again, pulled hard, extracted something and was nodding with satisfaction when Jean Chester came from the telephone.

"My step-father's still afraid something awful might happen to him," she murmured. "He doesn't trust Doctor Taylor, for some reason, and he wanted to know if Doctor Veach could help him in case of an emergency, because his place is only a quarter-of-a-mile from home, but of course Doctor Veach couldn't."

The two men tilted the operating-table, loosened the ropes, and slid the horse down upon a low truck. They wheeled it down a corridor. Its owner left and Dr. Veach, after scrubbing his hands, strode into the office, brisk and quick, peeling off his white jacket.

"I've a call to make, Jean," he said, nodding to Brent. "Must pick up Mrs. Morris's Pomeranian. Distemper. I appreciate your coming. You're not needed tonight, but new cultures must be started in the morning."

"Of course." Jean glanced at Brent and said: "If I could only have a minute before you go, Doctor."

Taking the hint, Brent wandered down the corridor. He paused at a door marked: *Laboratory—Miss Chester,* and looked into a typical array of beakers and flasks crowding bluestone benches, shelves loaded with bottled chemicals. A few canine yips and snorts echoed from another room beyond, and the tile walls acted as a resonant channel which brought him the anxious voice of the girl.

"Mother's holding my money back to punish me, Doctor, to make me let her alone. I know she won't give me a penny of Granddad's insurance money, either. Not having any money at all now, I'll have to sell my shares, Doctor—after wanting so much to help. I—I don't know what else I can do."

"Don't think of it, Jean," Veach answered, his words clipped. "I know you'll continue your participation whenever you're able, and to the greatest extent possible for you. I've no doubt that Simeon Taylor will be glad to increase his holdings by taking over your stock, in case you must part with it. It's unfortunate, but I'm sure I'll work it out, and please don't concern yourself too much. Better get some rest, Jean. Good-night." Carrying a cage in which to transport the ailing dog, Dr. Veach strode out.

"Doctor Taylor also has a piece of Doctor Veach's institution?" Brent inquired. "How come?"

"They were friends at the state university. Doctor Veach's time is so valuable, I do wish my step-father wouldn't bother the doctor with his ridiculous worries."

"Ridiculous or not, that man's scared out of his wits," Brent reminded her. "He's really afraid that he'll suddenly turn up dead. I'd like to find out whether it's only his warped imagination, or something real he fears. How about driving me over?"

"Then will you get in touch with Miss Lorne for me?" she asked eagerly.

"Yes," Brent solemnly promised.

All eagerness, she went out with him. At her car Brent paused, glancing about uneasily. He thought he had heard a furtive footstep. He sensed that they were not alone in the darkness.

The girl swung her car onto the pavement, lifting the headlight beams. They flooded the road. Brent peered at a puppet-like figure bouncing along the shoulder in their direction.

"Here he comes. Your step-father."

Bernard Dunbar, with jerky haste, was evidently bound for the veterinary college.

A roar swelled behind them. The swelling thunder of a motor broke upon the girl so suddenly that she instinctively swung aside. A car whizzed up from behind the coupe, a black, flashing mass traveling at an insane speed, and without lights. Swiftly it passed, swerved toward Bernard Dunbar. He stopped, stared as it rushed upon him. With a yell he jumped, leaped into the road in a wild effort to escape it. Again it veered—and Brent heard a dull, crushing impact.

Something hurtled through the air, tossed by the terrific force of the lightless car. Like a crazily twisting dummy, it struck the pavement, sprawled loosely. It fell inertly in front of Jean Chester's coupe, and she jammed on the brakes as the other car fled. She jumped out, Brent with her, and they heard tires screeching at the far intersection. As the juggernaut vanished, they stared down at the broken body of Bernard Dunbar.

CHAPTER SIX
DOUBLY DEAD

A MOAN quavered from Dunbar. The girl recoiled, her fingers pressing her lips against a horrified sob.

"Get back, phone the police," Brent said quickly. "I'll bring him."

She spun about and as she ran, her high heels tapping, toward the veterinary college, Brent slipped into her car, edged it off the pavement. Dunbar's face was cross-streaked with crimson—he was unconscious, though torn nerves caused his whole twisted frame to quiver. Brent gently gathered him up, carried him.

The girl was chattering over the phone when Brent lugged Dunbar to the metal table in the operating-room.

"They're sending an ambulance," Jean told him. "Coroner Middleton happened to be there. He's coming."

Brent flicked through the directory, looked up, saw headlights outside the window. The car stopped and Dr. Veach came in the entrance, carrying the cage in which a Pomeranian lay, rheumy-eyed and wheezing. Brent straightened, pointed to the operating-table, and the veterinarian stiffened.

"Good God!" he said.

He dropped the dog, hurried to Bernard Dunbar. The girl ventured after him, paused as he shook his head.

Turning back she came to Brent and impulsively closed both hands on his arm.

"Is—is he dead?"

"No. But it looks pretty bad. He was worrying about the wrong thing, poor guy. Worrying about a few grains of poison, and then two tons of steel hit him."

"Someone did it deliberately—deliberately ran him down!"

"Accidents happen," Brent observed wryly. "That's why insurance companies write double-indemnity clauses."

He dialed a number. "Doctor Taylor, please. Urgent."

"The doctor isn't here," a woman answered. "He's out on a case. Who's calling?"

"Out?" Brent clipped the word sharply. "Where?"

"I don't know. Several places, probably. He's always very busy. If you'll give me your name—"

"Ask him to come to the Veach Veterinary Hospital as soon as possible."

Dr. Veach came into the office, face gravely lined, to say: "Nothing I can do, nothing."

"He's still alive?"

"Yes." Veach peered back. "But prepare yourself, Jean. I'm sorry, but I'm afraid he can't last long."

"He was coming from his home when it happened," Brent said. "Coming here. I wonder why?"

"Was he?" Dr. Veach shook his head. "Not poison this time. Not poison."

He turned back to Dunbar, and Brent watched as he felt the shattered man's feeble pulse. The girl sank into a chair, sat motionless with shock. They waited for the ambulance. Looking for it up the road, Brent stared out a window. A faint movement surprised him. It flickered in the darkness, now was gone.

Brent shouldered out the entrance, ran along the edge of the pavement. There was a gasp, a scattering of gravel, and a girl was trying to out-distance him. She was near the diner when he caught up, gripped her arm, halted her. Val Randall's car was standing near the diner's door. She breathed hard, and the neon lights glimmered green in her eyes.

"I get it," he said accusingly. "You thought I'd got a hot lead, and I was holding out, so you trailed me This shows very clearly how unresourceful you are as a reporter. What you should be, Val, is a reporter's *wife*. In that capacity you'd really shine."

She was trying to pull herself loose from him. "Let me go, Bill! I've got a story to phone to the boss. As for marrying any reporter—first he'll have to show me he's better at the job than I am, and that'll take a lot of proving. Let go of me—Lora!"

BRENT MIGHT have socked her, except that two cars were turning toward the veterinary hospital. Angrily he turned her loose and followed them. Two internes were sliding a litter out of the ambulance. Coroner Middleton was already in the operating-room. Brent, at Veach's side, watched him make a deft examination. Veach straightened in amazement.

"Dead. But no hit-run driver killed him."

He peeled up Bernard Dunbar's lids, peered at the glazed eyeballs.

"If the car hadn't hit him, he would have died regardless, and in a few minutes. Look at his pupils. Pinpoints, both of them. Characteristic effect of belladonna. Powerful dose of it too, I think. He must have passed very quickly through the successive stages of great excitement—which probably sent him hurrying here—then coma and death." The coroner pursed his lips. "This man is dead of poison."

Brent stared. Poison after all, and this time a different kind. The poisoner was versatile as to his materials, could reach his victim in spite of every precaution.

Leaving Dr. Veach in consultation with the coroner, Brent went to the telephone. The number he called was that of the Dunbar home. The answer was a gruff growl.

"This is Bill Brent. Do I know you?"

"Sure, Bill, you know First-Class Patrolman Briggs. What else do you want to know?"

"Who's been at that place since you began casing it?"

"Nobody but the guy name of Dunbar. He stayed just a few minutes, on account of he got a phone call."

"Who called him?"

"Don't know, Bill. He just answered, kept saying yes, then went away."

"Did he eat anything?"

"Only one thing he did, except take that message. Went into the bathroom and, like he had a bad taste in his mouth, he brushed his teeth."

"Nobody else has been around?"

"Nary a soul."

Brent thanked Briggs, found the number of a Mrs. Ella Spye and dialed it.

"The *Reporter* calling, Mrs. Spye. We'll appreciate a little information, if you'll be so good. Has anyone been at the Dunbar house this evening?"

"Nobody but Mr. Bernard Dunbar," the woman cackled promptly. "And he stayed only ten minutes or so."

Brent also thanked Mrs. Spye, and he made a third call which brought him the voice of Captain Russo.

"A small favor desired, Captain. Has Mrs. Dunbar given herself up?"

"She walked into this office with her lawyer not sixty seconds ago," Russo answered. "Don't mention it."

Mulling over this, Brent turned from the phone as the entrance opened. Dr. Taylor appeared, fingering his bushy beard. Looking mussed and weary, he frowned at Brent.

"I called my home before starting back and was told—"

"In there," and Brent pointed in the direction of the second corpse in the case.

AS THE physician lumbered in its direction, Brent slipped from his chair and sidled outside. He walked a circle around Dr. Taylor's sedan, looking for crumpled fenders, dents, scratches, anything that might indicate a collision with a human body. Finding nothing of the sort, he reflected that a car would not inevitably show such marks. He returned to the office and sat intently eyeing Dr. Veach.

In the veterinarian he saw a first-class murder suspect. Dr. Veach was obviously in financial straits. All ordinary sources of funds had failed him, and he had been forced to abandon the construction of his college, an enterprise of paramount importance to him. Jean Chester might be considered his only hope of salvaging it. Worshiping him as a demigod, she had invested in the project all the money available to her. When more came into her hands, she would eagerly place it at Dr. Veach's disposal. What, then, were her chances of collecting, and his?

Two large insurance policies would now be payable to Bella Dunbar—unless she happened to be convicted of murdering her father and her husband. In that event the law, forbidding the criminal to profit by her crimes, would divert the proceeds to her next of kin—Jean, who would in turn promptly transfer the money to Dr. Veach.

A neat plan, Brent thought—to kill Samuel Elias and Bernard Dunbar in order to bring a fortune into the hands of Bella Dunbar—then to fasten the murders on Mrs. Dunbar so as to pass it on still further, to her daughter—finally to collect it intact and at will from Jean Chester.

But Brent did not elatedly pounce upon Dr. Veach and demand his arrest. He detected several things wrong in the picture.

In the first place, there was no conceivable manner whereby the veterinarian could have introduced the cyanide into the taffy which no one but the confectioners had touched before its delivery.

In the second, Dr. Veach could not have come even remotely within reach of Bernard Dunbar's toothpaste with the purpose of charging it with belladonna—if that was how it had been done—and it was even more unlikely that he could have poisoned the milk supply at Smitty's Dairy Bar, patronized by Bernard Dunbar.

In both instances it was utterly impossible that the veterinarian could have baited a poison trap for the victims.

The theory branding Dr. Chenery Veach as a murderer, Brent was forced to admit, was an excellent one except for that.

CHAPTER SEVEN
A SLUG ON THE HOUSE

VERIFICATION OF Coroner Middleton's judgment as to the cause of Bernard Dunbar's death was brought into the city-room during the busy morning by Val Randall. With typewriters and teletypes clattering, Brent couldn't overhear any of the news Val delivered to Garrett. Besides, he had another goddam Lora Lorne column to get out, not to mention the extra thirty-six still on order. At odd moments he managed to snitch a galley proof from Garrett's spike and glean the details.

Mention of Bella Dunbar, as Brent had expected, was at a minimum. She was being held for questioning, but Val had no official forecast of an indictment. Her husband's death had occurred just prior to her surrender. All the toothpaste discoverable in the Dunbar home had been analyzed and found to consist solely of the proper ingredients of toothpaste. No clues to the hit-run driver had been picked up. The coroner had extracted an appalling amount of belladonna from the mass of curds found in Bernard Dunbar's stomach. Except for the poison, he had partaken of nothing but milk. It was impossible that milk bought by the glass across a restaurant counter could be loaded with a toxic drug, but according to the evidence the milk bought at the restaurant *had* been loaded with a toxic drug.

Brent labored doggedly on the column while Val sped in and out, while Garrett shot copy down the tube, while all the staff steamed into the day's news, except Brent.

His mind departed far from Lora Lorne's erotica. Tempted from her duties to love by his own allegiance to crime, he remembered that as a rule almost everybody needed money. Dr. Veach was already noted. Martin Rumsey had a pressing problem in his advertising agency, and once Jean Chester acquired the face value of two insurance policies, he could get some of it by apologizing and marrying the girl. Brent also wondered about Roger

Jordan. He tackled the telephone, made careful inquiries, learned to his surprise that several of Jordan's hotels were close to bankruptcy. Though running a hotel required a great deal of money, and the sum which Mrs. Dunbar might provide would be comparatively trifling, it was nevertheless not hay.

Everybody in the case, Brent was finding, to his confusion, might conceivably profit—Mrs. Dunbar, Jean Chester, Dr. Veach, Roger Jordan, Martin Rumsey—everybody except Dr. Taylor, who remained an unknown quantity. And the discovery of a single dark detail might instantly change his position.

Brent realized with a start that the deadline was looming and he needed another letter before he could put Lora Lorne to bed. Brent found one dealing with the demon rum, halfheartedly prescribed a faith cure and carried the result to Garrett.

"Where's the other thirty-six?" the city editor demanded.

BRENT IGNORED the taunt. "Have you noticed that the police are not grabbing any poisoners? Are you satisfied to sit there and print the scribblings of a mere schoolgirl who's able to report only that a couple of men got mysteriously killed and after that nothing happens?" He bent closer. "Here's a proposition, Garrett. Put me back on police and I'll crack this case wide open."

Garrett said, his blue pencil jumping: "Thirty-six more, Lora."

"How would publisher Palmer like to hear that I could have brought in a murderer as our exclusive property," Brent asked, "but you didn't want any?"

Garrett's eyes narrowed at him. "You serious?"

"Never more serious in my life." Brent's tone was confidentially tense. "I've got leads. One of 'em has got to be right. I can't do it if I have to slave day and night in a cell that's all cluttered up with broken homes. But back on the police trick—easy. Shake?"

Garrett did not grasp Brent's proffered hand. "What've you got that Val hasn't got?"

"I don't spill a word of it unless it's my job. Not if you howl to high heaven. Not if you sue the socks off me. Good lord, this is the chance of a lifetime for both of us! I tell you, I can bring in the answer to this case so fast it'll make you dizzy—and Captain Russo even dizzier."

A voice behind Brent said: "Interesting, if true."

Captain Russo's unearthly black eyes were fixed on Brent as Brent warily straightened. He chose to ignore Brent for the moment and his spooky gaze turned on Garrett.

"You suggested I might drop in, and I'm glad to oblige. You're a very busy man, and I've only got a couple of homicides on my mind."

Garrett stood, pointed the blue pencil at him. "You've got a couple of homicides, and what the hell are you doing about them?"

Val Randall came from her desk, smiling sweetly. Brent knew that smile. She put it on whenever her beautiful white teeth were about to draw blood.

"Yes, Captain," she said calmly, "just what kind of a police department have we got in this town? This paper's going to spread the facts before the public. Fair warning! Once I get started, headquarters will be in for a housecleaning that'll go down in history."

"It's kind of dusty in places," Captain Russo said evenly.

"You've grabbed Mrs. Dunbar," Val continued in an ominous tone. "Well, if Mrs. Dunbar didn't murder those men, who did? Why are you handling her with kid gloves? Why don't you, or the chief, or the D.A., go before the grand jury? Why don't you ask for and get an indictment? Are you afraid of Jordan's influence? If you've got a good reason for this pussyfooting, we want to hear it. If we don't hear it right now, I'm going to ask these questions publicly and the Governor will get the answers in an investigation."

Russo said, his expression never changing: "Just listen to my teeth chatter," and turned away. Halfway to the door he paused, came quietly back and aimed his spectral gaze at Brent. "You might let Miss Randall and Garrett in on it. They want to see what's in the back of the book—and so do I. Yes, Brent. So do I. Well?"

Brent steadied himself, headed for Lora Lorne's cubicle with his shoulders sagging and muttered: "You dumb-heads can't take a joke."

AGAIN IT was late, the city-room was quiet and the only light shone in Brent's unhappy cell. He was still trying to get thirty-six columns ahead, and the number still to be written was thirty-six. Brows dark, he mulled over his problem, which was not anyone's domestic sorrows, but two poisoned men. He began digging into a stack of letters he had put aside for future reference, looking for one he had read just previous to Jean Chester's agitated arrival in the city-room.

Here it was—a letter signed with the initials of Bernard Dunbar, expressing fear that his wife meant to kill him.

Brent pored over it, then swiveled about and dug into his file. Lora Lorne conscientiously preserved the originals of all correspondence she answered in the *Reporter*. He produced two more letters, both written by "So Bewildered"—Jean Chester. He re-read them carefully, compared them with B.D.'s. His eyes lighted and he held the letters against his desk-lamp, finding the paper identically watermarked, that all three showed the same typographical defects—a leaning *t*, a *g* with a flattened lower loop. He sat thinking, slowly grinning, and he was grinning all over his face when Garrett strode in with Val Randall.

They ignored Brent again, but their lack of enthusiasm told him that no new breaks had developed in the case.

"I have three remarks to make," he announced. "The first is that this misguided young woman committed a tactical blunder when she threatened Russo. He's close-mouthed by nature, and from now on any clam will seem positively loquacious compared with him. You already see the effect, Miss Randall—no more news from headquarters. The captain, you see, is not crooked. He's going easy on Mrs. Dunbar for the simple reason that he's not convinced of her guilt. I mentioned this possibility twenty-four hours ago, but you paid no attention."

Val said despondently: "Oh, Bill, go away."

"Secondly," Brent continued to Garrett, "my offer still stands. Boot this young woman out of here, put me back on the police trick and I'll crack the case. But not otherwise. And not before I have your written agreement never again to make me write another line of Lora Lorne's guff."

"I know a bluff when I see one, Grandma," Garrett growled. "Where are those thirty-six—"

"O.K.," Brent said carelessly. "As you wish, chum. I'm going ahead on my own. I'll report results where they'll be properly appreciated. After all, I don't insist on the police trick and nothing else. I'll feel satisfied to be the new city editor."

Garrett sat up and Val eyed him narrowly. It was Brent's turn to do a little ignoring, and he sauntered out. He waited beside his car, watched the entrance long enough to be reasonably sure that Val wasn't shadowing him again. He drove rapidly, angled through Greengrove and stopped under the gaunt superstructure of the Veach veterinary hospital.

The lights were out in Veach's office and in the operating-room, but the windows of the laboratory shone. His steps echoed down the corridor and he went in. Jean Chester was alone in the building, but she didn't hear him. Clad in a stained smock, she was perched on a stool, head bent, hands covering her face, quietly sobbing.

"What's this?" Brent asked.

She dabbed a handkerchief at her eyes and her lips trembled. "I'm so terribly unhappy. Everything's gone wrong, everything." She lifted her chin indignantly. "You said you'd get in touch with Miss Lorne, but you haven't kept your promise, and I think you're mean."

"I'll do it right now, but on one condition. It will be a very special favor on Miss Lorne's part, you know. She intends her advice to be taken seriously, and if you don't do exactly as she recommends she'll never again try to help you. With that understanding, shall I call her?"

The girl's eyes widened expectantly. "Oh, yes! Really, I'll do just as she says, really I will! Please!"

BRENT NODDED soberly and poked his finger into the phone dial. The number he spun off was that of his own apartment. The distant bell began ringing, and though nobody answered, for the reason that nobody was there, Brent said into the transmitter: "The *Reporter*, calling Miss Lorne, very important."

Jean Chester exclaimed eagerly: "Let me talk to her!"

"No!" Brent said. "I've got to be careful as hell. Might get fired for doing this and—" He interrupted himself, while the bell rang on and on, to say: "Miss Lorne? This is an emergency, and your counsel is so badly needed, I'm sure you'll make an exception in this case—"

Keeping a straight face, he outlined the situation in careful detail to nobody. The ringing signal automatically continued and the girl listened, elated. He said finally: "I see, yes, I understand, yes, that's very wonderful of you, Miss Lorne, thank you, thank you so much." He disconnected with a sigh and the girl waited breathlessly to hear Lora Lorne's magical counsel.

"Please—"

"Miss Lorne feels very strongly that your attitude defeats your purposes. You must, she says, give your whole-hearted sympathy to the mother who desperately needs you. Go to her, tell her you understand her love. Help her with all your heart. As for your fiancé, Miss Lorne is sure your place is with him. Everything can be made right again so easily, but it's entirely up to you."

"Why, that—that's true!" Jean Chester exclaimed. "I can see it now—how stubborn I've been, how blind!" She jumped off the stool. "I'll do it! I'll go to Martin and Mr. Jordan and mother and— Oh, I'm so glad Miss Lorne has opened my eyes to it! Isn't she wonderful!"

Brent heard this grimly and watched Jean Chester toss off her smock, snatch up a hat, run buoyantly to the door and out. Her car whirred, and she was gone, wholeheartedly determined to carry out the injunctions of her nonexistent mentor. Brent wished her better luck this time and with a scowl bent over the typewriter.

He fed a sheet under the platen—tapped a few keys experimentally, then wrote:

> This is a sample of the work done on the machine on which So Bewildered wrote two letters to Lora Lorne, and on which the letter signed B.D. was also written. Here it sits in Jean Chester's office—a significant circumstance. Considered in conjunction with other known facts, it helps to clarify the case. In fact, I can now plainly see the entire situation. Jean Chester clinched the matter when, quite unaware of the real meaning of her words, she said

Suddenly the typewriter seemed to fly up, hit Brent in the face, and disintegrate. Then the desk bounced against his chin. Next the floor heaved like a stormy ocean and smacked him on the forehead. The whole building came apart, and crashed down....

It was dark, except for a dimly glowing blob of light, and Brent was on his feet again. His arms were stretched out, his legs were straddled. He was dizzy and wanted to lie down, but couldn't. He tried, and couldn't even manage to fall. He remained erect, realizing vaguely that he was fastened to something that was holding him up.

He heard echoing footfalls. Someone he couldn't see, was moving about and the gritty sounds reverberated. He was in the dark, tiled room, roped to the big metal table like an invalid horse.

The gritty feet prowled around him and suddenly his jaw was gripped. The hand was crushing his chin, pulling it down, pulling his mouth open. Something was hovering under his nose. It was a glass or a cup and it gave off pungent fumes. It was being pressed against his lips and his chin was being pried loose.

"Drink it!" a whisper came. "Drink it!"

OF COURSE the stuff was poison and it would trickle down his throat and kill him. In a little while he would be dead. Maybe Garrett would regret his ruthlessness, when he heard about it, and Val would drop a tear or two—then they'd bury him under a stone reading: *Here Lies Lora Lorne,* and that would be the end of him.

He kept his mouth closed so tightly that the talons left his jaw and the poison floated away.

Footfalls gritted on the floor again. He heard a peculiar sucking sound. His eyes were beginning to function. Now he could see that the blob of light was the hallway door. A shadow in the gloom moved toward him, but he couldn't make out who the shadow was. Then he looked down and saw the long, gleaming tube.

His shirt was ripped aside and his abdomen was bared and the point of the long thin tube poised on his skin just below his breastbone. Then it went in. Brent felt the sharp sting as it pierced the surface, but he couldn't feel it inside him. It sank deep until almost all its length was buried in his vitals. He sensed that something was flowing through the tube. Then the tube slowly slid out again.

Now his stomach felt hot. Its temperature went up and up and suddenly it seemed to burst into flame. It was the effect of the poison. A drug had been shot into his stomach and it was consuming him. At the same time it sent numbness through his whole frame. The numbness began in the exact middle of him and went out in circular waves, like the ripples on a pond when you toss a stone in.

The shadow-being was standing beside him feeling his pulse, waiting for him to die.

Brent stared at the door and saw a second shadow. It came from the hallway, a silent drifting cloud. It grew dimmer, but he could still discern it, creeping closer. It was horribly tall, as tall as two men. No—its height was normal, and its arms were stretched up, it was lifting something overhead.

He saw a swift movement, heard a crashing noise, a groan. Suddenly the lights were on, a blinding glare. Val Randall was trying desperately to loosen the ropes that bound Brent to the table. His arms dropped, then his ankles were free and he stood there under his own power. He was dying on his feet.

"I've been poisoned," he said.

He looked down, and forty feet beneath his head, on a level with his feet, he saw a broken toy chair, and a little bloody-faced doll who looked exactly like Dr. Chenery Veach.

Then he discovered, to his surprise, that he was running. He was outside, in the dark, running along the road. Now he was inside the diner. He saw himself jostling a customer off a stool, snatching up a cup of coffee, pouring an entire mug of mustard into it, stirring the ghastly mixture and gulping it down. It tasted swell, and never in all his life had he been so marvelously sick....

BRENT'S STOMACH still hurt. Probably for weeks it was going to feel like a hard ball of hamburger. This was tomorrow, and the arrival of the ambulance that Val had called, and the emergency room of the hospital, and everything that had happened afterward, was still a nightmare. He didn't feel like explaining things to anybody, but Captain Russo had to hear all about it.

He gazed about Captain Russo's office. There was Jean Chester sitting beside Martin Rumsey, and they were holding hands and looking foolishly happy. Bella Dunbar and Roger Jordan, also side by side, looked equally blissful.

Vaguely Brent realized that Lora Lorne's advice to the girl had worked like a charm. Everybody, even Dr. Taylor, was delighted, except Captain Russo, who still looked like a fugitive from a graveyard, and Dr. Veach, who was handcuffed.

"He'd been planning it," Brent said. "That's why he wrote the letter signed B.D.—to prepare the way by throwing suspicion on Mrs. Dunbar. I found out her husband simply couldn't have written that letter himself because, Miss Chester told me, he'd never been inside that laboratory. Doctor Veach didn't know that Miss Chester had also written several letters on that same typewriter to the same lovelorn column. The way he poisoned me, after I'd discovered that clue to his guilt, was the same way he'd staged those two poisonings.

"Samuel Elias wasn't murdered. He died a natural death from the heart disease that he'd been expected to die from for years. Being on the scene, Doctor Veach did some lightning thinking and took advantage of the corpse. When nobody else was near he removed a big hypodermic syringe from his case, loaded it with the cyanide solution he probably used for putting animals out of the way, and shot it into the corpse's stomach.

"He took the candy, and the card written by Miss Chester, and spirited them away in his case, because his whole plan would go haywire if the quote murder unquote were pinned on her.

"It worked so well that Veach immediately drew his second victim into a trap. That night he left the hospital, picked up the dog at a nearby house, phoned Dunbar, asked him to beat it right over. He slammed his car into Dunbar on the road, turned around a minute later and drove back. He liked it better because Dunbar wasn't quite dead. Again he shot poison directly into his victim's stomach, with the syringe, and this time the proper symptoms developed. Excuse me. I've got a horrible stomach-ache."

IT KEPT aching while a taxi transported Brent to the *Reporter* building. He labored up the stairs, paid no attention to the excited salutations of the staff and stopped at Val's desk.

"Have I thanked you for following me again and saving my life?"

"Don't mention it, Bill," and she went on pounding the keys.

"You're wasting your time," he pointed out. "Look, I'm a brave guy now. For weeks I've known nothing but broken homes and miserable marriages, but I'm all set to try it myself, regardless. Will you marry me?"

"What?" Val said, smiling sweetly. "And abandon my career?"

"What career? I'll fix that."

He strode to Garrett's desk and Garrett appraised him with a look of satisfaction which he was glad to see.

"Tell Val to get away from my desk," he urged. "Send her over into that little office where she belongs—now that I'm back on police."

"No," Garrett said.

"What!" Brent screeched. "I cracked this case, you hyena! I broke the biggest story of the year. I damn near got killed doing it. It's mine and nobody else's, mine—" He grinned. "You're kidding."

"Not at all," Garrett said calmly. "Here's a teletype just in from publisher Palmer. Read it yourself. He's delighted with the recent response to the love column. His warmest congratulations and by all means continue."

Brent clenched his fists. "I can't do it!" he snarled. "I tell you that column's driving me nuts and I can't do it!"

"I'll reserve a padded cell for you," Garrett said, taking up his blue pencil. "In the meantime you'll go on writing the column. Talk about it later. My police-reporter and I are busy on a big murder story. Let's have today's column in a hurry, and remember, we still want thirty-six ahead."

In a daze Brent drifted away, past busy Val, to his hated cell, back to his desk heaped with tinted, scented letters. Incredulously he pulled one of them out and stared at it. The words danced before his bleary eyes: *I'm so disillusioned and worried. I thought my boy-friend was real nice, but now I wonder if he really loves me because last night he made an improper—*

"God help me!" he moaned.

LET THE SKELETONS RATTLE

BILL BRENT, ALIAS LORA LORNE, THE *RECORDER'S* GENTLE AND MOTHERLY LOVE-COUNSELOR, DIGS INTO HIS VOLUMINOUS AND EROTIC MAILBAG AND COMES UP WITH A CLUE TO THE HEIGHTS HOSPITAL HOMICIDES THAT SUGGESTS THAT SOME OF THE STAFF'S AMBIDEXTROUS MEDICOS MAY BE PRESERVING LIFE WITH ONE HAND AND SNUFFING IT OUT WITH THE OTHER. SO HE INDULGES IN A BIT OF EXTRA-CURRICULAR ACTIVITY—FOR, AFTER ALL, BILL'S SPECIALTY IS BROKEN HEARTS, WHETHER THE HARM IS DONE BY CUPID'S DARTS OR SMALL-CALIBER BULLETS.

CHAPTER ONE
MURDERS ARRANGED FREE

THE THUNDER of the big cylinders in the basement softened to a rumble and stopped signaling throughout the *Recorder* plant that the mail edition was off the presses and the city final was due to roll.

The rest of the staff were racing the clock in an effort to meet the daily emergency of the deadline, but Bill Brent was preoccupied with a self-appointed task having nothing to do with getting the paper out on time. He was searching into the correspondence, some of it weeks old, that formed an everlasting heap on his table.

"You've been digging away for hours, Bill," Valerie Randall said, pausing at his door. "What in the world are you expecting to turn up?"

"Can't say exactly," Brent muttered, ripping open another envelope. "Don't know just who the letter's from or what it'll say or even if it's been written. But there ought to be something here—somewhere—"

Persistently hunting while Miss Randall hustled to her desk—while the battery of linotypes in the composing room sent up an urgent clatter and the advertising department rushed its late insertions and eight reporters belabored their typewriters to produce last-minute copy that went whiffing page by page down the pneumatic tube—he chucked each letter aside after a single worried glance.

There were hundreds, some pink, others lavender, many perfumed. All were addressed to Lora Lorne, the paper's mentor in matters of love—its own Dorothy Dix or Beatrice Fairfax, who counseled her distressed readers as to their wayward spouses, their shattered troths and unre-

quited raptures. None of them lightened the haunted expression on Brent's face. He reached the last without finding the thing he was hoping he wouldn't find.

Taking a new tack he strode from his cubbyhole of an office, which occupied a remote corner of the big littered room, and ran his anxious blue eyes down the galley proofs trailing from a spike on Garrett's rolltop desk. Almost at once a cold shock hit him. Here it was, finally—a brief item speaking of violence and a girl whose initials were O.Q.

"Well, at least," he consoled himself, poring over it, "she didn't get herself murdered."

He turned to Valerie Randall.

"You covered this, Val. What really happened? Let's hear the straight of it."

MISS RANDALL was probably the only girl police reporter and she was conscious of her distinction. She was also the loveliest brunette to be found in any city-room anywhere, in Brent's estimation, and she would seem even more beautiful to him if only she weren't to be found constantly in this one, particularly at the desk he considered rightfully his own.

"Why, Bill?" she asked, twirling a sheet of newspulp from her typewriter. "Do you know Odelle Quinn?"

"Never laid eyes on the lady," Brent answered, "but I've got to know how badly she's hurt, and what this guy had to do with it."

"Glen Carr, you mean?" Val was preoccupied with her copy—a more pressing matter, she obviously felt, than Brent's uneasy questions. "Is Carr a friend of yours?"

"Never heard of him until this minute," Brent said. "But whatever happened to that girl last night—especially if he did it—I'm concerned."

Val whisked her story to Garrett's desk and her blue-green eyes became curious.

"Odelle Quinn's her professional name. A night club singer, married to Carr, who's usually in the show with her as master of ceremonies. She's a beautiful girl, Bill, but why fret over another man's wife whom you've never met?"

"Is this true?" Brent insisted, tapping the news item. "She fell down stairs?"

"The boys at headquarters are pretty sure her husband tossed her down. But with a sprained wrist and an assortment of bruises she wouldn't admit it and wouldn't press charges."

"I was afraid of this," Brent said in a moaning tone. "Did it happen while they were having a spat?"

"That's putting it mildly. More likely he was flying at her throat. But how'd you know? I didn't mention it in the story."

"Never mind," Brent said. "Don't stop now."

"If you insist on the sordid details, Carr raised such a racket that the family next door phoned the cops. It might have developed into a swell front page yarn, but the prowl car got there too soon, I'm sorry to say."

"You're sorry no gore was spilled and I'm thankful!" Brent said fervently. "Because, Val, I'm responsible. This whole thing's on my conscience."

"Really, Bill? But how?"

"No able-bodied man ever had a screwier job. I tell you, Val"—he was intensely earnest about it—"this misbegotten column of mine is not only poisoning my very soul but driving me nuts."

"Don't take it so much to heart," Val said, smiling. "Why not simply pound out the stuff and forget it?"

"I wish I could," Brent said. "But it preys on my mind. I lie awake nights. I beat my brains all day over half a dozen letters of advice given with the very best of intentions, and all night I toss and wonder how many lives I've unwittingly wrecked. I—"

"Lora!" an imperious voice called. Garrett was shouting from his desk in the corner. "Miss Lorne, if you please!"

Blunt chin lowered, Bill Brent responded. He responded while the whole city staff grinned, because he, God help him, was the love oracle who hid behind the phoney name of Lora Lorne.

A portrait graced the column in which Lora Lorne publicly admonished her family of thousands as to their most intimate tribulations. It pictured her as a venerable soul with wise eyes peeping from kindly crinkles, combs in her snowy hair, eye-glasses dangling from a reel pinned to her sympathetic shoulder—whereas Brent, resembling her not in the least, was a husky who'd once smashed his nose against a Princeton goalpost, who wore size eleven brogues and liked his steaks rare.

"Don't call me by that name!" he said through his teeth, frowning down at his city editor.

SIX DAYS a week the copyrighted likeness of Lora Lorne turned a smug smile upon her readers—and nobody knew who the old dame actually was. Probably she was a creature living only in some forgotten artist's imagination. Non-existent or not, Brent had a definite feeling for her. He wholeheartedly hated her and he'd lie down under a five-ton truck rather than let the world learn that for months now he'd been forced to wear her saccharine false-face.

"Some day soon, Garrett," he threatened, "you're going to rub it in once too often and I'm going to pull you apart like a bug."

Having come out of the first World War a major at twenty-three, Garrett wasn't intimidated. A ruddy-featured man whose bearing was still stiffly military, his angular jaw was that of a disciplinarian.

"Where's today's column, Grandma?" he inquired in the same taunting tone.

Brent had four pages of copy in his hands and for a moment he fought an impulse to deliver them squarely between Garrett's granite-gray eyes. A long succession of seeresses had perpetrated the esoteric fiction of Lora Lorne since the column was begun twenty-two years ago, but Brent was the first man ever to wear her petticoats and the humiliation of it was getting to be more than he could bear. But he took a grip on himself.

"Here. Now let's be reasonable about this thing," he suggested, his manner becoming fraternal. "It's gone on too damned long and I've already suffered out of all proportion to my sins. Besides, look at the harm I'm doing." He placed the galley proof before Garrett. "There's a sample. It's just sheer good luck the girl wasn't killed."

"Ten days ago," Garrett reminded him, ignoring the evidence, "you received certain instructions from our publisher."

"Ten days ago I also received a letter from a worried young wife," Brent said. "She signed just her initials, O.Q. Her problem was one that's flung in my teeth twenty times a day. Her husband was cooling off on her, she wrote, and please, dear Miss Lorne, what could she do to revive the old love?"

"Our publisher, Mr. Palmer," Garrett said, "instructed you to write a six weeks' reserve supply of the column."

"Trying hard to help O.Q. keep her precious husband," Brent continued doggedly, "I answered that she should remind him she's still desirable to other men. In other words, arouse his jealousy. A hoary treatment, Garrett—and dangerous. I've been having nightmares ever since, about how it might be working out."

"So far you haven't even gotten started on those thirty-six extra columns," Garrett said.

"See for yourself just what my inspired guidance adds up to," Brent persisted. "A quarrel, a fight, the cops wading in, a public scandal, the girl hurt. Garrett, he might have broken her neck—murdered her. And if he had, I'd be the primary cause of her death. My God, I get a chill when I think of it—and you just take it as a matter of course, like a rockribbed gravedigger."

"You're over-straining your contract, you know, by neglecting to follow orders," Garrett added. "Do you want me to report that to Mr. Palmer?"

PALING A little, Brent earnestly bent over him. "Listen to me. The people who write in to Lora Lorne are bewildered, in serious trouble. Often their homes, their whole lives are at stake. Some of their problems would give Solomon a headache. I have to dash off hit-or-miss answers to questions that would stump a convention of psychiatrists and social workers."

"Arthur Brisbane once did it," Garrett said calmly. "And Dorothy Dix has more readers than Walter Lippmann, Dorothy Thompson, Hugh Johnson and Westbrook Pegler combined."

"That is not the point!" Brent asserted. "I spend all my spare time reading Freud, Jung and Adler, but the three of 'em working together personally couldn't do justice to the column I'm expected to concoct. It's all I can manage to sweat out one a day and you torture me with talk about thirty-six extras. Garrett, on my word of honor, this thing's got me punchdrunk. In the name of suffering humanity tell me I've turned in my last Lora Lorne, won't you?"

"Brent," Garrett said, unmoved by his sincerity, "you still need a lesson. I brought you here from New York and contracted to pay you a fancy salary because I wanted the best reporter I could get."

"And you got him," Brent said.

Garrett shook his head. "You let me down. You paid no attention when I warned you to lay off the liquor and three separate times you were missing the biggest part of a week. Your mind was on women instead of your work."

"This town is so dead compared with Manhattan there's hardly anything else—"

"When you finally go back to reporting, if you ever do—I have a very satisfactory police reporter at the moment, you see"—Garrett smiled at Val Randall—"you'll be cured for life and damned glad to handle your job properly."

"At this very minute I'm a reformed character in all departments, and you know it," Brent said. "I swear to you, Garrett, I wouldn't squawk if I weren't sure the lousy column is doing a lot more harm than good. It's an agency of evil, nothing less."

"Mr. Palmer thinks it's our most helpful and popular feature." Garrett's pencil left a blue gash across a page of copy. "And I'm too busy to argue."

"Then don't. Simply turn the column over to Val, put me back on the police trick where I belong," Brent persisted, "and I solemnly promise you—"

"Cut it out!" Garrett snapped. "You've already promised in writing to accept any and all assignments without question, but if you want to break your contract, get sued and blacklisted, go ahead. Otherwise you'll keep on being Lora Lorne exactly as long as I see fit. If that's clear, Lora, you can start rustling up those thirty-six extra columns."

"I warned you, don't call me—"

Brent clamped his jaw, snatched up the proof Garrett had brushed aside and resignedly carried his worries back to the cubicle, no more commodious than a broom closet, which relegated him to a position next to the morgue and isolated him from those privileged to handle the news.

He dug again into that mound of hated letters and uncovered a telephone directory. There was no listing under the names of Odelle Quinn or Glen Carr. Persisting, he called Information and was told: "The number is Heights, four-r thr-ree thr-ee ni-yun."

A woman's voice came over the wire with disconcerting vehemence. "It's not true, Glen! You're mad to think it. Especially of a man old enough to be— Hello?"

"Miss Quinn? The *Recorder* calling. We're making a survey of our services to our readers. Recently, I believe, you wrote to our Miss Lorne. Would you mind telling us whether you obtained satisfactory results, and if—"

"Results!" Miss Quinn wailed. "I'm so overwhelmed with them right now I ache all over and can't even talk!"

The connection crashed off in Brent's ear.

He wagged his head and asked for the number again. The distant bell rang and went unanswered and at the end of a full minute he was squirming in his chair. Suddenly he abandoned the phone and caught up his topcoat. Despite the scowl Garrett sent after him, he strode out the swinging doors—driven by the fear that his well-meant advice might even yet destroy the life of a young woman he'd never seen.

AS A MARCH twilight settled, gray and blustery, Brent veered to the curb and cut the ignition. The address printed in Val's report, he saw, was that of a duplex dwelling near the corner of Thirteenth and Maple Streets, a section posted with signs cautioning *Hospital—Quiet*. He was crossing the sidewalk when the entrance of the house swung open and a girl hurried out.

"I've had enough!" she flung over her shoulder to someone inside whom Brent couldn't see. "This time I'm through, finished! Say what you please, I'm answering that call, going straight to Doctor Dockery's office—and I'm not coming back. How do you like that, you hot-headed brute?"

Startled by her anger, Brent watched her run off the porch, her coat flying, clutching a purse in one hand, holding an insane hat on her head with the other. Furiously she kept running until, turning at the corner, her high heels flashed from sight.

Someone inside—probably the man she had so heatedly denounced—slammed the door. Not interested in him and assuming the young woman was Odelle Quinn, Brent purposefully started after her.

The name of Dr. Dockery, whom she had mentioned, had recently become known to him and fortunately the physician's office was nearby. He turned twice more, first into Twelfth Street and past the Heights Hospital, then to a doorway in the next building where a bronze plaque bore Dr. Seldon Dockery's name above that of Dr. Eric Kenelm. Another sign invited all comers to walk in, and Brent doggedly did so.

The luxurious reception-room was empty. The door of Dr. Dockery's consultation-room was closed and bore a card reading: *Will return at 3:00 P.M.* Another door connecting with a second office in the rear—Dr. Kenelm's, probably—stood open revealing an unoccupied desk. Miss Quinn was nowhere to be seen.

Though the silence in the suite hinted that it was deserted, Brent felt a strange sense of presences. Puzzled, he sat down impatiently to wait. Presently he heard whispers which somehow stirred his apprehension. They were a secretive, sibilant sound that seemed to issue from no certain point.

And suddenly he was chilled by a scream—a woman's choking, throaty screech of terror.

Its echoes ringing about him, Brent sprang up. Now there were scuffling noises in one of the other rooms—feet scraping on the floor, a thump, a clatter. And next—shots! A single cracking small caliber report jarred the walls, followed by two more, closely spaced.

Then a hush.

Brent stood rooted, full of a prickly dread that the thing he had wanted to forestall had already happened.

CHAPTER TWO
CORPSE WANTED

BRENT THRUST against the door of Dr. Dockery's office and found it locked. Quickly striding through a second door into the other office, he arrived at a third. From his previous visits he recalled that it connected with the treatment-room which separated Dr. Dockery's office from this one. Again Brent tried the knob and again a lock balked him.

Turning back, he stopped short. The middle door, through which he had entered this inner room, was moving. Propelled by an invisible hand, it swung shut. Even as

Brent stepped toward it he heard the squeak of a key in the lock.

He pulled at it and pushed. It was immovable. A sweeping glance, told him, moreover, that there was no window in the room. Someone had crept silently upon him and made him a prisoner.

His strap-watch read just 5:11, which agreed exactly with the clock on the desk. There was no noise—no slightest sound to indicate that Brent was anything but alone in the suite. He peered about, nerves tight, temperature soaring with the realization that he had a piece of front-page news by the tail—love specialist though he might be—and instinct brought his hand to the telephone.

The dial gave off a waspish whir. Urgently he murmured into the transmitter. "Police headquarters. Make it fast.... Homicide!" he said while the dead silence continued around him. "Captain Russo? Brent. There's been a shooting. Only one thing I can tell you. It happened in Doctor Seldon Dockery's office ten seconds ago. The sooner you get here—"

"Dockery? Lord!" the hollow voice of Captain Max Russo answered. "Coming!"

Feeling himself swinging into his old stride, Brent spun off the *Recorder's* number. "City desk.... Garrett, I've got something well worth an extra. While your pretty pet was probably off somewhere powdering her nose, I've been busy—"

"We never put out extras and neither did the sheet you decorated in New York," Garrett cut in. "Anything on police belongs to Val."

Brent alertly watched the door behind which the shots had blasted. "My department is still exclusively *l'amour,* is that what you think? You're going to be very much surprised when I tell you—"

"Quit clowning!" Garrett snapped. "If you've stumbled on any news, I'll send Val around."

"But this would frighten the child," Brent said. "She's never handled a major crime, you know. This is a job for a veteran, so tell her to clear out my desk, Garrett, because I'm going to take over."

"Not quite," Garrett said, his tone bored. "Val will pick it up in the usual way in the morning."

"By that time it'll be far beyond the reach of her lovely but incompetent fingers. If your personal solicitude for the young lady is so great as to mislead you into muffing a hot story, Garrett—well, that's your responsibility and fine with Bill Brent. I don't insist on the police trick exclusively, you see. In fact, I'll settle for your job as city editor."

He cradled the instrument, listened and heard nothing but the ticking of the clock on the desk. Afire with the hope that all this would mean his salvation, he looked about for a means of forcing his way out of this walnut-paneled trap.

There was a hat-tree. He could use it to batter a door down. He grasped it up, gave the nearest knob another tentative twist—and his breath stopped. He stared as the door connecting with the reception-room swung freely open!

BRENT STRAIGHTENED slowly and lowered the rack. The most promising object he could use as a weapon was a massive onyx ashtray. He gripped it and edged over the sill. The reception-room was still empty. It looked exactly the same as before. Cautiously working closer to the scene of the disturbance, he opened the way into Dr. Dockery's office.

It was also deserted. Nothing appeared to be disturbed. Freshly dusted, neatly arranged, it seemed to be waiting for the physician to hustle back to his chair for his evening appointments. Brent moved past a bank of file cabinets, advancing still nearer to the source of the gunshots, and looked into the treatment-room.

Its darkness held him back until, clutching the ashtray in one hand and reaching in with the other, he found the wall-switch. A brilliant ceiling reflected from a metal operating table covered with spotless sheets, from white cabinets containing glittering instruments on glass shelves. Every bottle was precisely aligned and the waxed floor shone. Nowhere was there a sign of disruption.

Nothing indicated that anyone had been here a few minutes ago, and Brent might have suspected he had dreamed the whole thing—except that there was a faint smell of burned gunpowder already fading out a partly opened window, and something green was wedged behind one of the enameled cabinets.

Brent went first to the window, raised the white curtain and gazed into a bare, sheer-walled shaftway. He turned back, then, to the green thing. Whatever it might be it had evidently fallen unnoticed and lodged against the wainscot, almost out of sight. He was tugging at it when he was surprised by a quick decisive clicking of heels on the floor.

The man who stopped to stare down at Brent was obviously a physician. He had appeared at Dr. Dockery's desk, was halted in the act of pulling several wrapped bottles of medicine from his overcoat. He and Brent, mutually startled, estimated each other warily, without moving.

Then, as a strained moment ended, the doctor swiftly about-faced and marched out.

Brent heard his heels beating through the reception-room and into the other office. Quickly there followed the noise of a drawer jerked open. Next, the opposite door of the treatment-room was flung wide and the young doctor reappeared, his right hand lifted waist-high.

Heart spurting, Brent found himself the focus of a huge black automatic's stare.

"I hope you won't move," said the doctor. "If you do, I'll have to shoot you."

His free hand groped for the phone. The deep creases around his mouth gave his face masculine character and a prematurely seasoned aspect. He appeared to be tired but dynamic, a doctor who worked diligently and long, without a thought of sparing himself. In his steady surgeon's hand the automatic had a particularly ominous look.

"I don't want to shoot you, because then I'd have to go to the trouble of patching you up." He said it briskly, nudged the phone so that it fell into its two parts and made ready to dial zero. "I'm too busy and as far as you're concerned, probing for the bullet usually hurts, you know."

"I can imagine," Brent said. "It's not necessary to call the cops." Though this wasn't the first time he'd contemplated the business end of a firearm, it was still a situation he couldn't face casually. "I've already called them."

The doctor's smile was quick, good-natured and skeptical. "If you're the thief who robbed these offices about two months ago, you shouldn't have thought you could get away with it twice."

"I'm Brent, from the *Recorder*. If Doctor Dockery were here, he'd verify that. I got acquainted with him in the

Chase case. Ducky Chase, who covered sports for us—killed by a hit-and-run driver. Remember him?"

Hesitating over the phone, the doctor considered this, but the automatic didn't waver. "Not personally. I was attending a medical convention in Chicago at the time. You might really be a newspaperman, as you say, and still be—"

"A burglar?" Brent turned his head, listening. "Hadn't thought of trying my hand at it."

"Then," the doctor demanded incisively, pointing to the costly ashtray which Brent was still holding, "what are you doing with that?"

Brent could only shrug and put it down. "It seems the cops are arriving right now. You might ask them for a character reference."

HARD SHOES ran across the sidewalk and the entrance opened. The two radio bureau men who hurried through the reception-room had their hands on their holstered service revolvers. They paused, glancing uncertainly from the doctor to Brent.

"Hello, Barnes, hello, Filiski," Brent greeted them. "Would you mind telling this chap that my racket is reporting crime not committing it?"

The doctor, in his astonishment lowered his gun a little. "I'm Eric Kenelm," he explained to the patrolmen. "Doctor Seldon Dockery and I share these offices. When I came in a moment ago I found this man sneaking about. Naturally I thought—in fact, I still do." To Brent he added: "Those rooms are left locked when nobody's here. Since the robbery we've kept everything closed up tight, except this reception-room. How'd you get in there? Just what were you doing?"

"I can't exactly say," Brent admitted, "but I thought at the time—"

He broke off at the sound of more footsteps. Again the door opened. Captain Max Russo appeared with three civilian-garbed members of the Homicide Squad at his heels. Prepared to go immediately to work, they reconnoitered through the two offices and the treatment-room and drifted to a pause with expressions as puzzled as those of the other two patrolmen.

"Well, Bill?" Captain Russo said. He was as gaunt and cadaverous as any dead man he had ever officially examined. With his dark, somber eyes and the sepulchral quality of his voice, he gave the impression of having just risen off a slab in the city morgue. "Well, Bill, where is it?"

"Damned if I know, Captain," Brent confessed.

Now Dr. Kenelm put his gun down. "I don't understand this! I come in here, find every door open and a stranger prowling around, and now the place is swarming with policemen. I think an explanation is in order." Of Brent he demanded: "You still haven't said just what you were looking for."

"A corpse," Brent answered.

Dr. Kenelm stared. "Whose corpse?"

"I'm not sure, but I think a lady's."

"Is this your idea of a joke? What led you to expect to find any lady's corpse in this place?"

"Three gunshots," Brent informed him. "When I came in, I'm reasonably certain there was a girl in this room with someone else. At exactly five eleven I heard the sounds of a struggle and the three reports, so I started looking for somebody who'd been shot. Doesn't sound unreasonable, does it?"

"Except for the fact that there's no victim of a shooting in here now, Bill," Captain Max Russo pointed out.

"I know, but don't ask me why not," Brent said. "You're not half as puzzled as I am."

"Who was the girl with?" Captain Russo asked.

"I've no idea."

"Who was the girl, then?"

Brent put on a blank expression and evaded the question with a shrug.

"You don't know anything about it," Max Russo commented dryly, "except you're sure somebody got killed."

"I'm not even sure of that much," Brent muttered, "— now."

Dr. Kenelm turned a baffled glance into every face, then, to Brent's relief, replaced the automatic in the drawer. Briskly entering the treatment-room, he gazed around while Captain Russo and the Homicide Squad crowded after him. None of them saw the green thing lodged behind the cabinet for the reason that Brent had quickly shifted so as to screen it with his legs.

"Not a sign of violence," Captain Russo said. "Not a single speck of blood. You haven't been your old self lately, Bill, but you haven't started having hallucinations, have you?"

"What about Doctor Dockery?" Brent asked, while Dr. Kenelm glanced into two supply closets where no dead body was to be found. "Isn't it possible the girl came here to keep an appointment with him? Wouldn't he know something about this?"

"Not likely," Dr. Kenelm answered. "He had an appendectomy scheduled for five o'clock. In any case, it's ridiculous to imagine he had anything to do with it. All his waking hours are devoted to saving lives, not destroying them."

"Where was the operation to be performed?" Captain Russo asked. "At the Heights Hospital, next door?"

"Yes," Dr. Kenelm said. "He's the head. Probably he's finished by now."

"Let's go over and talk to him," Max Russo suggested. "If he doesn't know anything about it, there'll be nothing left to do but ask him to treat you, Bill, as an advanced case of alcoholic dementia."

"Damn it, I might imagine whispers and even gunshots, but not locked doors," Brent retorted. "Besides, keep the record straight, Captain. I haven't so much as smelled a cork since Garrett made me—"

CHECKING HIMSELF there, he lingered as Dr. Kenelm went back to his desk. Brent was still interested in the green object lodged behind the cabinet, but he had no opportunity at the moment to give it a closer look. With Captain Russo glancing at him dubiously, he was obliged to follow and shut the door between.

"Do you want to examine my gun?" Dr. Kenelm asked.

"The shots I heard were fired by a smaller one," Brent said. "The pitch of the reports told me that much."

"Very helpful, Bill," Captain Russo said acridly, "but what we really need is some sort of victim. Unless we find one in a hurry, you'll be shown up as the same sort of maniac who turns in false fire-alarms."

Brent thrust his hands deep into his pockets and stalked out. The two radio patrolmen sped back to their tour and the three Homicide men ducked into their car while Brent walked between Russo and Dr. Kenelm. In a driveway that flanked the hospital and led past the accident ward, an ambulance was awaiting the next emergency call. They crossed it, the sharp wind tugging at their coats, and parted the glass doors of the street entrance.

"Who left those offices locked this after-noon?" Brent asked as they crossed the lobby. "Did you lock them, Doctor Kenelm?"

"Yes."

"Then who else but you or Doctor Dockery could have opened them?"

They entered an elevator before Dr. Kenelm answered. "I don't know. No one else has keys, except the cleaning woman who comes in every day—at least, as far as I can say. I hadn't been back since noon. As for Doctor Dockery—well, you'd better ask him yourself."

They encountered Dr. Dockery as they stepped from the elevator on the top floor. He was just emerging from the scrub-up room, a huge man with a shaggy gray-streaked head and jovial eyes twinkling behind his rimless glasses.

"Hullo, Eric, Captain Russo, Mr. Brent, hullo, hullo!" He hustled past, into the elevator and began peeling off his sterile jacket. "An officer of the law and a newspaper-man—what's up? Looking for me?"

They were starting down again.

"To ask if you've been back at your office within the past half hour or so," Brent explained.

"I've been operating," Dr. Dockery said, turning his starched cuffs over his hairy arms. "A mastoidectomy immediately followed by an appendectomy. Just finished, both patients doing splendidly."

"Then at five eleven you were in the operating-room," Brent persisted, "surrounded by nurses and assistants?"

"Of course." The elevator stopped at the ground floor level and, hustling again, Dr. Dockery led them into an office located opposite the admission desk. "Dear me, this sounds almost as if I'm being asked for an alibi. What's happened?"

"Nobody seems to know, Seldon, except Mr. Brent," Eric Kenelm answered with a smile, "and even he's a bit foggy about it. He insists he heard shots fired, but we don't seem to be able to learn at whom or why."

"Shots?" Struck with astonishment, Dr. Dockery nevertheless kept moving under the pressure of severe demands on his time. "In my office?" he asked, getting into his coat. "Good heavens, how is it possible? You weren't there, Eric?"

"I've been calling on patients all afternoon, busy every minute," Kenelm answered. "According to Mr. Brent, it was just before I came back—if it happened at all."

"It certainly happened!" Brent insisted. "Didn't either of you gentlemen make an appointment with a young woman for a few minutes after five at the office?"

Now Dr. Dockery was reading several notes left for him on the desk. "I've been operating, as I've said—since four thirty. Did you, Eric?"

"Not I." Dr. Kenelm was inclined to treat the whole matter as an absurdity. "Besides, I don't know, offhand, anyone I'd have liked to arrange to shoot."

"Then," Brent said, with dogged seriousness, "it was done by someone who came in from outside expressly for the purpose of shooting someone else. Do both of you have your keys?"

Dr. Kenelm promptly produced his key-case, and Dr. Dockery, getting into his huge overcoat, fished in his pockets.

"Never can find mine," he said, hustling from the room. "Captain, I've no explanation to offer." Abandoning his search, he impatiently threw up his hands. "Ah, the keys are probably in the car. All this is very puzzling, but so far as I know I can be of no help whatever."

"Tend to your sick, Doctor, by all means," Captain Russo said quietly, "and leave the dead to me—if any."

DR. DOCKERY squared his shoulders. "Thank you, Captain." In his voice Brent sensed a strain. "I make it a point to have an early and leisurely dinner with my wife. It's almost the only chance I have to visit with her, you know. Eric will give you what help he can, of course, and I—I'll be off."

He strode down the corridor, eyes so set and fired with such a strange, deep-burning fierceness that Brent was startled and prompted to follow him.

"Doctor Dockery!"

The physician turned at the emergency entrance, his strong jaw squared. "Yes, Brent?"

"Sorry to bother you with this," Brent said as they stepped out, "but do you have among your patients a young woman named Odelle Quinn, or Odelle Carr?"

"Quinn? Carr?" His bushy eyebrows leveled to a line, Dr. Dockery strode into the dark parking court behind the hospital. "Yes—yes, I have. Recently—two or three office calls, I think. Is she connected in some way with what you say happened?"

"Possibly," Brent answered, studying him. "Mind telling me whether there's anything seriously wrong with her? Anything, that is, to make her give up her night club job and settle down in this dull town?"

"No, nothing like that. An *ulsus ventriculi*—mild case of gastric erosion, common in persons as high-strung as she is. I prescribed antuitrin S and the condition was responding. At least, she hasn't come back within the past several weeks."

"Not last night or this morning, to have a sprained wrist strapped up?"

"Wrist?" Dr. Dockery opened the door of his black sedan. "No."

"Maybe Doctor Kenelm fixed it up for her."

With a scalpel-edged glance at Brent, the physician ducked into the car and found his keys dangling from the ignition lock. "Very unlikely," he answered. "Since she's my patient, he'd have referred her to me. He hasn't mentioned her—don't think he knows her."

"By the way," Brent said, "let me remind you again that you haven't sent us Ducky Chase's bill."

The engine hummed and Dr. Dockery impatiently released the handbrake.

"Don't intend to, Brent. Didn't leave a red cent, did he? His sister hasn't any money, I'm told. You'd have to take up another collection at the office, wouldn't you? Well, you newspaper chaps are underpaid but some of my clients have more money than they can use. Forget it."

"That's swell of you," Brent said sincerely, bending in the window, "considering that you stayed up all night, two nights running, trying to keep Ducky alive. We appreciate how hard you tried to save him."

"Nothing, Brent, nothing," the physician said brusquely, engaging the gears. "Sorry I didn't succeed. Goodnight."

Thoughtfully Brent watched the car glide up the driveway and turn into the street. He went slowly in the same direction and saw, through the glass entrance. Captain

Russo talking with Dr. Kenelm in the lobby. He turned to the next building, his manner casual for the benefit of the three detectives waiting in the Homicide car, and sidled into the reception-room used jointly by the Drs. Dockery and Kenelm.

Standing there in the quiet, he mentally retraced the daring moves made by a murderer who had held him just short of becoming an eye-witness.

He returned to the treatment-room with an ear kept cocked for the sounds of any approach. The green thing remained where he had seen it, lodged behind the cabinet, its existence unknown to anyone but him. He dropped to his knees, slid it upward, then pulled it free—a woman's purse.

IT CONTAINED, besides the usual feminine clutter—lipstick, handkerchief, comb, bobby-pins and vial of expensive perfume—a driver's license and an automobile registration issued to Odelle Carr, 715 West Thirteenth Street, blond, violet eyes, weight one hundred ten, age twenty-four.

Both, Brent saw, were dated only two weeks ago, and the car was a 1941 Cadillac convertible. There was also a purse wadded full of banknotes, but he didn't take time to count them. Instead, he stuffed everything back, replaced the purse exactly as he'd found it and, acting on a new impulse, shifted to Dr. Dockery's desk.

He dialed City 1515. "Criminal Identification Bureau... That you, Mike? Brent. I'm with Captain Russo on a rod case. He wants you to look into the pistol permit file. Is there a small gun—twenty-two or twenty-five caliber—on record under the name of Dockery or Kenelm?"

"Hold it a minute, Bill…. Here's a thirty-eight automatic licensed by Doctor Eric Kenelm. I remember, he bought it after his office got stuck up."

"Look again."

"Here's a twenty-five Colt auto, pocket model."

Brent's scalp tingled. "That may be it. Who—"

"Claudia Dockery."

"Claudia?"

"This one's dated years ago, Bill. Name changed. Used to be Claudia Lacroze. New address, too—four ten Sycamore Drive, same as the doctor's home."

"Reason for need?" Brent asked quickly.

"Says here, protection of valuables and sport."

"Sport?"

"We get lots of those, Bill. Usually people with pull. They just like to shoot at targets, that's all, including some dames. I don't mean dames as targets. Dames *at* targets. Think it's a bad idea, myself."

"So do I," Brent said. "Thanks."

His nerves felt like high potential wires. Eyes alert, he shifted to the file cabinets—a row of them packed with patients' case histories.

Under *C* there was no folder bearing Odelle Carr's name. Under *Q* there was no data that might apply to the same young woman under the name of Quinn. Brent even searched for additional reports in the drawers of the physician's desk, and there his purpose again failed.

Not a word of Odell Quinn Carr's pathological record was to be found in Dr. Dockery's office.

Leaving, absorbed in his reflections, Brent saw Captain Max Russo appear at the door of the Heights Hospital. Because he wanted to avoid any more embarrassing questions, he side-stepped and walked down the passageway until Russo's receding footfalls told him the coast was again clear.

Instead of retracing his steps then, he gazed across the parking space behind the hospital. A wall separated the cement court from the back yards of the houses on the next street. One of them, directly opposite, was the home of Odelle Quinn. The kitchen was lighted. Someone was circling about inside, casting a restless shadow on the window curtains.

Brent wound his way past a dozen cars and paused at the wall for a closer look. With a chilly tingle, he estimated a shortcut from the rear door of the Carr home, on Thirteenth, to the entrance of Dr. Dockery's office on Twelfth. Across the yard, over the wall, through the court, then along the driveway and finally a few paces up the sidewalk, and it was done—not more than three hundred feet, a distance easily covered in thirty seconds by a person in rapid motion.

CHAPTER THREE

DO KILLERS BAKE COOKIES?

BRENT HOISTED himself over the wall. Quietly approaching the rear porch, he crept up the steps and leaned over the rail in order to look into the window.

The man in the kitchen was a lean forty-odd, with a jaunty mustache and thin hair dyed a glistening black. His shirt-sleeves were rolled up, his collar open. Val had described Odelle Quinn's husband as a professional master of ceremonies, and though Brent couldn't guess why he was tarrying so far from Broadway, he looked the part.

Brent watched curiously as Glen Carr drew a shallow baking tin from the oven and shoveled cookies out of it. Carr then took up another tin filled with white discs and slid it into the oven in place of the first. Next, he spooned little balls of batter from a mixing bowl and flattened them with a tumbler over the mouth of which a piece of cloth was stretched. All the while he whistled a soft, peculiarly mournful tune.

This, Brent felt, was a strange activity for a night-club wit, particularly one who possibly had committed a vicious shooting only a few minutes ago.

His mind buzzing with questions, Brent crept off the porch and circled to the front door. He was about to thumb the bell-button when, again glancing through a window, he saw something that changed his tactics.

On the table lay an uncapped fountain pen, a blue envelope and a sheet of matching stationery half filled with a rapid scrawl. Tilting his head, Brent made out the all-too-familiar salutation, *Dear Lora Lorne*—

He couldn't read the rest because the letter was upside down, but Odelle Quinn had evidently written a new appeal for help. His concern prompted him to try the sash. Finding it unlatched, he raised it, making as little noise as possible, and hopefully put his head in.

Please, Miss Lorne, he read, leaning far over the sill, *answer right away or something terrible might happen. I'm frantic because your advice has worked out entirely too well. My husband has a beastly temper, and now that I've made him jealous he threatens horrible things and refuses to believe me when I tell him there really isn't any*—

There it came to a dark, abrupt stop, leaving Brent feeling miserably guilty.

Hearing a noise, he looked up. Glen Carr had stepped into the living-room. A bruise marked his chin and a scratch across his nose was healing. In one hand he had a gob of butter which he was applying to another pan. Standing still, he fixed his narrow-set eyes on Brent.

"Won't you come all the way in?" he asked.

Straightening from his embarrassing position, Brent grinned. "I'd like to. But I really came to see Miss Quinn—business reasons, of course."

Carr turned, vanished, then reappeared at the front door. "People usually enter through here," he remarked with an air of bohemian ease that belied the sharpness of his scrutiny.

"Reason I was reading that letter, I'm from the *Recorder*. Name's Brent. Mind talking with me a few minutes?"

"Why not?" Carr stepped back with a welcoming gesture. "But I've got to watch my cookies or they'll burn."

Brent followed him into the kitchen and sniffed the air. "I go for cookies. Cookies and coffee—nothing better."

"Have a chair," Carr invited. "Have a cookie. Glad you dropped in, even if you took an unconventional route. Up until now it's been a lonely evening."

"Thanks," Brent said, sitting and reaching into the crock Carr proffered him. The cookie was still warm. "Ah, peanut butter. Very good."

"I also have some of the walnut icebox kind. Thin as paper, crisp and delicious. Would you like one of those?"

"Thanks again." Brent took one of the walnut icebox kind in his other hand and nodded his complete approval. "Best I ever tasted. You see, I'm making a survey for the paper and your wife wouldn't talk to me over the phone."

"She's out," Carr said, peeking inside the oven. "Sorry there isn't any coffee ready, but I'll make some. Or how about a glass of milk?"

"Milk will be fine." Brent was estimating Carr and pretending to be unaware that Carr was estimating him. "You surprise me. I'd never expect to find a worldly chap like you puttering about a kitchen."

"Cooking is my hobby," Carr explained. "I love to cook and my wife hates it. Welsh rarebits and *crêpes Suzette* are really my specialties. Seldom found a chance to keep in practice until now, always being on the road. We're entertainers. To me a home is a dream come true."

"You seem to be very nicely settled." Glancing about as he munched, Brent saw that all the furnishings were new and expensive. "Been here long?"

CARR'S EYES grew black and pointed as needles. "We've been here a few weeks."

"Nice place. You had to sign a lease. Got a long engagement in the city?"

"We're retired," Carr said shortly.

"This your home town, or your wife's?"

"No." Carr's voice crackled. "And I can't say I like it here."

"Where'd you live before you moved into this house?"

"An apartment near our work—the Zombie Club." For a moment Carr's mask of geniality dropped and Brent saw a hint of the savagery that might flare up in him. "Just what did you come here to find out?"

"Wanted to ask your wife about a personal matter. Could I have another of those peanut butters?"

"Certainly." Carr brought the crock to Brent. "Help yourself to as many as you'd like. All I can tell you is that she's gone off somewhere and should be back by now."

"Does she often have reason to write to the lovelorn column?"

Carr was sullenly silent. He brought Brent a glass of milk from the refrigerator. He rubbed the scratch on his nose and frowned.

"This year's pastime," he answered at length. "Last year it was astrology. She's not for your survey. Count her out."

"Why?"

"She likes to act helpless and bewildered, but she always knows what she's doing. That woman never needed any help from Lora Lorne or anyone else. To look at her you'd think she's just an innocent child, but when it comes to figuring out a fast one she can give Lora Lorne cards and spades."

"I wouldn't question that," Brent said. "But why should she write to our Miss Lorne if it wasn't just what it seemed to be—worry over a rift between you and herself?"

Carr smiled thinly. "Maybe it was because she wanted the answer Lora Lorne gave her—to help her cover up."

"Cover up what?"

The gleam of Carr's too-white teeth vanished. Now he was scowling at Brent, breathing faster. "You want to know too much that's none of your business. I'm not talking to any newspapermen. And I don't think you came here just to ask about a letter."

Brent met his thrust with candor. "You are right, I didn't. It's a hell of a lot more serious than that."

"Just how serious?"

"As serious as anything can come."

Suddenly Carr was pale, his eyes wide. "Damn that—I told her she couldn't— If something's wrong, I had nothing to do with—" He pressed his lips, fear and fury on his thin face. "Don't play cat and mouse with me. Come out with it."

"O.K.," Brent said, sipping milk. "Where'd your wife go?"

"I don't know. But don't ask questions. Tell me—"

"You know, all right. She told you when she left. She went to Doctor Dockery's office. Why did she, since she's not one of his patients? And why hasn't she come back?"

"I'm a hoofer mostly," Carr said with a click, "not a mind-reader."

"You don't need to be psychic in order to tell me where *you've* been since five o'clock."

"Been?" Carr snapped. "Here. Where else?"

"Following your wife."

Carr's face was getting redder, the jet of his eyes more intense. "Look at the pile of cookies I've baked. It's a job you can't leave. I began right after my wife left and I've been at it every minute since." He took a menacing step toward Brent. "What is this? What's happened to Odelle?"

"She hasn't come back," Brent said levelly. "I don't think she'll ever come back—alive. Or maybe I'm telling you something you already know."

Carr stood still, hands hardened into lean fists, face sapped of all color, staring down.

"She was playing too dangerous a game," Brent said. "Too fast and loose and it got her. Or do you already know that?"

HE SAT with the glass half full of milk in one hand, a fragment of cookie in the other, tense under Carr's wild eyes. Both of them were utterly unprepared for the vicious noise that crashed between them.

A first sharp gunshot broke out of the silence bringing with it a tinkle of spattering glass particles. Brent began straining up, staring first at the amazed expression on Carr's face, then at the growing spot of red on the side of Carr's shirt. He was twisting to look behind him when the second shot cracked. He leaped away as white-yellow flame licked a third time through the shattered window.

Carr spun about, propelling himself toward the living-room. He stumbled against a chair, knocked it over, sagged against the wall. Scrambling for shelter, Brent saw that the wounded man was leaning across the door frame, blocking the only safe way out, that the whole kitchen was in the line of fire. There was a pantry standing open. Brent jumped in, pulled the door shut and shrank with a gasp against the loaded shelves.

It was a fearful retreat but Brent had no weapon, no other defense against the gun, and at least he was unscathed. He noticed that he was still holding the milk-filmed glass, that now it was empty. He dropped it. Then he heard quick footfalls somewhere in the rear. As they faded in an uncertain direction, he peered out the small pantry window and saw blackness—caught no glimpse of a killer making an escape.

Brent pushed the door and it wouldn't open. There must be a spring latch on the outside. He shoved harder and grew hot-faced. "Again!" he blurted.

Now there were faltering footfalls inside the house. Brent traced them as they moved across the living-room, then unsteadily up the stairs. In a moment they sounded almost directly overhead.

Drawing back, he lifted one leg and drove his heel against the door. He was out of the pantry a second after the latch tore off.

Bits of glass glittered beneath the broken window. The white streak across the floor was the milk Brent had spilled during his headlong retreat. Thin black fumes were pouring up from the oven. Brent ignored that and snatched open the rear door. The yard was full of quiet gloom. The high windows of the hospital cast down a glow that told him nothing.

He kicked the overturned chair aside and ran through the living-room. Guided by the noises continuing overhead, he mounted the stairs. In the front bedroom he found Glen Carr kneeling before a chest of drawers.

His movements quick, Carr was trying to twist a key that was stuck in the lock of the lowest drawer. He pushed himself up, turned about as Brent came near and left a few round dark drops on the rug. His side was bleeding. He seemed obsessed with a strange, frantic purpose, desperate to protect whatever the drawer contained. With a gurgling expulsion of breath he threw himself forward, jolted Brent backward against the bed.

Struggling to right himself, Brent saw the chair swinging down. It struck his upthrown arms with a crackling noise and came apart. The overhead light dimmed and swam in a glowing sea. When his vision cleared, Brent pushed the pieces of the chair off him, elbowed up, felt gingerly of the lump forming on his forehead and blinked. Everything was still, except for a thumping inside his skull.

Glen Carr was no longer there.

GETTING TO his feet, steadying himself, Brent smelled something burning. He felt his way down the stairs, then into the kitchen. The air there was thick with the pungent smoke streaming up from the charred cookies in the oven. He turned off the gas and, still groggy, set about making sure that Carr was nowhere about the house. He began by pulling the front door open, and there bewilderment halted him.

A girl standing just beyond the porch was gazing at him wide-eyed. It wasn't Odelle Quinn. This girl looked younger—about twenty. She was hatless and her honey-colored hair was stirring in the wind. Breath caught, lips parted, she held a red jacket tightly at her throat and concealed one hand inside it.

Suddenly spinning about, her legs flying, she sprang into the coupe she'd left on the opposite side of the street. It was spurting off when Brent jumped to the running-board.

"Hold it!" he gasped.

The girl, stiff with alarm, let the car roll a moment before she veered back to the curb. Brent clambered in and perched on the seat, estimating her while his forehead pulsed.

"Where is it?"

The girl was afraid but her eyes—they were a smoky gray flecked with gold, Brent saw now—were defiant. "Where's what?" she countered.

"The gun."

Her face pale but perfectly straight she asked: "Which one?"

"The one you used to shoot the man who was shot inside that house a moment ago."

With her left hand she was again clutching the neck of her red jacket and a diamond sparkled on her third finger. "I heard it," she said. "Just as I was about to knock. Not knowing exactly what had happened, I—" Brent could feel her trembling. "Do you really think I shot someone?"

He touched the pockets of her jacket and saw that she wasn't carrying a purse.

"Otherwise how did you happen to be at the Carr place just when the fireworks went off?"

"It's—it's a private matter." More than that, the lift of her chin made clear, she didn't intend to explain. "Shouldn't you be notifying the police instead of asking me all these questions, Mr. Bill Brent?"

"You're Gretchen Dockery," Brent said. "The doctor's daughter. If you were anyone else, I'd probably be turning you over to the cops right now. How does it happen you know my name?"

"I've been in the *Recorder* news-room three or four times in the past few weeks," Gretchen Dockery explained, earnestly searching his face. "You were off by yourself in a corner office, looking so miserable I couldn't help asking about you."

It was Brent's turn to put himself on the defensive. "I noticed you too. You brought in lists of guests. Something about your engagement. I even remember the guy's name. Raymond Lacroze. He's probably luckier than he deserves."

"You're getting off the subject, Mr. Bill Brent," Gretchen reminded him. "You found me running away from a house where a man had just been shot. You seem to think I did the shooting. Well, are you going to do something about it?"

"Yes—advise you to keep on running until you get home, then stay there," Brent answered. He stepped from the car but held the door open. "I'm not going to tell anyone about this, because I happen to think such a hell of a lot of your father—but I hope I'm not making a mistake."

She pressed her lips tightly together and shook her head.

"You came to the Carr place for a special reason—and I've a feeling you were pretty desperate about it. In fact, you still are. Off the record, what were you after?"

Backed in to a corner, she steadfastly met his gaze.

"You realize you're in a nasty jam, and if the cops should start digging into this it'll get a lot nastier," he insisted. "Why did you go?"

She lifted her chin. "I won't tell you."

"It'd be a big help if you'd trust me."

"I'll never tell you!" She was struggling against anxious tears. "You or anyone else—never. If that makes it even worse for me—well, I think I can take care of myself."

"Better expect to see me soon again," Brent warned her. "I'm going to find out exactly what you're hiding."

"You won't!"

She sent her car forward so swiftly that the door slammed shut. Standing in the gutter, Brent watched it swing from sight at the corner. He was left with a fleeting memory of Gretchen Dockery's white face turned back to him, her eyes wide and tormented.

The entrance of the Carr home was standing open, and Brent slowly crossed the sill. The intense quiet of the deserted rooms seemed secretive. The ache above his eyes spreading through his whole head, he climbed the stairs.

This was Odelle Quinn's bedroom, and Brent wondered dizzily why her husband's first shocked act upon being wounded had been to rush into it. Carr hadn't managed to open the lowest drawer in the chest. The key was still protruding from the lock. Half mad with pain, he'd evidently abandoned the purpose he'd considered so urgent.

Brent crouched and with a sharp wrench freed the key. He turned it in the reverse direction and the lock worked. Opening the drawer, he slowly took out the only thing it contained. It was a hat—a man's gray felt hat of expensive brand, dirty and crushed. And there were brown, crusty stains on it that might be blood—old, dried blood.

Bending over it, Brent felt an extra-sensory warning of a presence and lifted his throbbing eyes. Captain Max Russo was standing in the doorway, silent as a specter.

CHAPTER FOUR
DEAD ENOUGH

BRENT ROSE with a baffled shrug and with excessive deference placed the hat in Captain Russo's cadaverous hands.

"You can have it," he said.

"Much obliged," Russo answered in his hollow voice. "Always grateful for a bit of unofficial assistance. Whose is it?"

"Wouldn't know," Brent said. "Carr's, maybe. Maybe not. But it means something. He was anxious to do something with it even though he had a bullet in his guts. Seemed to think getting rid of it was even more important than dying."

"Another shooting, Bill?" the captain asked wryly. "While we're still hunting around for the victim of the first one? Well, so far I haven't noticed the second victim either."

"If you'd showed up a little sooner, you'd have seen him scramming out of here."

"All quiet when I came in," Russo said, his spooky eyes narrowing. "Found a purse in Doctor Dockery's office—first thing to suggest there might really be something behind the bedtime story you've been telling."

"You probably won't believe it, Captain," Brent said, "but I got locked in again. This time I did it myself, without intending to. There were more shots on the other side of the door—three, same as before. Can I help it if people disappear as fast as they get shot?" Grimly he grasped Russo's bony arm. "You'd better do your own looking."

They went down the stairs and with a sweeping gesture Brent invited the detective to view the disarray in the kitchen.

"Definitely not a fairy tale. If we ever find Glen Carr, he'll tell you it's real enough, because he's badly hurt—wherever he is."

Captain Russo stooped and touched his long-nailed forefinger to a dark spot on the linoleum.

"You're getting mixed up in too many shootings for one night, Bill," he said, his tone one of mild reproof. "It brings up a lot of questions. To begin with—"

"Look at this," Brent interrupted. He ran his hand over a round hole in the door-frame and another in the wall. "Two bullets missed Carr. Smaller than a thirty-two, but slightly larger than a twenty-two. A twenty-five caliber."

Max Russo's dismal eyes were studying him. "All right. I concede that somebody tried to stage a murder here. I want to talk to you—later."

He stepped out and stood on the back porch, peering about the murky yard. As Brent followed him he went down, walked along a bare, narrow garden plot at the base of the wall, then bent to examine a heel-print in the earth.

"Mine, probably," Brent admitted. "I shouldn't take time to explain now, should I? Whoever did the shooting probably got away through the court. If he isn't still inside the hospital, he's probably still going—or she is."

Russo straightened, eyeing him even more intently. "She?"

"I try to keep an open mind," Brent said pointedly. "And why couldn't it have been a woman? After all, it was done with a ladylike gun."

Brent hoped he would scoff at the theory but Captain Russo, busy with his own conjectures, offered no dissenting opinion. His taciturnity and his peculiar unearthly calm weren't helping the condition of Brent's nerves. Brent was further disconcerted when he abruptly ceased his search and, with an agility startling in one who looked so moribund, vaulted the wall.

Brent clambered after him as he turned his ghostly gaze into the cars he passed. All of them were empty. Going beyond the hospital's emergency entrance, they stopped beside the Homicide Squad car, which was still parked near the mouth of the passage.

"Anybody come out of here within the past few minutes?" Russo asked the men inside it.

"Nobody," the detective at the wheel answered, "except a couple of internes in the ambulance."

"Keep watching."

BRENT SWUNG open the street entrance of the hospital. Dr. Kenelm was striding from the elevator into the office opposite the admission desk. Seated when Brent and Russo entered, he glanced up from a clinical report, his smile quick and genial.

"Hello! Still trying to find your elusive corpse?"

"Cops are like firemen," Brent said. "They always expect the worst and answer every call whether it's a false alarm or not. Have you been busy here since we left?"

"Busy all over the place—being the house physician in Medical."

"Is Doctor Dockery still out?"

"He was called back as soon as he reached home. Critical pyrexia in one of his favorite patients." Dr. Kenelm rose. "I must ask you not to distract him any more than you can help. He's twice as busy as I am, with much more important work."

"Are you a married man?" Brent asked him abruptly.

"No." He paused in the door. "See here, isn't your investigation going rather far afield?"

"Looks like it's due to go even farther, and a lot deeper," Brent remarked. "I think Captain Russo wants to make sure you haven't been outside this hospital since he left it. Don't you, Captain?"

Max Russo said neither yes nor no.

Dr. Kenelm's face was fixed into stern lines. "I haven't been outside for even so long as a second, and you can believe me or not, as you choose. You know, you're being altogether too officious and I resent it."

"I don't blame you," Brent said. "But on the other hand there are a couple of people who probably resent having gotten shot up."

"A couple?" Dr. Kenelm's eyebrows arched. "Good Lord, do you actually mean—" He frowned across the admission desk. "Please don't raise your voice, Miss Ruthers. What's wrong?"

The white-capped girl at the switchboard looked exasperated. "Doctor Clark answered an ambulance call with

Doctor Adams a few minutes ago. He's saying they brought the patient out and found a body already inside the ambulance, but I can't make head or tail—"

Brent tightened and Captain Russo took a quick step as Dr. Kenelm echoed, "A body?"

"Give me that call!" Captain Russo ordered the girl and grasped up the phone on the counter. They listened as he spoke terse syllables. "Dead?… Don't touch it. Bring your patient if you must, but bring that body too, right away."

Brent's lips quirked as Russo disconnected and turned his night-black stare at him.

"Well?" Brent asked. "Which one is it?"

Captain Russo, looking gloomy, didn't answer, and Dr. Kenelm directed a bewildered gesture at Brent.

"Whichever it is," Brent said, "it's it."

"It must be it," Russo agreed ironically.

"Finally, anyway, there is a corpse."

"There's a corpse," and Russo moved to the entrance. "Stay right here, both of you. I'm going to watch for that ambulance."

Dr. Kenelm gazed at his watch as if calculating how much lost time this development would cost him, and looked up with his eyes anxiously darkened.

"Nothing to do," Brent said, "but follow orders. When it comes to cadavers, Russo's the doctor."

Kenelm shook his head in confusion and returned to the desk. Leaning casually on the counter, Brent waited.

The lump on his forehead was throbbing harder now. Through the street doors he saw Captain Russo pacing along the curb. Dr. Kenelm was busy in the adjoining office. One of the two elevators was open. Brent sauntered and was inside it, sliding the door shut, when Dr. Kenelm sprang after him.

"Just a minute!"

The panel was closed.

"Take me up," Brent ordered the attendant. "Police business and don't waste time asking questions. Wherever Doctor Dockery is, that's where I want to get off."

The operator hesitated. "I just took him back up to Surgery."

"Where from?" Brent asked as the car glided.

"The consultation-room."

"Anything unusual in that?"

"He's up and down, up and down, all hours of the day and night. Busiest doctor in town. And the best, if you ask me. A grand guy, Doctor Dockery is. All the kids love him."

"You're not telling me," Brent said. "What kids?"

"Patients. He's specially interested in rheumatic fever. It's enough to break your heart, watching him working over 'em. They don't live to be more than fifteen years old if it's not stopped right at the beginning. He's doing research too, and some day he'll have it licked."

"I hope so," Brent said sincerely.

STEPPING FROM the car, he saw a nurse entering a room far down the corridor. Other nurses were hustling about with an efficiency that indicated someone in authority was near. Brent hesitated under a sign reading *Isolation Ward—No Visitors,* then went on.

He peered past a screen door into a room where Dr. Dockery was bending over a bed and trimming the knots of a bulky packing bandaged about the knee of a tow-headed girl of ten.

"Continue the salicylate," the doctor instructed the nurse in a tone that suggested he regretted its inadequacy. "The dressing must not be removed." He placed his big hand gently on his little patient's hot forehead, and answered her drowsy smile.

"You'll be much better soon, Mary."

"I know I will, Doctor," Mary piped faintly. "I always feel better when you come to see me."

"Go to sleep now," Dr. Dockery murmured, "and I'll be back almost before you know it."

The nurse hurried out, brushing Brent aside, and caught the arm of an interne who was carrying several X-ray films down the hall.

"Doctor Dockery's in eight twelve and asked for the X's and I had to tell him they weren't taken yet, Doctor Beasley," she said in sharp rebuke.

Dr. Beasley snapped his fingers. "Sorry. Can't keep up with that man. I'll do it right away," he promised, and went on.

Emerging next, Dr. Dockery halted to gaze at Brent in alarm.

"You're not quite old enough to be immune to rheumatic fever, Brent," he said with genuine solicitude. "What are you doing here?"

"I came to tell you there's been more trouble."

Dr. Dockery set his mouth. "Were those more shots I heard behind the building a few minutes ago?"

"I hope you'll understand I'm not just trying to smell out a piece of sensational news. I'm really concerned. Damn it, I'm trying to say it might turn into a pretty nasty kind of business if you—well, if you hold back anything important."

"Brent," Dr. Dockery said forcefully. "What could I possibly have to conceal?"

"I'm afraid you've already done it. Odelle Quinn wasn't really your patient. You twisted the truth about her in order to cover up the fact that she'd been coming to your office for—for some other reason." Brent rubbed his chin. "Hiding things from me doesn't matter so much. But to try to deceive Captain Russo—as shrewd a detective as ever—"

Dr. Dockery was struck speechless and didn't hear the swift heel-beats coming down the corridor. Dr. Kenelm had burst from the elevator and was upon them, his hand clamping Brent's arm.

"What the devil do you mean by this!" he blurted. "You've no business here. I can't permit your damned snooping to interfere with Doctor Dockery's work!"

"It's all right, Eric," Dr. Dockery said, his tone husky. "Brent meant no harm. Please go down, both of you. I'll join you in a moment or two."

His face was drawn, pallid. Watching him enter the next room with drooping shoulders, Brent submitted to Kenelm's pull at his arm. They waited for the elevator and Kenelm remained indignant.

"Are you his watchdog?" Brent asked wryly.

"That, or his bootblack or anything else he might require me to be," Kenelm retorted. "His work is more important to me than my own. I'm damned if I'll let you worry him."

Their descent began in silence. Brent was astonished, the next moment, to find that Kenelm's good-natured grin had returned.

"Sorry, Brent. I was too harsh with you. It's simply that I can't help being a bit overzealous where Seldon Dockery is concerned."

"Very understandable," Brent answered. "I also want to spare him. Your way and mine are different, that's all. You seem anxious to side-track any trouble headed in his direction, whereas I think the best way to bring him into the clear is to uncover the underlying truth, even if it might mean a temporary upset."

"I feel very strongly that it's not necessary to disturb him at all. He hasn't the slightest connection with what happened. I insist on that."

BRENT SHOOK his head. "Even to the extent of placing yourself in a questionable light?"

"Knowing no more about it than Doctor Dockery does, I haven't given a thought to how I might become involved." Kenelm's smile yielded to lines of sternness. "Look at it from my point of view, Brent. My father was Seldon Dockery's closest friend. When he died I was left alone with nothing. God knows what would have become of me but for Seldon Dockery's generosity. He not only put me through medical school but shared his practice with me. I'll go to any lengths to repay him, Brent, and don't ever doubt it."

"I don't," Brent said, "but I wouldn't repeat that too loudly, if I were you, considering that your alibi's going to be a tough one to check."

Kenelm's eyes narrowed. "No matter. Even though you say your purpose is the same as mine, I'm going to stop your meddling. I can order you excluded from this hospital, you know—and I'll do it, unless you quit."

"It wouldn't stop me," Brent said.

Dr. Kenelm stared at him stonily, jaw set with resolution. Striding from the elevator, he turned to the accident ward. Brent, shrugging his regret, eased into the consultation-room as Max Russo pushed in from the street. The cold wind had brought no flush to the captain's sunken cheeks. Looking as if nothing could ever warm him again, he resumed his pacing inside.

Brent kept beyond Russo's sight and advanced upon the six or seven overcoats hanging in the corner. He found match-folders in the pockets, keys, a pack of cigarettes, nothing of interest. Still unobserved, he glanced sharply about, then began poking into the desk drawers. The sound of the sliding panel came from the elevator shaft. Quickly he closed the last drawer, his search unrewarded, and sauntered out to join Dr. Dockery.

"Brent tells me—"

"He does, does he?" Max Russo said, snapping a glance at Brent. "He was Johnny-on-the-spot twice tonight, and I keep wondering how come."

"I'm still completely in the dark," Dr. Dockery protested. "Is it necessary to disrupt my schedule?"

The captain's intensely dark eyes settled on him. "I can't believe a physician of your standing could be mixed up in a case of violent death. Besides, you have a perfect alibi— two of them, in fact. There's no good reason to keep you away from your patients."

"That's very decent of you, Captain," Dr. Dockery sighed. Again his jaw was strongly clenched, a dark fire smouldering in his eyes. Getting once more into his overcoat, he went to the entrance and flung over his massive shoulder: "Good-night, good-night."

The ambulance whirred past at the same moment. Immediately Captain Russo was following it. Brent went after him, noticing that its arrival had not delayed Dr. Dockery's departure, and stopped behind it in the driveway. One white-coated interne dropped from the seat and another opened the rear doors.

"There," the second announced to Captain Russo, pulling nervously on a cigarette. "Intact."

The captain stood gazing in and Brent peered over his shoulder. The dead girl lay huddled on the ambulance floor, her hat spilled off, her hair a yellow splash against her waxen cheek. Her left wrist was bound with bandages and her coat was twisted open, revealing three red-ringed holes in the front of her dress.

"A gun in there?" Captain Russo asked, his voice even more sepulchral.

"No gun," the interne answered.

"There wouldn't be, Captain." Brent pulled his topcoat closer about him. "The murderer saved it to use on her husband. We haven't found it yet, so he's probably saving it still."

"Or *she* is," Russo reminded him. "To use on whom next time?"

"Maybe me," Brent said. "Maybe me."

Odelle Quinn looked childlike in death, and alien to the scheming trait which her husband had hinted. Gazing at her still body, Brent shivered with a thought he couldn't shake off—the haunting wonder whether it still might be true that Lora Lorne's advice—his own bungling advice—had brought sudden death upon her.

CHAPTER FIVE

LIGHTNING IN THE DARK

MAX RUSSO'S face was bleak as a mummy's but his eyes turned upon Brent with a bright, black fire.

"Why is she dead?" he asked disconsolately. "Why?"

"Jealousy, perhaps," Brent said.

"Not her husband's. He was shot with the same gun—according to you."

Brent felt the uncanny force of the captain's gaze. "He could have killed his wife through jealousy, then the other man might have turned the same gun on him in retaliation."

"You know a lot about this," Russo said in a grieved tone. "Too much."

"I also know," Brent added grimly, "that while I was locked inside one room this body was carried out of the other, then along the sidewalk a few yards and put inside the ambulance."

"Why?"

"It wasn't much of a risk. Dark street—lonely. The idea may have been to confuse the investigation. Or to delay the discovery. Possibly the murderer wanted to get at Carr before Carr found out his wife had been killed. If so, he was afraid that otherwise Carr would name him."

"Or her," Russo murmured. "And Carr still might do it."

"That's right. He might."

Russo walked like an automaton to the sedan in which the Homicide Squad was still waiting. "Get to work," he said tonelessly, and turned back. Pausing again behind the ambulance he looked about with his ghostly eyes gleaming. "Bill!" he called in a voice which might have been that of Judgment Day itself. "Bill Brent!"

Brent had dodged beyond the cars in the parking court and was crouched behind the wall. Keeping in the shadows, he circled the dead woman's home. His sedan was still parked in front of it. He slid under the wheel and went off at an urgent speed....

Turning through a stone gate, Brent was immediately screened from Sycamore Drive by a hedge. The lane led across the landscaped grounds and brought him to the side of a stately Georgian house. Dr. Dockery's car, marked by its green cross, stood at the big garage beyond. Brent had scarcely stopped when a door opened and a young man ran with graceful swiftness down the steps.

"See here, Gret!" he burst out as he neared. "I've had enough of your snooping. I'll thank you to stop poking your pretty little nose into—" Halting, he seemed more annoyed than embarrassed by his mistake. "Oh—I thought you were my fiancé," he said with a faint accent.

Standing erect, he was so amazingly tall that he seemed almost to be in his own shadow. His sideburns were long in the Latin fashion, his hair curried to a gloss. Brent had never seen, except on a movie screen, any man so sharp in every crease, so impeccably groomed. Effortlessly he bounced back into the house, having shown no interest at all in Brent's identity or purpose.

Climbing after him, Brent saw him again, through a window of the spacious living-room.

"Now what about it?" Brent heard him ask petulantly. "Damned irritating, having that check pushed back at me. Didn't you know your account wouldn't cover it?"

Seldon Dockery was warming his big hands at the fireplace.

"A—an oversight, Ray," he said wearily. "I've been so busy I've neglected to keep my personal checkbook up to date. I—I'll arrange it in the morning."

A young woman rose from a chair near the blaze. Strikingly dark, her skin was the color of richly creamed coffee, and naturally long lashes veiled her eyes. She slipped her arm through Dr. Dockery's in a manner of loyal comradeship.

"Sometimes, Raymond, you're simply too much!" Her voice was throaty, her syllables faintly accented like those of the sleek young man to whom she spoke. "Never do you think of anyone but yourself, never! No matter how generous Seldon is to you, you must ask for more. After all, the check was for a thousand dollars."

"What of it?" Raymond Lacroze retorted. "He said he'd back me, didn't he? Well, I expect him to keep his word. Every day my bills pile up. Delays, delays, there's nothing else. It's enough to drive me mad. I don't ask what becomes of all your money. I merely insist—"

"On having too much of it. You are too selfish, Raymond!" There was dark lightning in the young woman's eyes. "You can't see that Seldon has more important things on his mind tonight."

"More important!" Lacroze scoffed. "What could be—"

'Al villiano dadle el dedo, tomará la mano!—Give him an inch and he'll take a mile. Already you have spent twice as much as you said you would need. Perhaps we will lose all patience with you, then where will you be left? Go away, please! We've had enough of your insolence."

LACROZE STRAIGHTENED indignantly to his towering height, made a spiteful sound through his teeth and strode into another room. Brenz, realizing that Lacroze hadn't mentioned him, touched the bell-button as Dr. Dockery turned to frown into the fire.

"Where is Gretchen?"

"I don't know, Seldon. Perhaps she has been trying to learn where all the money is going. It makes Raymond furious when she questions any expense. It may be why he's so unreasonable tonight."

A maid opened the door and Brent identified himself, still listening.

"I regret so many things, Seldon, and urging you to help Raymond with his silly Villa Mañana is one of them," the young woman was saying. "You're so worried tonight. It is something at the Heights? Would you rather hurry back?"

"How you've changed!" and Brent heard the doctor chuckle. "No—you were right. You're young and I'm tied down too closely. Sometimes I think— Well, I'll never again take the risk of losing you, my dear."

"But Seldon, you know it will never happen again. You see, my eyes are open now to the true values of our life together and—Susan?"

The maid whispered and Dr. Dockery exclaimed: "Brent? Here? Why—why, ask him to come in."

They were standing at the fire, the physician seeming even more of a worried bear beside the vital young woman whose slender arm still clung to his.

"Mr. Brent is from the *Recorder*, Claudia," Dr. Dockery said. "You've never met my wife?… Is it the same matter you mentioned at the hospital?"

Mrs. Dockery was not many years older than her stepdaughter and certainly as lovely as Gretchen. Brent's fascinated gaze clung to her and he reluctantly nodded.

"The police may not be far behind me. I wanted to forewarn you."

With lifted head, the doctor asked: "Why do you think it's necessary, Brent?"

"The shooting in your office was done with a small caliber gun." He spoke frankly, watching their faces. "And your wife owns one that fills the bill."

Instantly Dr. Dockery challenged him. "And suppose she does?"

"Seldon, you didn't tell me of this!" Claudia said. "What could it have to do with my husband, Mr. Brent—or me?"

Brent pawed his face. "I feel like a fool. This thing's really none of my business. I thought I'd help keep you out of it if I could, that's all. But now that I'm here, may I see the gun?"

"You may," Dr. Dockery assented, his voice deep in his throat. "Do you remember where you keep it, Claudia?"

"I—I think so."

Claudia sent a troubled glance at Brent as she hurried from the room. With questions pressing to his lips, he remained silent. The doctor stood with hands clasped behind his back, profoundly disturbed, eyeing Brent in wordless reproof until his wife returned, walking quickly.

"I had to look for it. It hasn't been touched in a long while, I think. There."

It lay tiny and black on her palm. Brent took it, smelled of the bore and released the clip. It contained six cartridges. Evidently they had been inserted months or even years ago. Several of them were touched with green corrosion.

It would be a smart trick, Brent reflected, to remove the old bullets from the clip, insert new, fire them, then replace the old in order to rule out at a glance an otherwise suspicious piece of evidence—but he shook the thought from his head.

"Now I feel a lot better!" he said. "I'm sorry for this intrusion, Doctor."

"Not at all, Brent," Dr. Dockery answered. "If there's sound reason why we should be investigated, I suppose we must put up with it." He seemed to shrink from the gun. "Please put it away, Claudia."

"Yes," Claudia said. "Once I thought it was such fun to shoot, but somehow I do not like this thing any more."

As she carried it from the room her husband lowered his shaggy eyebrows at Brent. "Now, is there something else on your mind?"

"A great deal, but I'm keeping you from your dinner and it's high time I made a discreet exit," Brent said. "Thanks for not throwing me out. Good-night."

Dr. Dockery took him to the door, sent him off with a slap on the shoulder. He was running down the steps when he caught sight of the tall figure waiting beside his car.

"You're quite right," Raymond Lacroze said, his lids drooping. "You've no excuse for meddling in this family's affairs."

"Listening in, were you?" Brent asked.

"I don't like that."

"O.K. You don't like it and I don't think I like you."

Unexpectedly Lacroze smiled—a mirthless thinning of his mouth. It was the ominous smile of a man filled with a confident sense of power. He turned away, bounded up the steps, paused for dramatic effect. "Don't do it again," he said softly. Then he disappeared into the house, leaving Brent more coldly impressed with his simple warning than if he had threatened violence.

Puzzled and apprehensive, Brent swung his car out the gate. He was a block away when light struck into his eyes from the rear-view mirror. Another car was leaving the Dockery home. Within the space of two blocks his suspicion that it was trailing him grew strong. As he drove across the city it chose the corners he chose. Not until he swung toward the Heights Hospital did it change its tactics.

There at the last intersection, as if the driver were either satisfied as to Brent's destination or wary of following him farther, the other car hummed straight ahead. A huge neon sign near the center of town seemed to guide it like a beacon. The shining red letters announced: *Opening Soon— Villa Mañana.*

THE AMBULANCE was turning out of the hospital driveway. Having finished their field work, the Homicide Squad were getting back into their car—all except Max Russo. The captain stood alone in the gloom, head bowed, calculating his next move.

Avoiding him, Brent crossed the lobby. The consultation-room was empty and Dr. Kenelm's overcoat was gone from the rack in the corner. A directory was posted opposite the elevators and Brent consulted it. "Second floor," he read to himself out loud.

He chose the stairs and came into a corridor where an arrow pointed to *Roentography*. Following it, he opened a door bearing the same word and entered a room filled with weird electrical apparatus. He was alone there.

Another door was marked *Darkroom—Do Not Enter.* Brent knocked on it and there was no answer. Venturing a preliminary peek inward, he stepped into a black-walled light-trap—a short maze which led him into a smaller room filled with an acrid smell and the glow of a single deep-red bulb.

Brent paused, thinking he had heard a quick movement, while his eyes adjusted themselves to the crimson-tinted darkness. Details slowly sketched themselves in—a bench bearing a stack of aluminum film-holders beside a row of developer and fixer tanks—but no one was at work there. Eyebrows knit, Brent saw, resting on the rim of one of the tanks, the handles of half a dozen film-hangers. He took one up, held the dripping negative over the hypo solution—and again his ears caught a quick, furtive noise behind him.

Suddenly the ruby light seemed soundlessly to explode. It became a shapeless blur, a dim scarlet flare floating off....

Brent found that his face was pressing against the black floor. Reverberating as if from far away he heard rapidly fading footfalls. The pain in his head was so overwhelming that all his other senses flickered and he groped feebly in the air, not knowing what had happened to him.

He rolled over, found his knees, then his feet. The red blob swam before him again and he tottered to the light-trap. Groping into a white brilliance that blinded him, he heard an exclamation, felt someone grasp his arm.

"What's the matter with you?" a voice boomed through his skull.

Then he was slumped in a chair, squinting into a face he vaguely remembered. It belonged to the interne he had seen earlier that evening in the corridor on the top floor—Dr. Beasley. A wet, chill cloth was pressed over his face, and when it was taken away he saw more people in the room. Before him, as if risen from a neighboring grave, stood Captain Max Russo.

"Am I hurt?" Brent asked him.

"Just knocked galley-west," the captain answered despondently. "Your hat probably saved you from a cracked cranium."

It was lying on the floor, looking strangely like the bloody hat Brent had found under lock in Odelle Quinn's bedroom.

"What brought you up here, Bill?" Russo was asking in his empty tone. "Who did you run into?"

"I think—" Brent said, "I think he—he would've killed me if he could."

"Or she," said Russo dryly.

Brent pressed his hands over his head, trying to force its shattered parts back together. "I went in the darkroom. Somebody was already there—probably hiding under the bench, but I didn't know that—and let me have it from behind. How long was I out?"

"Why should anyone jump you in there, Bill?" Russo asked.

"I interfered—interrupted something." He found Dr. Beasley's face. "Better take a look inside—see if everything's as you left it."

Captain Russo remained unmoving, sorrowfully estimating Brent, until Dr. Beasley returned.

"There were six films in the hypo, and now there are only five," he reported.

"Ah!" Brent said, a glimmer returning to his eyes.

"One missing," Dr. Beasley added. "The patient's in eight twelve."

"Why?" Russo asked.

Nobody answered but everybody looked at Brent. He undertook the risk of standing up and pushed away the hands that tried to help him.

"Please, let's skip the whole thing. Maybe I just fainted and fell. Anyway, God knows I've had enough for one

night. Would anybody mind if I just sort of went peacefully away from here?"

"The sooner the better, Bill—before you turn this thing
into a massacre," Captain Russo said. "Swallow a handful
of aspirin and put that head of yours to bed. I want you
to be able to answer a lot of questions at headquarters
bright and early in the morning. Did you hear that clearly?"

"I got it," Brent mumbled, and went.

CHAPTER SIX
FIND ANOTHER GUN

THE CITY-ROOM came to bustling life while
Brent labored, alone in his faintly scented cubbyhole,
to bring forth another of Lora Lorne's admonitions to the
amorous. His persistent headache wasn't alleviated by the
too-familiar problem of a married woman who had taken
to coveting her neighbor's husband. While he endeavored
to repair the dizzy dame's moral outlook—"The wages of
sin are certain to be hard, dear"—he sent side-long glances
at Garrett and awaited the inevitable sarcastic call.

"Lora!" it came. "Here, please, madam."

Gritting his teeth, Brent finished his sentence—"clutches
of a mad passion that sweeps aside all thought of honor,
responsibility, right and wrong"—and took with him a
letter he had found in the morning's mail. A rare thing, it
was addressed not to a non-existent Miss Lorne, but to
him, William Coleridge Brent, Esquire, personally. Unfold-
ing it as he arrived at the city editor's desk, he chose to
ignore Valerie Randall.

Val had already hustled in and out and breathlessly in
again. Her cheeks flushed, she had handfuls of notes and
her smile at Brent was expectant.

"Val's all set to hear your angle on the murder story, Grandma," Garrett said.

"Is she?" Brent remarked. "Here's another letter from Middletown, where Ducky Chase's sister teaches school. Is it possible you're so nearly human that you sent her some more bucks without telling anybody?"

"Never mind that," Garrett said.

"Val—"

"I'm interested in this phenomenon," Brent interrupted. "When Ducky died we took up a collection and sent his sister Amy the coffin money she needed for him, and she duly thanked us. But here she writes: 'I didn't expect a second gift, and certainly not such an enormous sum, even larger than the insurance policy Harry dropped a few weeks before he died.' I'll gladly revise my low opinion of you, Garrett, if—"

"I know nothing about it," Garrett said impatiently. "Get busy and tell Val—"

" 'Though it was sent in cash,' Amy Chase goes on, 'without a letter or even a return address on the envelope, I know it must have come from Harry's friends on the paper.' Well, this is the first I've heard about it. So, Garrett, your heart isn't completely ossified after all?"

"Please, Bill!" Val implored him. "There's so much to cover today, I'm half crazy already!"

"I don't wonder," and Brent eyed her scornfully. "The job's too big and tough for your dainty hands. This is a fine racket you're working, Garrett. Instead of showing this lovely girl your etchings, you gave her the police trick. You spend practically every evening at her apartment, teaching her journalism. Under the same conditions I'd enjoy enlightening her as to how to break this murder story, but as it is—"

"Brent!" Garrett grated, and leveled a threatening finger.

"Besides, you've given me other work to do—remember? I have a large family of readers to guide past the shoals of wrecked homes, illicit desires and past wrongs. Has the chief of the Homicide Squad clammed up on you, Val? Then ask Glen Carr. The guy certainly knows more about these shootings than anybody else."

"He's still missing, Bill, wounded as he is," Val said quickly. "Russo thinks he's keeping under cover in fear of his life."

"Probably he fears exposure even more," Brent said. "If he recovers from those bullets he knows he'll probably wind up in jail. But there are lots of angles you haven't thought of yet, Val, of course. For example, did the Carrs rent that particular house simply because it's in a good, quiet neighborhood, or for some other obscure reason? Probably the former, but I haven't time—"

"You're wasting plenty of it, Brent," Garrett cut in. "Sit down and talk to Val."

"Then too," Brent continued, "the post-mortem has shown, as it must, that Odelle Quinn had no stomach ulcer. For another thing, there's only one place where the weapon of murder can be. And that hat I discovered—though there are no initials stamped in the band, it's easy to tell who owns it. Not Glen Carr, and the blood on it's too old, of course, to be Miss Quinn's. Do you now why any of this is true, my child?"

"Why—why no, Bill," Val confessed, wide-eyed.

"I'm glad you don't," Brent said. "I'm sincerely happy that you've got an amateur on the police trick, Garrett. I devoutly hope you never got around to teaching her how to find out all the answers."

"Brent," Garrett said vehemently, rising, "you're to turn all your information over to Val, here and now—and that's an assignment."

Brent shook his head and immediately regretted that he hadn't chosen some other manner of signifying his refusal.

"I won't do it," he stated flatly. "You can rant your loudest. You can fire me, sue for breach of contract. You can even promise in writing to put me permanently back on police and I'll still tell you to go to hell. That's how I feel about the situation now, Garrett."

The city editor's eyes were cold as stone. "You're putting yourself on the blacklist—kicking yourself out of the newspaper game forever."

"If that's my choice," and Brent grimly nodded, "I'd rather sweep gutters. Because I know whom the evidence incriminates—incriminates so conclusively that there'd be scarcely any hope of an acquittal—and I'm damned if I'll smear it all over our front page or any other. As matters stand, Garrett, that's final."

He turned away while Val Randall gaped at him and Garrett's wrathful stare burned his back, and disappeared into the morgue.

SPLITTING OPEN the bound volume of the *Recorder* for February, Brent pored over an item headlined: *CHASE HIT-RUN DEATH ADMITTED BY EX-DENTIST.*

On the seventeenth, the day Ducky Chase died, after being accidentally run down at the corner of Fourth and Maple, Leslie Danforth confessed. No longer practising, Danforth was employed in the Coombs Dental Laboratory, suppliers to the profession. Upon his surrender it was ascertained that a fragment of yellow lens found at the scene had been broken from the fog-lights of his car.

Brent thought he heard his telephone ringing but reviewed, regardless, several peculiar aspects of the accident. The driver had halted long enough to learn that Ducky Chase gravely needed medical aid. Then fleeing, he had again stopped to phone the Heights Hospital for an ambulance. These extenuating circumstances, pleaded by the city's most prominent and expensive attorney, had served to reduce Danforth's sentence to one year.

Checking backward to the first news of the accident—though his telephone was ringing—Brent reread these sentences:

> Chase was struck within ten yards of the small apartment building where he lived. The lack of eye-witnesses is accounted for by the late hour and the fact that retail stores stand on the other three corners. Only one room on the street side of the apartment was occupied. When questioned by police, Mr. and Mrs. Olin Dorr said that at the time of the accident they had not yet returned from the roadhouse where they spent the evening.

Olin Dorr? Could Val, stumbling in one of her early assignments, have gotten the name wrong?

Still ignoring his telephone, Brent referred to the small ad run daily by the Zombie Club. Odelle Quinn was featured as "Radio's Sweetest Thrush," while Glen Carr was described as "Your Favorite M.C." A week later both their names had disappeared from the Zombie Club's entertainment bill and the chief attraction was, "Francine—Our Own Dancer Divine."

Tantalized by a feeling that the name of Francine was also somehow familiar, Brent now responded to the persistent clamor of his phone.

"I said bright and early," the unearthly voice of Max Russo reminded him. "Or do I send a troop of strong-arm dicks after you?"

"Coming!" Brent promised.

As he crossed to the swinging doors he saw Garrett glaring over his rolltop desk. Deciding that the city editor was holding his fate in abeyance while giving him a last chance to surrender his inside information, he answered with a dogged wag of his head, pushed out and ran down to the street.

Reaching the lobby of a building two blocks away, he read on the directory board: *Gregory Walsh, Architect—Third Floor*. He was turning to the elevators when a panel slid open and a woman emerged. She was thirty-odd, quietly dressed, pretty and hurried. Her appearance caused Brent to change his plans. Turning about, he followed her out.

She entered the City Trust Company and went directly to the window marked *Savings*. Pretending to be a depositor, Brent stood behind her. She pushed five twenty-dollar bills under the grille and the teller entered the amount in a growing three-figured column. He said, "Thank you, Mrs. Danforth," and she stuffed the passbook into her purse.

Still dogging her, Brent went thoughtfully as far as the entrance of the office building to which she directly returned. There a glass display case was affixed to the wall. Also bearing the name of Gregory Walsh, it framed the front elevations of several of the architect's recent projects. One of them, which Brent intently studied, pictured a remodeled building with an extremely modernized Spanish motif, decorated with a sign proclaiming sweepingly, *Villa Mañana*.

Haunted by the portentous voice of Captain Russo, Brent went on. When he slid into his sedan, which was sitting in front of the *Recorder* plant, he found something more to puzzle over. A note was attached to the steering-wheel with a bobby-pin. The brief message left him baffled.

> Bill Brent—You ask me to trust you and now I must.
>
> Please don't print this or mention it to anyone except Father.
>
> Tell him he mustn't worry—I'm all right.—Gretchen D.

CAPTAIN RUSSO was not at his desk. An inner room of the Homicide Squad's offices was closed, and through the door came voices. The first Brent heard was a man's, raised in petulant complaint.

"Warrants, searches, stupid questions! You interrupt my practice, and why? What could I have to do with this ridiculous murder?"

Claudia Dockery's throaty voice answered. "If you have nothing to fear, why must you behave like a guilty spoiled child, Raymond? Do be quiet!"

"I've never yet encountered a homicide I could call ridiculous, Mr. Lacroze," Brent heard Max Russo observe. "The fact is that the gun was within your reach. You'll wait here, please, until I've had the report from the ballistic lab."

"This will cost you your job, you fool," Raymond Lacroze warned him levelly. "You'll regret it, I promise you!"

"Oh, hush, Raymond!" said Claudia Dockery.

Captain Russo appeared in the doorway and his spooky eyes settled on Brent. He sank into his desk chair, his gaunt face sorrowful, contemplating the gray, blood-stained hat lying on his blotter.

"Bill, you know a lot more about this than you pretend. You're holding out."

"I've learned a few things I'd rather not know," Brent admitted. "I don't think I'm going to tell anybody what they are. Not unless the situation takes a turn for the better."

Russo sighed. "I like you, Bill. I don't want to jail you—for obstructing justice, at the very least."

Brent smiled wryly. "The justice of the case is what I want most to preserve—but don't ask me what I mean. About that hat. Do you know whose blood is on it?"

"Ducky Chase's," Russo answered.

"That's right," Brent said quietly. "And it's Ducky Chase's hat, of course?"

"No."

Wary of Max Russo's sagacity, Brent chose his words with care. "Then it belongs to the man who ran him down, you think? Dropped or brushed off while he bent over Ducky? If so, Leslie Danforth unknowingly left it there on the bloody pavement when he rushed away."

"Officially that case is closed," Russo reminded him. "Danforth's doing time now. So why should this hat, if it's his, be so very important to Glen Carr?"

"Danforth's second offense, as I remember," Brent said. "Wasn't he in trouble with the law several years ago?"

"In a different way. It had something to do with the administration of an estate. He was the executor. Under charges of embezzlement lodged by one of the inheritors he was brought to trial. My own opinion is that it was mismanagement instead of theft, but he was found guilty."

"All that has nothing to do with Ducky Chase or Odelle Quinn, though," Brent said.

Max Russo shook his head. "Under the state law Danforth's conviction for the felony automatically revoked his license to practice dentistry, even though he was released on probation. He had to go to work as a laboratory assistant. Having a record, he couldn't hope to get off again when he confessed to hitting Chase."

"Danforth's wife has found herself a job in an architect's office," Brent added. "And though her salary must be small, she's been depositing one hundred dollars in cash in her savings account regularly every week."

Russo's eyes were darkly alive in his dead face. "Blackmail? But how could that be?" Taking up a pencil, he made a note.

"No use grilling her about it," Brent said. "She knows that if she talks she'll lose that income and her husband will stay in jail anyway, under a new conviction for criminal conspiracy."

"What?" Russo stared keenly at him. "Bill, are you deliberately trying to cloud the issue?"

BRENT WAS watching the detective's reactions. "I'm hoping the truth will turn out to be something different than it seems now. Do you know that Glen Carr was more than ordinarily jealous of his wife? She'd written to Lora Lorne. Acting on our dear Miss Lorne's advice, she may have been pretending to play around in order to keep her husband's interest up. On the other hand, her letter may have been a shrewd feminine trick. Her husband felt she was using it to hide a real affair."

"In that case, who's the other man?" Russo asked. "Or the other man's woman?"

"Have you checked everyone's alibis?" Brent countered.

Max Russo sat back. "Unquestionably Doctor Dockery was operating when the Quinn woman was killed. He says he was in the hospital when Carr was shot, but there happens to be nobody who can verify that. Doctor Kenelm saw all the patients on the list he gave me, but it's hard to say just when he arrived at and left each one's home. The second time, he was also just somewhere in the hospital. Mrs. Dockery says she was downtown, shopping. No corroboration."

"What about the daughter, Gretchen?" Brent asked as casually as he could manage.

"Haven't even seen her. They keep telling me she's expected home any minute, but she hasn't shown up. As for our hot-headed friend, Lacroze, he says he was at the new night club he's going to open soon which will feature his own dancing. But that was after the decorators had knocked off for the day—no one else was there. Coming right down to it, Bill, there's only one person I'm sure was at each place when the violence was done. You."

"And of course," Brent said uneasily, "I had a powerful motive for shooting two people I'd never seen before."

Russo leaned forward, his eyes black as the depths of a tomb at midnight. "How can I be sure you didn't know them? If Odelle Quinn and Glen Carr were playing some sort of crooked game, what proof is there that you weren't a party to it? With both of them out of the way now, there's no one else you have to cut in."

"I can truthfully say I'm not unfriendly with anyone concerned," Brent answered quietly, "except Raymond Lacroze, whom I'd like to smack on the jaw for a reason not directly connected with the case."

Russo's face was inscrutable. "What were you doing in that darkroom? Where's the film that disappeared?"

"Gone by now," Brent said. "Gone forever."

"You know the reason for it," Russo asserted bleakly. "I think you're covering yourself with your story about someone hiding under the bench. Isn't it true you went in there with the purpose of destroying that film?"

"Why should I?" A chill crawled up and down Brent's spine, and testing the depths of Russo's knowledge he asked again: "Why in the world should I?"

Max Russo was silent and the door opened. A bald man wearing a stained smock brought to his desk a brown envelope on which a memorandum was pasted. The man withdrew and as Russo read the typewritten lines Brent could look into the gaping mouth of the envelope. It contained a twenty-five caliber automatic.

Russo rose with almost an audible creaking of his joints and opened the connecting door.

"I have the report now," he said, "and you may go."

Raymond Lacroze uttered a triumphant "Hah!" Indignantly swinging his long legs, he strode from the office without waiting for Claudia Dockery. Pale, she paused at Captain Russo's desk.

"For myself I do not care," she said earnestly, "but I hope this means you will not again worry my husband."

Max Russo looked profoundly regretful and placed the automatic in her hands.

"Your property."

Claudia Dockery turned from him with her chin resolutely lifted. After she closed the door there was a moment of uncertain silence.

"The death bullets weren't fired from that gun, then," Brent surmised.

"You may go too, Bill," Captain Russo murmured. "Even you may go—at least this time."

CHAPTER SEVEN
DYING DECLARATION

THE NECESSITY remained that today's paper must contain not only a murder story but another Lora Lorne column. While the tension in the city-room heightened and Val Randall hammered her inadequate notes together on her typewriter, Brent sweated over the tribulations of a husband who felt impelled to leave his wife because she loved contract bridge more passionately than him.

Advising against a tragic fracture of their home—though in Brent's private opinion it would probably be a godsend—then fishing about for the one more short letter he needed to fill out the day's stint, he heard quick footfalls and looked up into the hotly annoyed face of Raymond Lacroze.

"Where's Gretchen?" Lacroze demanded. "Will you tell me or must I beat it out of you? I can do it, you know."

Brent seized Lacroze's arm and led him to another desk. "That's not my office," he took pains to point out first. "What makes you think I know more about your fiancé's whereabouts than you do?"

Lacroze's jaw was confidently pointed. "No one else knows. Not I, the man who's going to marry her. Claudia doesn't, or the doctor. But you! You've meddled from the very beginning. Now, where is she?"

Sliding his hand into his pocket, Brent closed it over the note he'd found in his car. "After all, it's rather early in the day. If she simply went out this morning and hasn't come back—"

"She's been gone since yesterday afternoon," Lacroze interjected. "Missing all night. No phone call—no word at all. I warn you, my practice has been interrupted too much. Don't waste my time. Don't lie."

"Frankly, Raymond," Brent said, "every time I see you I like you less. Damned if I can figure out why such a swell girl ever let you give her that ring, especially since her father probably paid for it. Anyway, why come to me? Tell the cops."

Lacroze towered over Brent, his eyes narrowing. "I've already had too much trouble from the stupid police. Doctor Dockery doesn't know Gret is gone. Claudia has put him off with excuses. She's trying to find Gret before he must be told. If something's happened to her—if you know—"

"I wish I did," Brent said sincerely, "but I can't help you."

Lacroze's dark lids lowered. "I hope you're telling me the truth," he said in the same ominous tone that had chilled Brent last night. "And I hope you won't make the mistake of putting this into print." He turned, then, and his graceful, long-swinging stride took him out of the city-room.

Brent still had his Lora Lorne column to finish, but he followed. Reaching the street, he saw Lacroze rapidly driving off. The note in his pocket was a strange trust he wanted to keep, but it wouldn't prevent his questioning Claudia Dockery about Gretchen's disappearance. He ducked into his car—and as he turned from the curb the back of his neck prickled, warning him somehow of a presence.

Glancing into the mirror, watching the rear seat and seeing nothing suspicious, he drove slowly. After rounding another corner he found himself passing the colorful but incompleted front of the Villa Mañana. Lacroze's car was now sitting there, his selfish impatience having probably prompted him to abandon the search for his fiancé. Another sign held Brent's eyes—*Lacroze and Francine, Stylists of the Dance.*

He turned twice more, reconsidering his destination, and stopped at the entrance of the building where he had a one-room apartment.

"It's safer here," he said, cutting the ignition. "You can come up for air now."

He was answered by a soft gasp, a movement, and Gretchen Dockery's face appeared in the mirror.

SHE ASKED quickly: "How did you know I was back here?"

"I just sort of sense it when you're around," Brent said, turning to smile at her. "Where've you been hiding yourself?"

"In a movie, until it closed last night," she confessed. "In parked cars since then. I was watching and saw you get out of this one early this morning. I'll go crazy if I don't talk to somebody, and you're my best bet."

As Brent got out she came to him, her cold hands thrust into the pockets of her red jacket. He led her into his apartment and she sank to the studio couch, searching his face. On the card table, still set up, were his percolator and toaster. He plugged in both.

"You're a tired and hungry young woman—and a scared one, though you've got plenty of stuff, at that." Brent brought a cup from the kitchenette, cream from the refrigerator. "Thinking the cops might force you to say too much, you've been keeping out of their reach."

"They use blinding lights and black-jacks, don't they?" Gretchen asked with a shiver. "And don't they tap telephone wires? That's why I haven't even phoned home."

Brent didn't grin. "You're protecting somebody," he said. "Not yourself, I hope. Who is it?"

"You've got to tell me what's been happening!" Gretchen said suddenly. "Have the police—"

"No arrests so far. But something's due to break very soon now. I feel sure of it. You still won't tell me what you're so worried about, will you? You needn't, though. I think I know."

Distraitly she ran her fingers through her honey-colored hair. "But you couldn't!" Alarm flashed in her eyes. "You—you're not putting it in the paper!"

"Unlike the *Recorder's* present police reporter, I wouldn't wreck anybody's life for the sake of a little news," Brent assured her. "There's more I've got to find out—not for publication. Insurance against disaster, sort of. About Doctor Kenelm, for example. Is he the type who makes passes at married women?"

An incredulous laugh forced itself from Gretchen's lips. "He has no time even for unmarried ones. I thought I was in love with him once, but I couldn't get to first base. He's wedded to his work."

"You came off a bit better with Ray Lacroze, who's equally wedded to himself," Brent observed with a grimace of distaste. "Who the hell *is* that guy?"

"Claudia's cousin. Their fathers were brothers—Argentine cattle ranchers—their mothers American. I'm sure you've heard of Ray—Lacroze and Roselle, the dancing team that made a big hit in New York last year. He split with Roselle and has a new partner now. He's always been ambitious to have his own night club, and Father's backing him."

"Latins are reputed to have tempers hotter than tamales," Brent observed. "They're capable of fierce jealousies. Your step-mother, for example. There must be many beautiful women among your father's patients."

"Once Claudia was that foolish," Gretchen said. "But now—" Her voice whispered off.

"Orange juice?" Brent suggested, bringing her a glass from the kitchenette. "You like Claudia?"

"I'm suddenly crazy about her. She's become so swell, Father's so much in love with her, and she's so devoted to him—now. But at first— About a month ago there was almost a terrific bust-up."

"What stopped it?" Brent was watching the brown bubbles in the percolator. "What changed things so greatly and so suddenly?"

Gretchen hesitated. "At first Claudia thought of nothing but entertaining, flitting about to parties. She was jealous of Father's work, furious because he took her out so little. Some trifling thing—a country club dance Father couldn't make—brought it to a head. Claudia had a tantrum, threw her clothes into her bags and started off for Reno."

"While your father was doctoring some poor kid at the Heights, no doubt?"

"Exactly. She left a note and I found it. I remember it began: 'This is a horrible valentine to leave for you, but I'm so terribly unhappy—' Really, she was breaking her own heart by doing it. I phoned Father and he rushed to the airport, reached the plane a second before it was due to take off—luckily, because he couldn't possibly have followed her any farther—and brought her back."

BRENT SOBERLY put a cup of coffee in Gretchen's trembling hands. "A near thing that brought them a new understanding."

"You see, one of Father's patients developed a dangerous condition at that very time, and the hospital couldn't reach him. A grand little boy, and he almost died. Father had a hard fight, saving him. Claudia felt it was her fault and it impressed her deeply. Since then she's been really wonderful—wholeheartedly devoted to Father and his work."

Brent earnestly estimated Gretchen. "It's no new feeling for you. You've always been for him, in the biggest way possible."

"Of course." She gazed at Brent over her cup. "The look in your eyes! It makes me go cold all over. They seem to know so much! But do you understand how desperately I—I've wanted to—"

Brent came quickly to his feet. There were footfalls in the hall—uncertain, stumbling steps moving closer to his door. They stopped directly outside. Then there were scratching noises—the scrape of fingernails against the panel. Gretchen was breathless and Brent moved cautiously. He gripped the knob, swung the door open.

Glen Carr fell into his arms.

He held Carr a startled moment as Gretchen sprang up. Carr was gasping, his face haggard. His coat sagged open, releasing a bloodstained towel that fell to the floor. The whole side of his shirt was a crusty brown. There was no strength left in him. Trying to speak, he made breathy, meaningless sounds.

Brent carried him to the couch. Gretchen was already hunting in the pantry. She brought a tumbler half full of Scotch and Brent forced a trickle through Carr's pressed lips. Carr was racked with pain. His hand clutched Brent's wrist and he strained up, striving again to speak.

"Easy," Brent cautioned. "You've been on your feet, dodging the cops, when you should have been on an operating table."

"Not—not Doctor Dockery!" Carr gasped. "He'd—he'd kill me!"

Gretchen was still, her fingers pressing against the protest on her lips. Brent stuffed a pillow under Carr's head. Carr's were the white-rimmed, terrified eyes of a dying man. A throaty rattle mixed with his words.

"I told her—she was crazy to do it. But she wouldn't listen. She schemed—found him—I told her there were others—others besides Dockery—to watch out for. Told her they'd get her—one of them would. I tried—tried to stop her but—"

Exhaustion blurred Carr's voice. His fingers frantically gripped Brent's wrist as if to cling to life itself. He pushed the whiskey away and his lips worked.

"Listen, man!" Brent said. "You may not stand much of a chance. If you know who shot you, now's the time to spill it."

"Dockery—"

Brent stiffened. "Do you actually mean Seldon Dockey killed your wife and tried to kill you?"

"Dockery—"

"Listen, Carr! *Do you mean that?*"

Carr sputtered and went limp. Brent held him a long moment before getting up. He had died with an accusation on his lips, and Brent turned to gaze at Dr. Dockery's white-faced daughter.

"He was wrong!" she flung out. "It isn't true!"

Eyes pinched, Brent crossed the room to the telephone. He spun the zero and said, gazing miserably at Gretchen: "Police headquarters…. Homicide…. Brent calling, Captain. You'll find Glen Carr's dead body in my apartment. I'll leave the door unlocked for your men. I'm going straight to the Heights Hospital."

He disconnected on Russo's startled silence and firmly took Gretchen's arm.

"I'm sorry. I wanted you to be able to keep your secret. But maybe it's got to come out. The whole thing—now."

CHAPTER EIGHT
SORRY, KILLER

BRENT ESCORTED Gretchen Dockery into the lobby of the Heights Hospital and his nerves suffered a new shock. Max Russo was already there, standing by the door of the consultation-room, cadaverous and solemn.

"I think you'd better wait here, Gret," Brent said. "And look. This might seem to be turning out all wrong, but so far you've trusted me. Don't stop now, will you?"

She lifted her imploring eyes, not answering, and Brent left her. Max Russo went with him into the elevator. As the car carried them upward the captain uttered a profoundly morose sigh.

"Doctor Dockery is on the op floor," he said.

Brent couldn't look at him. "I think you know all the answers. You even feel the same about it now as I do."

"I've learned more than I like," Russo nodded. "But it's a job to be done—a job I hate."

They walked side by side along the corridor and paused when Dr. Dockery appeared. He strode from one of the rooms and without noticing them entered the next—812. They turned after him and paused just inside. He was bent over the little girl in the bed, snipping the knots of the dressing packed about her knees. A moment passed before he glanced up.

"What is it?" he said, his deft hands never hesitating. "You shouldn't be here, you know. Is the matter so important?"

"What I'm about to say may lead you to suspect me of bad faith, Doctor," Brent answered. "But it isn't that. It's more of a— Well, sometimes you must cause a patient pain in order to help him."

The drowsy youngster lay quiet under the touch of Dr. Dockery's gentle hands. He worked skillfully while his broad forehead took on a few beads of feverish perspiration.

"The corner where Ducky Chase was run down the night of the fourteenth is on a direct line between this hospital and the airport," Brent said. "You were desperate to get there before your wife's plane left and you struck Ducky with such force that he was flung dying into the gutter. It was an agonizing dilemma you faced then, and seconds counted. You chose to hurry on after the woman you loved."

Dr. Dockery bent to his task, seeming scarcely to hear.

"Odelle Quinn and Glen Carr denied witnessing the accident, but they'd seen you from the window of the apartment they occupied then in the same building where Ducky lived. They'd seen the green cross on your car and perhaps even the license number. And they'd found the hat you'd unknowingly left behind—an unusually large one, to fit a big, shaggy-headed man. It was Odelle Quinn who learned your identity and schemed to bleed you."

Max Russo was sorrowfully silent, watching as the doctor loosened the little patient's dressing.

"You were forced to pay her the price she demanded for her silence because exposure was an unthinkable alternative. Hit-and-run driving, particularly when it costs the victim's life, is a felony, and a conviction would mean that your license to practise medicine would be revoked. But you couldn't keep on submitting to blackmail and living under the threat of that danger. It had to be stopped. So Odelle Quinn was called by phone to your office, and the purpose behind the message was to kill her."

Dr. Dockery's fingers were probing into the fluffy cotton.

"As a precaution she'd taken to carrying a little gun in her purse. She was an itinerant entertainer, so it wasn't registered locally. I heard her scream when it was snatched from her hands and turned upon her. But simply killing the woman wasn't enough. Her husband, though an unwilling party to the blackmail, must also be eliminated. He was shot with the same gun, and then—"

Max Russo, silent as a ghost, was moving closer to the bed.

"You know who has been concealing the weapon since then, Captain," Brent said. "*She* has—that little patient."

Now Dr. Dockery's hands were still. "You'd ordered her knee to be X-rayed, Doctor, and it hadn't been done. At the time you weren't aware of the delay. Once the X-ray picture was taken, a few minutes afterward, there was nothing to do but get rid of the film. Of course it would show very distinctly the silhouette of the weapon concealed—"

Dr. Dockery's hands were deep in the cotton, and Max Russo was jerking toward him. The struggle was sharp and brief. The captain pried open the physician's fingers, and the gun lay there—a vest-pocket automatic, short-snouted and small enough to be concealed in his palm. Russo tore it from his grasp.

Seldon Dockery's great shoulders sagged with defeat and his face was wanly drawn as the detective said: "There's not much more, Doctor. We'll go down to your office now."

FILLED WITH regret as he was, Brent felt a crazy surge of relief as the elevator carried them down—relief because it wasn't Lora Lorne's advice, after all, that had caused the death of Odelle Quinn.

Dr. Dockery, crossing the lobby, turned his wretched gaze on his daughter and could not speak to her. He strode out heavily, followed by Max Russo. Brent took Gretchen's arm.

"Chin up, Gret," he said gently. "This is it—the thing you've been hoping would never come out—and it's going to be tough. The best you can do now is keep a stiff upper lip—say nothing."

She ran after her father. Brent accompanied her into the reception-room. Dr. Kenelm had left his desk in the inner office and had come anxiously to his associate's side. Dr. Dockery was now seated tensely in one of the chairs, and Captain Russo's spectral eyes were fixed upon him.

"But there's one fact we can't ignore, Captain," Brent said. "The person who killed Odelle Quinn is undoubtedly the same one who next killed Carr at the first opportunity. She was shot at exactly five eleven, and at that time Seldon Dockery was operating, surrounded by half a dozen witnesses. His alibi is unassailable. He's absolved of these murders."

But there was no hope in the gray lines of Dr. Dockery's face—only anguish.

"They were shot by someone who knew Seldon Dockery was being mercilessly blackmailed, who meant to stop it. The murders were an act of protection, undertaken, of course, without his knowledge."

Brent gazed at Eric Kenelm.

"There's a man, Captain, who hasn't tried to conceal his high esteem for Seldon Dockery, his deep gratitude for everything his friend has done for him. His alibi is weak and he hasn't tried to strengthen it in any way. When he found me prowling about this office after the first shooting, his actions convinced me. If Doctor Kenelm is a murderer, he's far smarter than most—intelligent enough to leave almost no clues at all, to resort to no artifice in order to ward off suspicion. In other words, his behavior has been that of a man innocently involved. What do you think of him, Captain?"

Max Russo said nothing, and Eric Kenelm was as wordless.

"Only one person really knew from the very beginning that Doctor Dockery had accidentally caused Ducky Chase's death. There she sits—his daughter."

Gretchen's hands gripped the arms of her chair.

"Being deeply sympathetic with her father, she sensed the real meaning of the deep agitation in him that night. She must have noticed that when he came back from the airport with his wife, he lacked his hat. The newspaper stories of Ducky's death confirmed her fears, and his drained bank accounts told her he was being bled. Perhaps by watching her father's office she learned who was blackmailing him. Last night she even set out for Odelle Quinn's home in a desperate effort to find some way of releasing him, and—"

The outer door quickly opened. Claudia Dockery's quick steps slowed and she gazed uncertainly from face to face. Her husband's warned her of a crisis. Raymond Lacroze, entering behind her, ignored everyone else after an impatient glance around the room and frowned his annoyance at Gretchen.

"It's high time you decided to give a thought to someone besides yourself. Claudia was coming to tell the doctor—"

"Please, Ray, not now!" Claudia interrupted. "Seldon, what are they doing to you?"

She hurried to her husband, fell to her knees at his side and clasped his hand. He managed a smile for her and his tortured eyes again turned to Brent.

"No one, certainly, feels a stronger devotion for Doctor Dockery than his wife," Brent said. "And nothing that Gretchen learned was beyond the scope of her own observations. Perhaps she felt even more strongly protective, suspecting that another woman was threatening not only her husband's life-work but her home. Doctor Dockery is a man who inspires staunch loyalties—even loyalty of a sort in his prospective son-in-law."

Lacroze flushed. "Whatever you're driving at, be careful of what you say to *me*."

"I'm being as careful as I know how. So painfully careful that I wish Captain Russo wouldn't let me go on with this—but I've got to. Being an entertainer like Odelle Quinn, did you know her?"

"Slightly," Lacroze snapped.

"And who is Francine?"

"Fah! A cow."

"She's a lovely, talented young woman," Claudia Dockery said at once. "A local girl, a dancer. Francine Danforth is the daughter of one of my husband's dearest friends."

BRENT STILL confronted Lacroze. "You were more than slightly aware of what was happening. At least Gretchen confided her fears in you. You saw the money you needed for your Villa Mañana—and you could look to no one but Doctor Dockery for it—being drained away by someone else. You could safeguard your own interests only by cutting off the flow. To a man of your selfish ambitions, a mere murder or two—"

There was a quick knock, and again the door opened. Brent suppressed a moan at sight of Valerie Randall. Directed by Garrett, beyond doubt, she was seeking to pick up the crumbs of Brent's information. Grimly gratified that she hadn't come sooner, Brent led her to Dr. Kenelm's desk, where she would be not too conspicuous an interloper.

"A reporter from the *Recorder*," he said, "and I suppose we must put up with her."

Lacroze caught his arm. "I don't care for the way you talk. You can't speak to *me* like that. I won't let you accuse *me*—"

"I haven't accused you," Brent retorted, "and frankly, I'm almost sorry to admit that with all your self-centered ruthlessness, you haven't the intelligence to have done it so well."

He turned his back on Lacroze, while Gretchen and Claudia watched him closely, and met the eyes of Captain Russo.

"There's only one person who could have convincingly called Odelle Quinn to this office. Next, when Doctor

Dockery heard the shots fired behind the hospital and realized what had happened, there was only one person from whom he could have taken the gun for the purpose of concealing it. Only one person who could have learned about the X-ray, who could have gone into the darkroom confident of not being noticed—"

Eric Kenelm spun about. Before Captain Russo could move, the door of his office was closed, the key was twisting in the lock. Brent's last glimpse was of Val's startled face. At once he ran past Dr. Dockery's desk and into the treatment-room. There he was stopped. A lock also fastened the connecting door.

"Val!" Brent called. "Are you all right?"

Russo's bony hand stopped him. "Take it easy, Bill. He's got a gun in his desk."

"Val!" Brent insisted. "Can you get out?"

There was no answer.

"Captain," Brent said quietly, "some of the fault of that accident must have been Ducky Chase's. He liked his night-caps and was always wandering around in an absent-minded fog. Certainly no one could have regretted it more than Seldon Dockery, a man who day and night fights sickness and death. I'll never believe it's right that one mishap should condemn a physician of his stature and rob us all of the good he can do."

Russo watched the door and there was silence in Eric Kenelm's office.

"Seldon Dockery called an ambulance at once and was very soon doing everything in his power to save Ducky's life. He sent Ducky's sister a small fortune. A friend agreed that it would be a tragedy if he should lose his license, and went to jail in his place—switched the broken fog-lamp to his own car and confessed. Doctor Dockery retained the best attorney in the city for him, and Danforth is being paid more money now than he earned as a laboratory assistant, and his sentence is short. Besides that, the doctor negotiated a good job for Mrs. Danforth. Even more, he's backing Lacroze's Villa Mañana only on condition that Danforth's daughter dance there. God knows the man has made retribution."

The shot was a heavy, muffled boom. A wailing cry followed it and the knob of the connecting door frantically rattled. With the turn of the key Val Randall appeared, so stricken with fear that she could scarcely stumble across the sill. Brent caught her, steered her to a chair.

"He—he warned me not to move and kept aiming the gun at me!" Val gasped, clinging to Brent's arm. "All the while he was writing and pointing the gun. Then he turned his back—"

Brent closed the door behind him. Max Russo was bending over the desk, reading the scrawled page that lay within an inch of Eric Kenelm's lifeless hand.

"It's a confession," Brent said. "He's taken everything on his own shoulders—not only the two murders, but the accidental death of Ducky Chase. What answer can you make to that, Captain?"

"I can't doubt a dead man's word," Max Russo said.

THE ROAR of the big presses in the basement decreased to a rumble, warning the *Recorder's* staff that again the deadline for the city final was at hand.

While eight newsmen pounded their typewriters and Val Randall, still deeply shaken, rapped out a new lead to her murder story, Bill Brent dug into his everlasting pile of correspondence. The day's Lorne column was still unfinished. He still needed one brief letter to fill it. He was chucking aside one missive after another when the copy boy pushed a telegram into his hands.

As he read it his eyebrows climbed. It was the first time anyone had ever appealed to Lora Lorne's wisdom by wire.

DEAR MISS LORNE: I NEED YOUR HELP. I'VE JUST LEARNED THAT I DON'T REALLY LOVE THE MAN I'M ENGAGED TO MARRY. ANOTHER MAN HAS CAPTURED MY HEART AND THIS TIME I KNOW I CAN'T BE WRONG. TELL ME QUICKLY, MISS LORNE, WHAT SHALL I DO?

—G.D.

Brent stared at it, remembering that Gretchen Dockery had called at the city-room, had even asked questions about him. And had someone betrayed him by divulging the horrible truth that he and Lora Lorne were one and the same?

Garrett interrupted Brent's conjectures. This time the city editor hadn't called derisively over the heads of the rest of the staff. He had personally come on a mission so earnest that he even used Brent's right name.

"Listen, Brent. Val's so upset she's writing practically nothing but typographical errors. Compared with Russo right now, a clam is positively garrulous. The paper's going to be late. This story's the biggest in years and you know all the inside of it. Get busy, will you? Give me one of your old humdingers!"

"You forget, Garrett," Brent said, smiling slowly. "This is the rapture department."

"Don't quibble, man! I've got a feeling about that story as Val's handling it. It sounds straight, but somehow it isn't. There's more behind it than she dreams. I want the real lowdown, a story twice as big as she's giving me. Write

it for me, Brent, and you'll go back on police tomorrow—
you'll never be Lora Lorne again. I give you my solemn
word."

Brent dabbed paste on the back of the telegram, slapped
it on a sheet of copy paper and under it scrawled his in-
junction to G.D.

*By all means follow the dictates of your heart, dear. Break
your engagement at once and let nature take its course.*

"Here's today's column, Garrett, and no, thanks," he said
with a grin. "I prefer to stay right here in this flowery little
cubbyhole. You see, I'm just finding out that after all there
are certain peculiar advantages to being Lora Lorne."

KILLER, STAY AWAY FROM MY DOOR!

LORA LORNE, THE *RECORDER'S* GENTLE ORACLE ON AFFAIRES DE L'AMOUR (WEIGHT 200 LBS., CHEST HAIRY, AND ANSWERING ALSO TO THE MANLY MONIKER OF BILL BRENT), GOES OUT TO HIS CAR ONE RAINY NIGHT AND FINDS: ONE FLAT TIRE, ONE NICE FRESH CORPSE, AND ONE JAR OF "AUNT MARTHA'S MARMALADE." CAUGHT LIKE A FLY IN THE UNSAVORY MURDER-JAM, BRENT FOLLOWS A STICKY TRAIL TO THE "SPOTLESS" KITCHEN WHERE THE TASTY MUFFIN SPREAD IS MORE CAREFULLY PRESERVED THAN HUMAN LIFE—BEARING ALWAYS IN MIND THE ADMONITION OF RUSSO OF HOMICIDE: "A NEWSPAPERMAN IS NO MORE COMFORTABLE THAN ANYONE ELSE WHEN HE SITS DOWN ON 2000 VOLTS."

CHAPTER ONE
DEAD LETTER

RAIN SPATTERED on the windows of Bill
Brent's cubbyhole in the remotest corner of the
Recorder's city room while he worked with paste-pot and
sheers. He was plucking letters from the inexhaustible
accumulation on his desk, composing answers to the problems they raised and assembling them into a full column
of type. His sour expression testified that he was sick of
the wacky job, and particularly sick of the interrupting
clamor of his telephone.

"Deposit five cents for five minutes, pul-ease," he heard
the operator say.

A bell bonged and a man's voice requested of Brent,
urgently: "Miss Lora Lorne—I must speak to Miss Lorne
at once."

"Very sorry," Brent muttered, as he did some forty or
fifty times every day. "Our Miss Lorne never answers
questions over the phone."

"But I don't want her advice," the voice said quickly.
"Just the opposite. I want to tell *her* something."

Brent's bushy eyebrows bent upward. This was an un-
precedented anomaly. Lora Lorne was the *Recorder's* love
expert—its own Dorothy Dix or Beatrice Fairfax—whose
guidance was anxiously sought at all weird hours of the

day and night by a woeful assortment of abandoned wives, jealous fiancés, torch-bearing spinsters and young girls more or less ruined. Prayers to Miss Lorne's fabulous wisdom came in an unrelenting flood from her large, harassed family of readers, and Bill Brent was tired unto

his very soul of them all. But this call was different. Never before had anyone undertaken to turn the tables and advise the paper's wise old seeress as to what *she* must do.

"Let's get this straight," Brent suggested, mildly amazed. "You mean you wish to enlighten our enlightened Miss Lorne?"

As the man answered, a mournful *whoo-oo-whoo* came over the wire—perhaps the horn of a river barge somewhere in the background.

"Not exactly that. I wrote Miss Lorne a letter. I expected her to use it in her column right away, but she hasn't printed it."

"That's to be expected," Brent answered. "After all, Miss Lorne receives about a thousand letters a week. She can print only six or seven a day at the most. It just happens that she didn't select yours."

"But—but I need her advice—" the man said, "need it desperately!" He sounded breathless, and the tension in him was growing even tighter. "She *must* print my letter. There's no one else I can turn to, and unless I have her advice something terrible might happen!"

"Well, tell me about it," Brent said dubiously, "and maybe I could—"

"Not you," the man protested. "You wouldn't understand, whoever you are. Please connect me with Miss Lorne—let me talk to her personally. I tell you, it—it's really a matter of life and death."

Bill Brent lapsed into silence. He couldn't connect Miss Lorne with this unknown man. Lora Lorne, as visualized by the thousands who trustingly turned to her in their amatory distress, was unable to answer the telephone simply because she did not exist. She was merely a phoney name plus a copyrighted picture which graced the *Recorder's* daily column of admonitions to the ardent. Actually her grandmotherly wisdom came out of the hard head of a two-hundred-pound, broken-nosed, big-hoofed guy named William Coleridge Brent, who liked his liquor neat.

THIS WAS a humiliating situation which Brent was unable to explain to the man on the phone.

Brent had come to the *Recorder* from a New York daily, under contract as a special reporter. He had scarcely learned the local ropes when Garrett, the hard-bitten city editor, had jerked him off the police trick and assigned him to the love column.

Garrett was a militaristic disciplinarian, and this was a punitive measure. Brent had missed a total of two or three weeks' work, due to wine and women. Even though he had since taken the vow as to both alcohol and step-ins, Garrett was still determined to teach him a lasting lesson. Until further notice, which was not forthcoming as yet, Brent must continue to masquerade as the *Recorder's* aged oracle of *affaires de l'amour,* whom he did not resemble in any particular.

Lora Lorne's portrait, printed atop the column every day, depicted her as a sweet old soul with combs in her snowy hair, wise eyes almost lost in kindly crinkles, eyeglasses dangling from a reel pinned to her sympathetic shoulder. Though this creature's heart-warming likeness had appeared every day since the column was begun twenty-two years ago, nobody remembered who the old dame really was. A long series of female busybodies had hidden behind that saccharine false-face. Brent, heaven help him, was the first male ever to function as Lora Lorne, and he would rather swallow cyanide than allow the mortifying secret to leak out.

"Miss Lorne is not in the office," he mumbled to the man on the phone. "She never comes. I don't know her address—nobody does. The demands on her time are so heavy, you know—she must be protected for the sake of *all* her huge family of readers."

He grimaced, remembering that no matter how sickening his crazy job might become, he couldn't chuck it. He was being paid too much. Besides, it would mean a fracture of his contract. In that event Garrett would take a sadistic delight in suing the pants off him and blacklisting him as well.

He could, however, pray for a chance to get back on the police trick where, by reason of his big-town training and his sex, he properly belonged. Though he had lived his hermaphroditic life for too many months now, his news-hawking instincts were still alive. Sensing an ulterior motive in the anxiety of the unknown man, he began to dig for it.

"But I can get a message through to Miss Lorne," he suggested. "If you'll describe your letter—"

"I can't trust anyone but Miss Lorne herself," the man said flatly, his agitation growing sharper. "I know *she'll* keep faith with me. *She'll* understand that I must have her advice so as to avoid the—the heartaches, the horrible things that will happen to half a dozen people who don't deserve such—such punishment. I've got to talk to her."

Punishment? Was this man hinting at something criminal? With the thought Brent shed his mental petticoats. Becoming his old self again—a police reporter scenting something similar to blood—he tried rapidly to think of a subterfuge which would draw out the secret the unknown man was guarding. Silent another moment, he heard another sound on the wire—a faint click-clatter as of freight cars rolling over a long stretch of track.

"Well, I'm damned," he said, simulating pleased surprise. "Miss Lorne has just come into the news room for the first time in months. I'll ask her if she'll speak to you. Maybe you'll get a break."

"Tell her the matter is vital," the man urged hopefully. "Vital!"

Brent wedged himself from his cramped office. The nightly deadline was near, bringing the city staff to its busiest pitch. The clatter of typewriters mingled with the rattle of the rain on the windows while eight newsmen labored over their copy. Brent turned to the desk which he still considered rightly his own and seized Valerie Randall's arm, stopping her in mid-sentence.

"A man on my wire, Val," he said, tugging her away from her machine. "You're going to talk to him, as Lora Lorne. Use a high-pitched, quavering voice—make yourself sound older and wiser than God. Get it?"

She didn't quite, so Brent kept explaining while he steered her to his phone. Though Val Randall was by all odds the loveliest brunette he had ever desired to kick out of a newspaper plant—working his old trick, she was trying to make herself famous as a female police reporter—she was the only confederate he could enlist on short notice. Now she was nodding her pretty head, signifying that she understood what he meant her to do.

"He-ll-o," she cackled, when Brent brought the transmitter to her lips. "Lo-ra Lorne is speak-ing to you. Let me li-ft the weight from your poo-oor troubled heart, de-ar friend."

The voice on the wire said quietly: "I'm very grateful, Miss Lorne. The matter's desperately important, and unless I have your advice I know the results will be tragic—really tragic. If you'll be so good as to print my letter in tomorrow morning's editions—"

"But tell me, de-ar friend," Valerie said in her senile tone, "how will I recognize it?"

"By the color of the paper. It's orange. But—"The man hesitated. His voice lowered. "On second thought, Miss Lorne, let me speak again to the man who brought you to the phone."

Puzzled, Brent took it—and immediately hot words burst into his ear.

"That wasn't Lora Lorne! She's a rank fake! She sounded like some kid trying to act like an old woman in a high school play. I'll not say another word to you, you trickster—except this. If that letter is not published the tragedy will be on your head. Any terrible thing may come of it now—anything—even murder!"

A crash and the vehement voice was gone, leaving that ominous word echoing in Bill Brent's mind—*murder.*

CHAPTER TWO

DEATH UNDER THE LID

"**WHAT IS** it, Bill?"Val Randall asked quickly. "News? If so, remember *I'm* a reporter."

"A screwball, probably, that's all,"Brent answered, eyeing her. "Nothing's coming of it, thanks to the way you messed it up, so scram!"

She wrinkled her shapely nose at him. "After all," she said, *"I've* important news to handle on the Winston case."

Having goaded him twice in his sorest spot, she turned away, but she got no farther than a single step. A man was blocking her path.

"Just a minute!" the man said with a snap.

Brent recognized him as Walter Eastwell, a special investigator attached to the district attorney's office. He had just pushed in through the swinging doors of the city room and his slicker was trickling rainwater on the littered floor. He had a bristling mustache and an outthrust chin. His eyes burning with an irate fire, he leveled an accusing finger at Val Randall.

"You've been spying on me."

"Why, Mr. Eastwell," Val said ingenuously. "Whatever in the world are you talking about?"

"Don't deny it, and don't tell me this is no way to talk to a lady," Eastwell retorted. "When it comes to getting news, you're as gentle and innocent as a starved tigress. We're going to have this out, Miss Randall, right now!"

Brent watched Miss Randall hurry after Eastwell to the city desk. Eastwell whacked a hand on it so emphatically that Garrett, whose nerves were tough as rawhide, sat up like a jack-in-the-box. Again the investigator leveled an indignant finger, this time at a copy of the *Recorder's* mail edition, which had just come up from the press room. A front page headline shouted: *D.A.'s SEARCH FOR WINSTON SHIFTS TO SOUTH SIDE.*

"Still missing!" Eastwell blurted. "Missing while we're doing our damndest to smoke him out. He'll stay missing as long as this lousy sheet keeps tipping him off by printing these public warnings, telling him where we're hunting for him day by day!"

The Winston case was none of Brent's business, but he recalled that Timothy Winston was a chemist who had been engaged in research on a new commercial product. As a result of a disastrous fire in his private laboratory, he had been forced into bankruptcy. One of his backers had brought charges against him, accusing him of concealing certain assets.

A week ago Winston had suddenly made himself scarce, evidently fearing the results of his trial, which was called for next Monday morning. Since then the D.A.'s investigators had been scurrying about in an effort to flush him out of cover. So far, as Walter Eastwell was making plain, they had failed.

"Eastwell," Garrett said, coming to his feet in defense of Val Randall, "we've done nothing but print the news you've given out yourself."

"I have given out this stuff?" Eastwell protested. "Are you balmy? I haven't passed you a jot of information about the Winston case, or any other, for that matter."

"Why, *Mr.* Eastwell!" Val said in a hurt tone. "Five or six times since Winston scrammed you called me on the phone and told me just where you were hunting for him. Really you did. Don't you remember?"

"Damn right he remembers!" Garrett was scowling. Having come out of the first World War a major at twenty-three, Garrett could work up a formidable scowl. "Trying to get from under, are you, Eastwell? Your boss is squawking because you've gotten yourself too much publicity, is that it? Well, don't try to pass the buck to Miss Randall. Because it won't work."

Eastwell stiffened. "I never called you, young woman, never! Don't try to becloud the issue, Garrett. Unless this she-wolf of yours stops trailing me around—broadcasting every move I make—obstructing justice—"

The argument degenerated into more heated denials and counter-denials, and Brent was satisfied to let Val Randall remain in the middle. At the moment he was more concerned with a certain letter. Hopefully he began digging into the correspondence piled and scattered about his cramped office.

There were letters perfumed with violet, with heliotrope or exotic musk. There were baby blue letters, faintly mauve letters, letters written in blood-red ink on pale pink paper. Searching for an orange one, Brent tossed the others aside and dug steadily deeper into the accumulation. At last he came up with a bright envelope.

IT WAS addressed to Lora Lorne in a peculiarly neat hand. The printed return card in the upper left corner had been scratched out so heavily that Brent couldn't decipher a single character beneath the pen-strokes. Noting that it bore the postmark of Substation D, Brent ripped it open, found inside a sheet of the same color—evidently a letterhead from which the imprint had been sheared—and plunged into the message which the unknown man had considered so urgent.

> Dear Miss Lorne:
>
> For many years I have kept a dreadful secret. It is the secret of an old crime which the world has forgotten, yet it will not let me rest. I hope you will understand that it happened when I was much younger, through circumstances which I could not control. I cannot tell the details even to you, Miss Lorne, for I must not let the truth become known. But even now, in spite of all my precautions, my past is threatening to ruin my new life. That is why I am so desperately in need of your guidance.
>
> My secret has begun to leak out. I am sure it is known to several persons. I fear a scandal, but even more deeply I fear that in my anxiety to keep my secret I may do something unforgivable.
>
> In order to understand my feelings, dear Miss Lorne, you must think of me as two selves. My one self is quiet, honest, a

conservative business man. My other self is impulsive, rash, even reckless. You see, I am really two different persons who are constantly in conflict. At moments when I am hard-pressed by many troubles, as I am now, my evil half dominates me and fills me with fear of the vicious things I may do.

In order clearly to differentiate my two personalities, Miss Lorne, I will call the quiet one Tom and the reckless one Mike.

Frowning over the letter, Bill Brent muttered to himself: "This guy definitely needs to have his valves ground."

Tom is content to make the best of a bad situation. If my secret becomes known, he will uncomplainingly face the consequences. Not so with Mike. Mike will go to any extreme to protect Tom. Determined that the truth must never be learned, Mike will not only scheme shrewdly to guard it, but will strenuously fight to destroy the dangers that threaten Tom. That is my great fear, Miss Lorne—that Mike will contrive to conceal my old crime by committing new ones—even the worst.

Mike's hot-blooded audacity must be mastered. He must be prevailed upon to control himself, or he must be removed from the temptation to strike back, or in some other way the savage in him must be kept from running amuck. I am at my wit's end, Miss Lorne, because I realize I cannot conquer him alone. I must have help, quickly, before something disastrous happens. Tell me, Miss Lorne, what can I do?

The letter was signed, *Fearful*.

Mulling over it, Brent reconsidered. It wasn't what it seemed. Apparently a psychopath's babbling, it was nevertheless literate. Any man who could analyze his case so clearly as this, Brent thought, would be intelligent enough to take himself to a psychiatrist rather than appeal to the rapture department of a three-cent newspaper. The writer of this letter, Brent surmised, was not really seeking Lora

Lorne's advice. Some hidden purpose lay behind his demand that it be published.

Did it, then, conceal a message intended for some reader of the Lorne column? If so, Brent thought he might squeeze out its real meaning. Suspecting the whole setup, his mind began tracing it from its beginning.

The phone call had come from a pay-station within the five-cent zone. Brent had heard the hoot of a river barge in the background, then the clatter of a passing freight train. The river curved through the outskirts of the city, and the railroad tracks crossed a bridge on their direct way to the Central Terminal. There was only one place where a telephone might have picked up the noises of both rails and river—the vicinity of the South Side Bridge.

Brent stared at the front page headlines—*D.A.'s SEARCH FOR WINSTON SHIFTS TO SOUTH SIDE.*

His blood pressure climbing. Brent recalled that Timothy Winston was in a tight spot. For a week now the chemist had been lurking under cover while investigators and an army of cops fine-combed the city for him. It was an intensive, systematic manhunt, getting steadily hotter. Winston was due to get grabbed the moment he made a move that would betray his hiding place. But suppose, hard-pressed as he was, that he had found it necessary to send an important message to someone. How could he do it without bringing the cops down on his neck?

He couldn't approach his home, which was probably under surveillance, or keep a rendezvous with his wife, who would be trailed in case she made a suspicious move. Brent had heard from Val Randall that Winston's telephone wire was tapped. To use the mails would be much too risky, and to send a telegram would be practically an open invitation for the dicks to call. Winston was cut off from every ordinary means of communication, in fact, including the personal column of the *Recorder,* the use of which would also leave a broad trail. But the Lorne pillar!

That was a shrewd idea. It could have been easily prearranged—Winston to write, if necessary, to Lora Lorne, couching the letter in such a manner that its real meaning could be read only by the person for whom it was intended—his wife, most probably. The flaw in the plan was that there was only one chance in several hundred that any given letter would actually see print. When this particular one had failed to appear, the unknown man had been obliged to phone his insistence that it be published. If Brent's reasoning was right, then the voice on the wire had been that of the fugitive Winston.

HIS HOPES soaring, he studied the letter. Superficially it had no connection with Winston, except that the neat handwriting might be the meticulous script of a scientist. So far as Brent knew, however, nobody involved in the case was named Tom or Mike. After half an hour of cogitation it still didn't make sense to Brent.

Abruptly he gave up, stuffing the letter in his pocket and realizing that the message itself was less important than its source. No matter what it meant, he had found a clearcut trail which promised to lead straight to the man for whom the police had been vainly searching for seven days and nights.

He had only to ask the clerks at Post-office Substation D if they recalled a person or firm that used stationery of this unusual orange color. Undoubtedly they would remember—but if not, he could canvass the printing shops located near the South Side Bridge. One further step and Brent would then not only have run down Winston, but he'd also have a major news story—one that would enable him to shed Lora Lorne's hated bustle and win his salvation as a newsman.

Already out of his chair, he grabbed his hat, his trenchcoat and his pasted-up copy. Walter Eastwell, he noticed as he wedged himself out of his office, had left. He slapped today's column on Garrett's desk and ignored Garrett's acidulous comment: "It's about time, Grandma."

Knowing that if he tipped his hand prematurely Garrett would order him off and turn the story over to Val, but that once he had the whole sensational coup sewed up nobody would be able to rob him of it, he ran down six flights of iron stairs to the ground floor and pushed out into the downpour.

His car was parked near the loading dock, in the street at the rear of the plant. Raindrops snapped out of the murk and pelted his face as he slid under the wheel. His plan of action was mapped and the motor hummed, but he hadn't yet rolled six feet when something crunched under a tire and the car's rear end sagged.

He piled out into the drenching rain. It was the right rear tire and it was flat as hell. Growling blasphemy, he bent, shielded the flame of a match and saw that the trouble was no mere puncture but a gaping gash. In the flowing gutter lay the broken glass jar that had done him this inopportune damage. He muttered at the jagged pieces and demanded of God to know how in the name of justice they had ever come here.

It was a thick-walled quart jar and it had not been empty. A sticky yellowish stuff had flowed out of the fragments. Gobs of it were dissolving in the swirling gutter water. The rain was also causing the jar's label to slough off. As Brent read it—*Aunt Martha's Marmalade, Hand-Packed in Her Own Spotless Kitchen*—it floated away and plunged out of sight through the grating of a sewer—where, Brent felt, Aunt Martha herself deserved to wind up.

The rain sluiced down and Brent had to change a wheel. He gripped the handle of the baggage compartment, was glad he hadn't left it locked, and yanked it up. Another match flickering, he stooped in to free the spare. After a moment he straightened, dropped the match and drew a soughing breath.

Another car, he realized with a start, had just stopped and was flanking his. He recognized it from the days when he had happily done police. It was the power-packed limousine of the Homicide Squad. The man who had just alighted from it was Captain Russo, the squad's chief, who was as cadaverous as any corpse he had ever smelled out. Brent was reminded that Russo possessed the uncanny instincts of a buzzard, and Russo was gazing at Brent now with unreadable eyes that were the dull, depthless black of a sepulcher.

Brent looked again into the baggage compartment of his car—at the body of Walter Eastwell lying huddled, his face almost unrecognizable, the top of his head very messy.

"There you are, Russo," Brent said. "He's as dead as he'll ever get. The D.A.'s really got something to complain about now."

CHAPTER THREE

MURDER AND MARMALADE

THE DISTRICT ATTORNEY was in the managing editor's office, with Garrett and Val Randall, declaring that the *Recorder* was responsible for the murder of his ablest investigator. He blamed the paper as a whole because of its damned snooping, its unethical exposure of official confidence—meaning its coverage of the Winston manhunt. The hands of at least one of the news staff were morally stained with Eastwell's blood and somebody, the D.A. asserted, would suffer.

Bill Brent got the gist of this while pacing back and forth near the managing editor's door. Uneasily recalling the warning of murder which he still attributed to the fugitive Timothy Winston, he shrank into Lora Lorne's padded chair and apprehensively awaited developments.

A burst of consternation in the city room had followed the news that Eastwell had turned up dead in Brent's car, but now the Homicide Squad's investigation was bogging down.

"You're the one who phoned my office—told us just where we could find Eastwell's body—weren't you, Brent?" Captain Russo inquired in his peculiar lifeless tone.

Brent shook his head and tried to figure out the circumstances. Eastwell had left Garrett, Van Randall and the news room in a huff, but he had not been killed immediately thereafter. Evidently in pursuit of the missing Winston, he had first gone to some place unknown even to the D.A., where he had been beaten down with a hammer.

The dust remaining on Eastwell's clothing was foreign to the *Recorder's* plant and not to be found anywhere outdoors in this rainstorm. The hammer was indicated by the marks left on his crushed skull. His cooling body had been transported back as far as Brent's car, and for reasons best known to himself the murderer had anonymously phoned police headquarters to tell the Homicide Squad where it could be found, which accounted for Russo's timely arrival.

"Your car," Russo said hollowly. "Why yours?"

"The killer evidently couldn't let the corpse be found at the scene of the crime," Brent surmised. "I don't know why, exactly, but he had to move it out of a danger zone. So he began driving it around, looking for a place suitable for publicity purposes."

"But why *your* car?"

"Mine was probably the only car in the block that didn't have its baggage compartment locked. I give you my word of honor, Russo," Brent said earnestly, "I'll never be so careless about it again. I need my bus. You're not going to hold it as evidence, are you?"

"So much rain," Russo complained morbidly. "No fingerprints."

"Besides," Brent pointed out, "you've taken a good look into my tool kit. My hammer is clean and dry, definitely not the one used to beat the life out of Eastwell."

"I hope you're an innocent bystander," Russo answered. "I'll take a chance that you won't turn up any more murdered bodies. I don't like too many."

"You mean I can go?"

"Not too far," the captain said sadly.

The conference in the managing editor's room was continuing when Brent went quietly out. Pausing behind his car, he first made sure that Russo's squad had removed the corpse from it. The rain had driven them inside. Brent had the spot to himself. After changing the damaged tire he securely locked the trunk, then turned his attention to the broken glass in the gutter.

All the marmalade had now dissolved away. Nothing remained but the fragments of the jar, washed clean by the rain. The Homicide Squad either had not noticed them, or had thought them unimportant. Brent felt differently about it. A full quart of marmalade dropped into a gutter near a murdered body was, in his opinion, not a matter to be ignored.

Through the slackening rain he drove first to Post-office Substation D. It was closed and as dark as the warehouses and factories surrounding it. At this hour no printer would be open either. Both Brent's leads were temporarily blocked. But a few delicatessens and grocery stores might still be doing business. He set off again.

The drowsy clerks in the first two stores said: "Never heard of it." The third and fourth said: "Don't carry it—no call for it." The fifth thought hard and told Brent, "Had some once—maybe I got a little left somewhere," and after several minutes of searching produced a dusty tin-capped tumbler selling for nineteen cents. Brent felt it was worth the price to learn that Aunt Martha's own spotless kitchen was a local institution.

HE TOURED. Winding in and out of the deserted streets of the South Side, he returned again and again to the foot of the bridge. He followed the river, which was rising under the rain, and shuttled back and forth, hunting advertising signs and nameplates, straining to read them through the flashing wig-wag of his windshield wipers. After what seemed an interminable hunt, he veered suddenly to the curb and ducked out.

Above him on a cracked brick wall were the sooty words, *Aunt Martha's Marmalade,* above the line, *Thomas Stone, Distributor.*

"Tom!" Brent murmured.

Hoo-whooo! mourned a passing barge.

The ancient building sat directly on the river. The crumbling foundation perched on a bank of rock and its sheer rear wall rose directly above the water's swirling edge. Walking quietly into the cinder-packed yard, Brent saw that the windows were begrimed and dark. Trying the door of the garage, his hand found a padlock dangling loose. He struck a match and discovered that the hasp had been pried off. Unweathered splinters told him that a job of breaking and entering had been done here, possibly tonight.

He sidled into the garage, paused and listened. Another match showed him a motorcycle dozing in a stall. Instead of a sidecar it had a small delivery cab. Time had dimmed the painted gold of Aunt Martha's name. Brent went to it, pawed it and felt heat. The motorcycle had been used within the past several hours.

He opened the cab. Still another match showed him several jars of marmalade on its floor. They'd been bounced onto their sides, probably by the quick turns of a fast trip, and one of them, containing a pint of Aunt Martha's concoction, had cracked. Wondering just how good it was, Brent reached inside as the flame winked out, touched a sticky spot and brought his fingers to his tongue.

He spat violently.

Another match and Brent put his head into the cab. He had missed the jar. Gingerly trying again, he found that the stuff oozing from its cracks was, in fact, quite tasty. The sticky brown spot on the floorboards near it, however, was not.

Since the cab could accommodate a dead human body, folded up, the dark stuff was definitely not anything that Brent liked on toast for breakfast.

Brent could now account for the broken marmalade jar in the gutter. Someone, while hastily transferring a corpse to his car, had inadvertently nudged the jar out of this motorcycle cab.

He found the motorcycle's tool kit. The hammer it contained was small, clean and dry—obviously not the weapon of murder.

He peered about. High stacks of corrugated paper cartons surrounded him. Opening one of them he saw that it contained, as he had expected, marmalade. There were hundreds of boxes here, each packed with jars of various sizes, crowding the garage to the roof.

Striking more matches, Brent moved into the adjacent rooms. They were also chock full of marmalade—marmalade that had been stored here so long that the boxes were disintegrating. Mounting a flight of wooden stairs, igniting one match after another, Brent encountered more and more of Aunt Martha's product.

The age of the boxes progressed inversely as he climbed. The newest were on the highest floors. In the largest room at the top of the flight the supply of boxes had evidently become exhausted. The loose jars were stacked, piled and heaped helter-skelter and in bulk in all the corners. The whole building, to Brent's amazement, was crammed with the stuff—a reserve prodigious beyond a small boy's sweetest dreams.

Jars suddenly began skittering, clinking and rolling at Brent's feet—an avalanche of marmalade precipitated by his step upon a loose board—and as it subsided he sensed an echoing movement in another part of the building.

Brent trailed it quickly along a dusty hallway. Evidently the noise of the cascading jars had alarmed someone. The sound of his steps produced more noises—noises that fled as he approached.

He ran toward a streak of light shining under a closed door. He squeezed through, saw nobody, crossed an office, then pushed into a room which was empty except for a cot covered with old blankets. Now the fast noises were below Brent, indicating that someone was fleeing the building.

Handicapped by the darkness, he stumbled down another flight of stairs which took him past two landings, at each of which more marmalade was piled. A loud slam echoed from somewhere beyond. Brent presently found another door on the ground floor—the entrance. Jerking it open, he sidled into the rain and ran across the yard to the street.

Everything was quiet. If Brent was right in surmising that his quarry had mistaken him for an investigator from the district attorney's office, then Timothy Winston had just slipped through his fingers.

BRENT RETURNED to the rooms on the top floor. The cot gave point to his theory that this was Winston's hiding place. In the adjoining office the floor was tracked. Dust covered the rolltop desk, a swivel chair and an ancient black safe.

The top drawer of the desk contained a supply of stationery printed with the card, *Aunt Martha's Marmalade, Thomas Stone, Distributor.* They matched the cryptic letter written to Lora Lorne, and the reason for their tint was now obvious, since marmalade and the color orange both spring from the same natural source.

Brent peered into the wastebasket. It was empty except for several scraps of paper. Fishing them out, he fitted them together into an ordinary envelope and a page torn from a scratch pad, both white. The name of Thomas Stone was typewritten on the envelope. The message, which was also neatly typed, had no salutation and no signature.

> Stay inside. Don't let them scare you out. That might wreck the works. You're safer here. They're getting closer, but they won't reach you. They can be kept away, if only you'll stay strictly where you are. Remember how much depends on you.

Brent tucked it in his pocket alongside the orange letter and, turning next to the safe, he noticed that the windows were painted black—painted recently, to judge from the smell.

The safe was closed, but not locked. Inside it he found a pack of printed slips bound by a rubber band.

They were receipts. Beginning with March 7, 1936, the dates on them progressed at weekly intervals up to the present month. Each was made out in payment for a quantity of marmalade received, and the amounts paid for the consignments averaged between fifty and sixty dollars.

They were all written in the same precise hand that had penned the letter to Lora Lorne and all were signed, in quite a different script, *Payment Received, Martha Kelsie.*

Looking further, Brent found a cash box. It contained so much money that he involuntarily whistled. There were handfuls of coin plus sheaves of tens and twenties, the whole totaling, at a rough guess, ten or twelve thousand dollars. And Brent recalled that the fugitive Winston was wanted under charges of concealing assets in bankruptcy.

Suddenly Brent was pushing his whole head into the safe. Something had hit him on the nape with vicious force. He felt no pain, but chagrin because his preoccupation with the safe had permitted an assailant to attack from the rear. He did not remember pulling his head out of the safe again.

When he became cloudily conscious he was being dragged across a floor. He heard rusty hinges squeak a hundred miles away. Rain spat at him, cold wind puffed in his face, the river gurgled. He was being rolled like a keg of beer. His legs were sticking out into wet space and the rest of him was tumbling after them.

Somewhere in the night a note of lament rose: *Whoo-oo-hoo-oo!*

Instinctively Brent whipped his arms about, seeking support. He flung them down against a flat surface—the floor. He was hanging outside an old loading floor, dangling against the sheer rear wall of the building.

He looked up at a towering phantom-like figure. It was stooping, preparing to beat at him, to force him to let go. He clung there unable to defend himself, knowing that when the blow fell he'd plunge unconscious into the dark river swirling far below.

He knew, too, that the thing poised to whip down at his head was a hammer.

CHAPTER FOUR

DARK WALLS WATCH

BRENT CLOSED his eyes and hung on. After a moment he realized dimly that somehow the hammer wasn't coming down. He blinked and the menacing shadow-figure was gone. It had been scared off. There was a bright shine now at the far end of the room, beyond the heaps of marmalade—the beam of a flash-light.

The light was on the steps. It had come from below and was going up. In the reflected glow Brent saw a girl. She was a very pretty girl. Twenty and blond, she had lovely legs. She paused, startled, as an inarticulate call burst from Brent's pressed lips.

As she turned back with a little gasp her light swung over Brent's head. She didn't see him. Her attention turned instead to someone who was coming up the stairs after her—a man holding a flaming paper match. The man halted as the girl's torch beamed into his face. He was a dark, jaunty chap, and handsome, though there were deep lines of dissipation around his mouth.

"Hello, Lila, darling," he said.

"Roy!" the girl exclaimed. "What are you doing here?"

Brent was slipping. He couldn't shift his arms, hot breath was locked in his lungs despite his effort to call again. He was wondering how sharp were those rocks at the water's edge three stories down when, quickly, the light swung back.

"What was that?" Roy said.

Brent's excruciating effort to hang on had wrung a groan from him. The beam struck full in his eyes. He heard exclamations, running footfalls. Roy's hands dug under his armpits. Lila helped. Brent flopped flat on his back on the floor, gulping in air, the aching tension going out of his muscles.

"Thanks!" he gasped, grinning up into two faces that were the pleasantest he had ever seen. "Thanks!"

"Don't mention it," Roy said. "Maybe you can do the same for us sometime. What the hell happened to you?"

"Tell you about it—when I get my breath back!"

Lila and Roy gazed down at Brent. He was obviously all right now, and they evidently had troubles of their own on their minds. They turned to each other—Lila puzzled, Roy with a disarming smile.

"What *are* you doing here, Roy?" she asked.

"I followed you, of course, Lila, darling," Roy said.

"Followed me?" The girl was concerned. "But nobody knew I was coming. I didn't tell anyone."

"You see, Lila, sweet," Roy explained, "I arrived at your home just as you drove off. Didn't you notice me trailing you? And when I saw you go into this spooky place I had to come in right at your pretty heels because I simply don't want anything to happen to my darling Lila."

Though somehow he sounded familiar to Brent, his voice was richer and more cultivated than that of the man who had cried murder over the phone wire.

"Roy," Lila said, "you've been drinking."

"I think so, Lila," Roy said contritely. "I'm just a no-good rum-hound, that's what I am."

"Oh, Roy!" the girl cried. "I told you what would happen if you did it again! And besides—why aren't you at work?"

"Been fired, Lila," Roy confessed.

"Fired!" the girl blurted. She was really angry now, and Brent thought it made her seem even lovelier. "Fired again?"

"Yes, Lila," Roy said. "I showed up late again, that's why. I really couldn't help it, though, Lila. I'd wandered into a bar somewhere, and I'd gotten my foot caught in the rail."

"Roy, Roy!" There were tears in Lila's eyes now. "I love you, really I do, but we can't go on like this!"

"I was afraid you'd say that," Roy answered solemnly. "But if you'll give me one more chance—"

"It's no use," Lila said, her voice breaking. "I'm terribly sorry, but this time I'm going to do just what I swore I would."

SHE REMOVED a diamond ring from the third finger of her left hand. A little sob broke from her lips as she gave it to Roy. He stared at it sadly, then tucked it into his vest pocket. They seemed to have forgotten Brent. He elbowed up, feeling that as Lora Lorne he had a right to intervene.

"Lila," Brent said, "aren't you making a mistake? Roy seems to be an all-right guy. Look what he just did for me—saved me from a fatal fall. Fired or drunk, you really ought to help straighten him out. Go on, Lila, take his ring back."

"She won't," Roy told him. "She's much too good for me anyway." For all his bantering speech, there was such profound pain in his eyes that Brent felt sorry for him. "Well, what the hell did happen to you?"

Remembering that he had almost found Timothy Winston, almost at the cost of his life, Brent felt he had earned the right to keep the story exclusively his own.

"Slipped," he said. "Floor's wet, you see. The roof leaks. Skidded and fell against the door. Very old door—it gave way. But I'm O.K. now, thanks to you."

He found his feet, while Lila studied him, and Roy gazed at her with the lines growing deeper and darker around his wry mouth.

"Lila," Roy said quietly, "why did you come to this place?"

"To see Mr. Stone," Lila said, still estimating Brent. *"You're* Mr. Stone, aren't you?" Before Brent could find the breath to deny it, she rushed on. "Your phone call tonight upset Mother, Mr. Stone. She didn't understand. You said she must stop making marmalade for a while, and yet she'll keep on getting her checks just the same."

Lila's anxiety was so real, and Lora Lorne's homely counsel had become so deeply a part of Brent, that he felt he must reassure her. "You needn't worry about that. Have you glanced around? The stock on hand is enough to cover all the muffins in town for many months to come."

"Mr. Stone, Mother's been doing so well, and she's been so happy in her success, and I don't know what in the world we'd have done otherwise, but—well, I never find any of her marmalade in the stores, and everybody I ask says no, they don't buy it."

"It's a big city, Lila," Brent reminded her.

"Be honest with me, Mr. Stone! I've thought for a long time now that something—well, something strange is going on that Mother and Richard and I don't know about. I've worried for fear it might be—dishonest. Please, Mr. Stone—I can face the truth!"

"Lila," Brent said, "what on earth could be crooked about Aunt Martha's Marmalade, Hand-Packed in Her Own Spotless Kitchen?"

"That's absolutely right," Roy said. "Forget it, Lila."

"But it would be perfectly terrible if something happened to the business now, because so much depends on it!" Lila said. "Richard and me and Mother's happiness—everything!"

"Look, Lila, darling," Roy said. *"I'm* the guy who watches out for you."

"Everything *will* be all right, Mr. Stone!" Lila asserted with a forcefulness that astonished Brent. Her eyes were taking fire and her lips were pinched together. Pretty as she was, her face began to shine with an indefinable fierceness. "I'll see to that—somehow!"

She walked rapidly across the cavernous room. Roy lingered. In the glow Brent saw that he was smiling an oddly quiet smile.

"Maybe you're really Thomas Stone," Roy murmured in a tone so low that Lila could not hear, "and maybe not. I don't really care. But there's one thing I want you to understand clearly. Though she'll probably never marry me, Lila will always be my whole world. I'm going to keep her safe. If you pull a fast one on her I'll kill you."

Still smiling his oddly sad smile, he turned, left Brent in the dark and went quietly down the stairs.

REFLECTING THAT the deeper he went into the Winston case the wackier it became, Brent stopped trying to figure it out. Alone now, and with a few matches left, he used them for a return trip to the office.

This was unquestionably Winston's hide-out. Tonight the D.A.'s investigation had pressed so close as to throw him into a panic. Brent could not doubt that Walter Eastwell's search had somehow led him to this building. Eastwell's real lead might never be known, but in any event the trail had led him to his death.

Having narrowly missed a similar fate, Brent felt it could fairly be attributed to Winston's desperate desire to avoid facing trial for concealing assets in bankruptcy, which charge the money in the safe could evidently substantiate.

Feeling that to wait here for the fugitive to return would be a waste of time—being also a trespasser and guilty of illegal entry of a sort—he lighted his way down the stairs. The garage door, he found, was provided with cleats on the inside, and there was a stout bar. He dropped it in place, turned back, let himself out the entrance. Stooping, he gathered a handful of cinders and scattered them finely over the sill.

The rain was letting up when he left the bleak building behind him. Back in the *Recorder* plant, he found that the activity in the news-room had subsided. The last edition had been put to bed. Val Randall was not there, having evidently gone to headquarters to follow developments. Garrett was winding up a busy night at his desk. His cold gray eyes fixed on Brent.

"Before you even begin," the city editor said flatly, "the answer is no."

"Look," Brent said. "Val's fragile hands were never meant to toy with homicide and gore. Mine were never meant to guide the wayward steps of unmarried mothers. After all, the *Recorder's* business is news, and as a news digger-upper I am locally unsurpassed."

"That's a matter of opinion," Garrett remarked.

"I'm speaking of news of sensational importance," Brent persisted. "Suppose I can reveal certain circumstances of the Eastwell murder which will virtually solve it. My unusual merit as a reporter would then put me back on police, would it not?"

"My dear Miss Lorne," Garrett said, "it would not. The police don't need your guidance as much as your immense family of rapturous readers does. Leave the law alone and confine yourself to the vagaries of Venus."

"Do you mean to say that if I served up that story piping hot you'd keep me on the heart-throb column regardless, you sadist?"

"Miss Lorne," Garrett said with a rasp, "our police department will soon crack the case. The facts will then be available to our Miss Randall. The *Recorder* will thereupon make haste to print them. I do not believe we need your assistance, except as a patroness of the passionate."

"The hell you don't," Brent said. "I'm telling you, Garrett, I've got the story by the tail. But that's all I'm telling you until I have your word of honor that you'll put me back on the police trick as soon as I've cracked—"

"You're going to stay strictly off news," Garrett declared, "and that's final. In fact, I'll see to it. I'm warning you, Grandma—stick to your knitting, or I'll expand your column to one full page every day."

"A full page!" Brent gulped. "Oh God! You couldn't! Nobody could be so utterly inhuman—"

But Garrett could be, and Brent knew it well. He sat in agonized silence, grimly thinking that his only chance of salvation was to risk the punishment Garrett was threatening—split the Winston case so wide open that Garrett must relent and reward him. As he doggedly planned his next move, the copy boy tossed a copy of the latest edition on the desk.

The headline jolted him: *EASTWELL MURDER BRINGS WINSTON SEARCH NEAR END!* Captain Russo and the D.A. were jointly promising that it was only a matter of hours until they would capture the fugitive.

"Listen, Garrett!" Brent blurted. "I'll spill it right now— the whole works! We'll beat 'em to Winston and score the biggest scoop—"

"Calm yourself, Grandma," Garrett said. "Quite aside from the fact that Winston doesn't remotely concern you, you know we never put out extras. The final has just come off the presses. There won't be another edition until tomorrow afternoon, by which time Val will probably have the whole authentic story direct from Russo himself."

CHAPTER FIVE
ONE CORPSE WAS PLENTY

BRENT STOPPED his car near the Winston residence. Upstairs and down its windows were lighted. The night wind eddying past it brought the acrid smell of something burnt.

The charred remains of a low frame building stood in the rear yard. The tangled metallic mass amid the ashes was the remains of certain equipment. This was all that was left of Timothy Winston's private research laboratory.

Brent thoughtfully rang the bell at the front door. Though he saw no sign of the district attorney's spotters, he felt he was being watched. After a moment quick steps approached, the door opened and a young woman looked out.

Brent recognized her, from pictures printed in the *Recorder*, as Ann Winston, the fugitive's wife. Her dark brown eyes were bewildered and alarmed, but her chin was lifted and her self-possessed bearing left no doubt that she was completely capable of taking care of herself. Judging at once that her loyalty to her husband was withstanding a crushing strain, Brent liked her.

"From the *Recorder*," he said. "I think you'll want to talk with me. I've picked up certain information concerning your husband."

Ann Winston paled, a flicker of consternation showed in her eyes. She did not answer, but neither did she avoid Brent's gaze. For that he liked her still more. She turned quickly and he followed her into the living-room. As she waited anxiously for him to speak, he brought the orange letter from his pocket, held it before her widened eyes and gave her time to read it through.

"Important message," Brent said, taking a shot in the dark. "One you can't ignore."

If the fugitive's wife knew what it meant she gave no sign. Her drawn expression did not change, and she said nothing.

"Don't be afraid of me," Brent said. "As a reporter I was once a very tough guy, but life has mellowed me." Life as it flooded upon him in the shape of Lora Lorne's mail, he meant. "I wouldn't wreck anybody's life for the sake of a few headlines. For example, I know as well as you do that ever since your husband disappeared he's been hiding in the office of Aunt Martha's distributor—but I haven't told anybody yet."

Ann Winston's teeth pinched her lip. Quickly she asked: "Why are you doing this?"

"I'm trying to squeeze a big story out of it, but I also think everybody else is out of step. After doing a serious job of thinking, I've decided that Timothy Winston is no murderer."

Mrs. Winston smiled in a comradely way that won Brent all over again. "You and I are right about that," she said, "but why do *you* believe it?"

"The weapon of murder apparently wasn't available to him," Brent explained. "Then too, there's no reason why he'd be eager for the police to find the body so soon. Just the opposite. He'd want it to stay out of sight as long as possible, for reasons which the headlines make obvious. Also, your husband wouldn't have had to break into his own garage, as the murderer had to do in order to get at the motorcycle."

"Of course Tim hasn't killed anyone!" Ann Winston said. "It isn't in his makeup to do such a horrible thing. He's so completely unselfish—so generous he often suffers for it."

"I think the real murderer is someone who's tried to protect your husband—somebody who wanted the corpse uncovered in a hurry so that the news would warn him to watch out and dig deeper. But," Brent went on, "I'm afraid he did actually conceal those assets, and he's still pretty desperate to keep them under cover."

"He didn't! Really, he didn't."

"Look here," Brent said. "You put up this house as security for your husband's bail. If he's still missing on Monday morning you'll forfeit it—but I think you're actually hoping he'll remain a fugitive. You used to be a registered nurse, and you're going back to work as soon as you can, hoping that some day you can be with your husband again. You simply don't believe he took that money, even though there are strong reasons to believe he did take it—perhaps because of another woman."

"That's too absurd!"

"I hope so, for your sake. But let's look at it from the beginning. Your husband carried on his researches in the lab he built in the back yard here. He was getting at something really big."

"A synthetic mica."

THE SUBSTANCE which Winston had nearly perfected, Brent recalled from Val's accounts in the *Recorder*, would make the United States independent of the failing supply of natural mica from India. Necessary as insulation in electrical devices, and also useful as a protective film on corrosive metals, it would be vastly advantageous in the country's defense program.

"A big thing," Brent said, "and in order to develop it your husband got backing from his friend Gordon Lane and from a business woman who has a reputation for never missing a trick—Adaire Barclay."

At the mention of Adaire Barclay's name, Ann Winston's lips thinned.

"The fire destroyed your husband's lab. The insurance covered only the building, not the costly equipment that was totally destroyed and only partly paid for. Winston said he was wiped out and asked for more backing. Miss Barclay refused, doubting that the funds already advanced were exhausted. She demanded an accounting. Your husband couldn't satisfy her because his books were destroyed in the fire. Without money, he was not only obliged to abandon his researches but also forced into bankruptcy."

Brent recalled further that Miss Barclay, convinced that she'd been swindled, had hired a private detective to snoop into Winston's affairs. The detective had reported having seen Winston drawing money at a bank where he evidently had an account under a false name.

When Winston denied this, Adaire Barclay had filed charges with the district attorney. According to reports, Winston had countered by shaking the shamus, closing out the account and caching the money somewhere, all before the D.A. could get within reach of him. The D.A.'s investigators had then begun digging for those concealed assets.

"Your husband must have felt pretty certain he'd be convicted, Mrs. Winston, or otherwise he wouldn't have scrammed," Brent said. "And I know it to be a fact that he is concealing a sizable sum in cash."

The doorbell rang, but Ann Winston seemed not to hear it. Lowering herself stiffly into a chair, she gazed at Brent with something like terror in her eyes.

"You know?" she asked in a whisper.

"I'm also sure that the D.A. will argue that it was your husband's desire to keep the money hidden that drove him to murder the investigator who was about to bring it to light."

The bell rang again, but still Mrs. Winston paid no attention. Dismayed by Brent's statement she rose suddenly and came to him with a gesture of entreaty.

"It's something I can't explain—something I can't let anyone else learn, ever! The money is so terribly important, but once the truth about it comes out it will be worthless. It's really not what you think it is—please believe that!"

"If it belongs to your husband and he didn't include it among his assets—"

"But he couldn't! It—it's a sort of secret trust. Tim pledged himself—he's doing his best to keep that trust, in spite of all the hardships he's suffering now because of it!" Ann Winston was trying earnestly to make Brent understand. "You see, Tim knows that if the money's found it will be mistaken for the concealed assets the police are hunting for—just as you've mistaken it. And of all places, he can't let it be found at the Aunt Martha office."

"You're admitting that he *is* hiding certain money," Brent pointed out, "and that it's not his own."

A new, brittle voice broke in: "Of course it doesn't belong to him! At last I've heard you admit it!"

THE WOMAN who had paused in the living-room door was regally tall, coldly dark. A successful executive, she operated the city's snootiest beauty salon, Brent knew, and marketed a line of *chi chi* cosmetics under her own name of Adaire. Jealous of her reputation for business acumen, Miss Barclay evidently bent over backwards in her resolve to be nobody's fool. The troubles embroiling Timothy Winston sprang directly from this trait in her. As she gazed at Ann Winston her expression was forbidding, even merciless.

The man who had appeared at her side, however, was plainly of a more tolerant disposition.

"I beg your pardon for breaking in on you like this, Ann," he said gently. "We saw you here in the living-room, but you didn't hear the bell and— Well, there's no stopping Adaire once she gets started, you know. We came, really, to tell you how sorry we are about this latest development."

Gordon Lane, unlike Adaire Barclay, evidently prized friendship above money. It was generally known that he had sunk all his available capital in Winston's researches. His generosity was probably the reason why his string of haberdasheries, though prosperous enough, were less successful than Miss Barclay's glamor parlors. His concern for Timothy Winston was deep and real.

"As soon as I heard about it, I went to Adaire," he explained to the fugitive's wife. "She agreed it must be a horrible mistake—this thing about the murder. I brought her here believing I'd convinced her that the only way to save our investments is to save Tim himself. But apparently she's changed her mind."

"I mean to do what's just," Adaire Barclay stated flatly. She came forward, her brilliant eyes narrowing. "It's high time you came to your senses, Ann Winston. You've been blinded and duped by an unfaithful man who—"

"Adaire!" Gordon Lane blurted. "Good lord, I'd never have brought you here if I'd thought you'd turn on Ann like this!"

"If you like, Gordon, you may allow yourself to be cheated," Miss Barclay snapped. "But not I! And you, Ann

Winston, you may go on believing in your husband if you're foolish enough, even though all this trouble is due to his infatuation for another woman—a mere girl!"

Brent stood by in astonishment while Gordon Lane angrily seized Miss Barclay's trim arm.

"That's enough, Adaire! I'll remind you that Tim and Ann are my best and oldest friends. If you're going to be so unreasonable and cruel—we'd better leave."

"Not yet, Gordon," Adaire Barclay retorted. "Not until I've gotten to the bottom of this, as I mean to do, right here and now."

Gordon Lane turned quickly to Ann Winston. "I'm sorry. I came here to say I'm sure I can raise a little money *for* Tim. Please don't refuse it. I'm as determined to fight for Tim as Adaire is determined to fight against him." As Ann Winston's eyes thanked him, he turned back sharply. "As for you, Adaire, I'm damned if I'll stand for any more of your cruelty. I'm leaving. Will you come?"

"If you'll wait until I've said what I'm going to say, Gordon," Adaire Barclay answered with chill firmness, "I'll drop you off—on my way to the district attorney's office."

Gordon Lane's eyes flared at her. "Thank you, no. I'll walk. Good night, Ann—and count on me to the limit."

Indignantly Lane strode out. Adaire Barclay was so intent on Ann Winston that she seemed unaware of Brent's presence.

"Now I know how to prove that my charges against your husband are true! I heard you admit that Tim Winston actually is hiding money—*my* money, of course. He doesn't dare let it be found, you said—and of course he doesn't! But it *will* be found. At a certain office you mentioned. Whose office was it, Ann, if you please?"

Ann Winston's face was deathly white.

"Aunt Someone, wasn't it?" Adaire Barclay insisted. "Aunt Mary, perhaps? Aunt Margaret? I didn't hear the name clearly, but it doesn't matter. The district attorney will be able to trace it down easily. I'm going to him right now."

Coldly righteous, Adaire Barclay turned from the room. Ann Winston was too stricken with consternation to move. The door slammed. In the street the starter of a car ground. Suddenly the fugitive's wife was running to the porch, calling wildly: "Adaire, let me explain! Adaire, come back, come back!"

Through the window Brent saw Adaire Barclay's car accelerating toward the corner. Ann Winston's anxiety drove her around the house at a run. Following her, Brent immediately met the glare of a pair of headlights. A car left the garage with a rush and swept past him. Mrs. Winston veered it, tires whining, in the direction Adaire Barclay had gone.

It was a race—the fugitive's wife trying desperately to reach the district attorney's office ahead of Adaire Barclay so as to prevent, if possible, a damning revelation.

Brent strode to his own car, hoping that Ann Winston would succeed. Miss Barclay's information placed so soon before the D.A. would snatch Brent's lead out of his hands. It would break the story tonight, give it completely to Val, strip him of his hope of escaping Lora Lorne's damnable apron strings. He wanted to help Ann Winston to dissuade Adaire Barclay, but at once he found his purpose frustrated.

Hunched under the steering wheel, jamming his thumb against the starter button, Brent growled with wrath because the damned motor couldn't catch.

AFTER HALF a dozen tries Brent slid out, muttering blackly, and lifted the hood. Rain pelted on him. The wind was gusty and his supply of matches was almost depleted. Precious minutes slipped by while he hunted for the trouble.

His last match but one revealed it. The wire leading from the ignition coil was loose in its socket. It had not worked itself out, Brent judged. A scheming hand had broken the connection for the purpose of delaying him. Realizing that with a start, he thought of Gordon Lane.

He sank the wire back in place and heard the swift approach of a car. It surprised him by swinging into the Winston driveway. There it slid to a stop. Ann Winston sprang from it. She had had time to drive to the district attorney's office and back. Brent heard her sob as she ran into the house.

Now there were footsteps on the sidewalk. A man appeared, paused and eyed Brent, swaying a little. He was wearing a raincoat and a low-pulled hat. He lifted one arm, proffering Brent something.

"Have some," he said.

It was a bottle. It was very good rye. It was exactly what Brent needed.

"Thanks," Brent said, returning it.

"I live here." It was Roy's voice. "Don't you live any-where?"

In celebration of his lost job and his broken engagement, no doubt, Roy had practically emptied the pint. Swaying again, he leaned closer to grin at Brent. And again, behind his mask of pleasantry, Brent saw sincere suffering.

"I'm trying to place you," Brent said, "and I can't quite."

"Surely," Roy said, "you realize that on many and many an occasion my dulcet voice has bored the bejeezes out of you? May I remind you of the gentle but reliable cleansing

action of Doctor Minerva's Mineral Water? Your an-
nouncer is Roy Burrows, and what of it? This is Station
WTOP, God help you."

"So that's why you sound so familiar. I'll also come clean.
Name's Brent. On the *Recorder*."

"I regret that," Burrows said. "Your sheet has painted
entirely too black a picture of Tim. Doesn't deserve such
treatment. Salt of the earth, Tim. You've caused too much
pain here. Ann—Mrs. Winston—good soldier—the best—
my sister. I think I should sock you."

"Don't get me wrong," Brent said quickly. "I have a
screwy theory that Tim is an innocent man."

"Have you really? That's fine," Burrows said. "Now we're
pals again. Look, this bottle's empty. In the kitchen I have
another in a condition of unsullied virginity. Come on in
and let's ravish it."

Brent followed Burrows' uncertain steps into the house.
As promised, Burrows produced another pint from the
pantry—in which, Brent saw, many jars of Aunt Martha's
marmalade were stored. In appreciative silence they each
had a shot.

"Your engagement still broken?" Brent inquired.

"Shattered beyond repair."

"Would it be possible that Lila is really more interested in another man?"

Burrows squinted at him. "If she were, who could blame
her? I, sir, am a heel."

"Tim Winston?"

Burrows had another neat one, quickly. He eyed Brent
but said nothing.

"Tim Winston is no doubt a tragically misunderstood
man," Brent said thoughtfully. "Through no fault of his

own, evidently, he's in desperate need of protection from the law. So what about Tim's great and good friend, Gordon Lane, for example?"

Burrows meditated. "So far as I know, Gordon's never murdered anybody, but you never can tell about these quiet chaps, can you?"

FOOTFALLS CROSSED the next room and Ann Winston appeared, her eyes now cleared of tears, her chin again firmly lifted.

"Please don't, Roy. We all need to keep our wits about us now."

Brent asked: "Does that mean you didn't manage to head off Adaire Barclay?"

Her brown gaze turned to him squarely.

"When I arrived at the building, Adaire's car was sitting in front of the steps. I was too late—so I didn't go in after her, but came back. Of course by now she—she's already told—"

"Adaire," Burrows said with sudden feeling, "is a —————. The hell with her." He went on in a tone of acrid self-censure. "Ann, my dear, I have now been hired and fired by every last radio station in town. So far as the local radio industry is concerned, I'm a pariah. You and Tim have already supported me in indigence too much, bum that I am, and you're alone now—but what can I do? I shall have to consider the problem very seriously. In the meantime, however, I am going to bed."

He cheerfully stumbled up the rear stairs. Brent's last glimpse of him underscored the deep grief he felt the man was trying to conceal. Ann Winston hurried after him. Left alone, Brent went out the kitchen door and paused beside Ann's car.

In her haste she had left the key-folder dangling in the ignition lock. He removed it, opened the trunk, found the tool kit. After a moment he replaced it. The usual tools were present, he'd found—except the hammer.

He drove rapidly into the South Side. Parked a safe distance away, he walked into the bleak yard of the building bearing Aunt Martha's name. He spent his last match for an examination of the entrance sill. The cinders he had sprinkled there were undisturbed. Timothy Winston, Brent surmised, was still fearfully seeking cover elsewhere, probably in the dark doorways so plentiful in this neighborhood. In any event the fugitive had not yet ventured back.

Brent drove next to the plaza around which the municipal buildings clustered. The windows of the district attorney's office were still bright squares in a white façade. At the broad steps sat a car adorned with Adaire Barclay's trademarked crest. Deciding to wait for her, in order to check her suspicions of Winston against his belief in Winston's innocence, Brent leaned against it. Abruptly shocked cold, he gripped a handle, pulled a door open.

Adaire Barclay lay huddled on the front seat. The crown of her trimly coiffured head was crushed. Her face was no longer a model of elegance. It was horribly streaked with a color more vividly bright than any rouge her factory had ever produced.

Brent wondered if Ann Winston had actually thought this car empty, or if, resorting to desperate means—

Stiffly he bent in to feel of Adaire Barclay's dangling wrist. He was vaguely aware of a shadow looming up behind the front seat. Before he could jerk back, the blade of a guillotine seemed to cleave down on his neck. Desperately striving to escape the next blows, he dived to the floor.

His blood turning to printer's ink, flooding thickly over the lights of his mind, the last thing he realized was that the hammer couldn't reach him as long as he crouched with his head pushed under the dead woman's glamorized legs.

CHAPTER SIX
DEADLINE FOR MURDER

THE FACE that Brent saw when he pulled himself up was the gaunt, spooky face of Captain Russo.

"You discover too many bodies, Brent," the chief of the Homicide Squad complained tonelessly. "And it's never necessary for you to deliver them to the district attorney's door."

"Correction," Brent muttered. "This one delivered itself."

His mind full of fog, Brent saw the Homicide Squad going to work on the conveniently placed corpse. As he allowed Russo to lead him across the plaza and into police headquarters, he wondered if the murderer of Adaire Barclay had left him in the car under the impression that he was likewise dead. Slumped in a chair in the Homicide Squad's suite and listening to Russo's grieved questions, he gathered that the killer had again phoned the captain a helpful message mentioning at least Miss Barclay's demise.

Parrying the captain's questions, Brent tried to give Russo a plausible explanation of his corpse-finding proclivities. As a newspaperman, he said, he'd merely intended going up to the D.A.'s office to glean a few new facts as to Walt Eastwell's murder. Glancing inside Miss Barclay's car, he had found her in a battered condition. As regards any subsequent incidents, he didn't know from nothing.

"Brent," Russo said sadly, "I like you when you are not in proximity to a corpse. I do not like you when I suspect you're gumming me up. If you're holding out on me, I'll have to take drastic steps."

"Steps?" Brent said.

Russo nodded, the pivot of his cadaverous head seeming to creak. "It's possible that a snooping newspaperman can cause two murders. Murder is something I deeply regret, particularly when two of them are caused by a snooping newspaperman."

Brent grew cold.

"Let me remind you of two facts, one legal, the other scientific," Russo continued. "First, in the event that A incites B to commit murder, A thereby becomes guilty of the crime of homicide. Second, a newspaperman is no more comfortable than anyone else where he sits down on two thousand volts."

"You think I'm mixed up in these killings?" Brent asked, sitting straight. "You mean you think I'm making myself technically an accessory—or something?"

"For the present, Brent, I assume that you're free to leave," Russo said sorrowfully. "For the present."

Not waiting for further permission, Brent went in haste.

WHEN HE returned to the *Recorder's* room next morning, Brent glanced into his cubbyhole and winced at sight of a fresh heap of mail. It stiffened his resolution to divorce himself from Lora Lorne no matter how serious the risk.

The only two desks occupied at this hour were Val Randall's and Garrett's. Val was feverishly writing up the new facts available on the Barclay homicide, and the city editor was dressing up her copy for a sensational spread for the first editions. Neither of them deigned to notice Brent.

The murder of Adaire Barclay had one aspect which Brent found reassuring. It had temporarily distracted the attention of the D.A. and Russo from the Winston search, and as a result they had not yet made good their promise to capture the fugitive.

Meaning to take advantage of the delay, Brent looked into the telephone book for the name of Martha Kelsie, then quietly left. Driving into Maple Street, on the opposite side of the city, he stopped in front of a bungalow. Brent's ring at the doorbell was quickly answered by a young man. Evidently about to hasten out, he was wearing the white uniform of an interne under a light raincoat.

"From the *Recorder*," Brent informed him. "We'd like to get a feature story about Mrs. Kelsie's marmalade business."

The young man's eyes, sharply narrowed, were those of a shrewd diagnostician. "Why, yes," he said. "Perhaps some publicity would help. Come in."

Brent inquired, going in: "Which hospital are you with?"

"Surgeons. Two more months and my interneship is finished. You may say in your story that my medical education would have been absolutely impossible without my mother's industry and resourcefulness. It should be a fine inspiration to others."

Young Kelsie's smile did not apologize for the admiration he felt for his mother but, rather, challenged Brent to question it.

"My sister," he said with the same burning pride. "Lila."

Lila Kelsie looked up from a canvas before which she was standing in the front room. Her eyes grew round, and again Brent saw in them a certain indescribable fierceness.

"Lila is outstanding at the Academy—again all thanks to Mother," her brother said. "In a few years Lila is certain to be one of the finest portraitists of children in the country. This is Mr. Brent, from the *Recorder,* Lila."

"Brent?" Lila repeated softly. "Did you say the *Recorder,* Richard?"

Richard was peering at Brent and Brent felt the keen force of his stare.

"Mother isn't here at the moment," he said quietly. "She went to market. But I'll be glad to show you around."

Brent winced under Lila's stinging gaze as he stepped into the spotless kitchen where Aunt Martha's marmalade was made and hand-packed. Richard Kelsie showed him the crate of ripe oranges, the bags of purest sugar, the great shining copper kettles. Since apparently Mrs. Kelsie had been cooking her marmalade day in and day out for years, Brent shuddered to remember the carloads of the stuff moldering in the warehouse.

"It has been a great satisfaction to Mother to know that she's been able to fulfill the heart's desires of her children," Richard said evenly.

Going through the motions of making notes, Brent felt Richard keenly studying him. Lila was also watching him—almost stalking him, in fact. When he said he had enough data for a fine feature article, and would send a photographer later to get a picture of Mrs. Kelsie, they followed him to the door. He paused for one last question.

"How did all this begin? Was your mother left a widow?"

Richard Kelsie's face hardened. "Please don't print any mention of my father!" he said with a snap. "No good can come of opening old wounds. Loving him and admiring him as we still do, I insist that his name be left to rest in silence."

The eyes of Lila and Richard shone in the dusk inside the door as Brent turned uneasily from it.

In the *Recorder's* morgue, half an hour later, he found the answer. It was a bundle of old clippings in a file marked with the name of Owen Kelsie. The last headline read: *KELSIE, ELDERLY EMBEZZLER, DIES IN STATE PRISON HOSPITAL.*

BRENT FINGERED rapidly through the clippings, piecing the story together. Owen Kelsie, Lila's and Richard's father, had embezzled about $20,000 from his employer, Simon Harkey, of Harkey and Company, paint wholesalers, after working as a bookkeeper for thirty-two years. His motive was rather obscure. It was said that knowing he was ill of an incurable heart ailment, he'd wanted to take his family abroad to enjoy life for the few months or years left him. Simon Harkey, however, had discovered the false entries in Kelsie's books before he could fulfill this dream.

It was believed, though no proof of it was available, that Owen Kelsie had speculated with the stolen funds and lost them. Despite his protestations and Mrs. Kelsie's staunch faith in his innocence, Harkey had pressed the case, with the result that Kelsie was convicted.

In prison Owen Kelsie's health had rapidly failed. By special dispensation of the warden, Kelsie's family, as well as his two boyhood friends, Gordon Lane and Timothy Winston, had come to his bedside a scant hour before his death. The final news story ended with the statement that Simon Harkey, the plaintiff in the case, had died of pneumonia the previous year, leaving his paint business to his two sons, whose management had ended in failure soon thereafter.

With this picture in mind, Brent returned to his perfumed cubicle. Mulling over it, he was unaware of the heightening activity in the news room until the swinging doors parted and Val Randall's high heels tap-tapped rapidly to Garrett's desk. Her cheeks were flushed, her eyes sparkling with excitement. Reading this as a danger signal, Brent sat up and cocked his ears.

"Off the record, chief, the break's coming any time now!" Val drew a breath. "As soon as the news of Adaire Barclay's murder got around, Winston made the mistake of phoning his home. He must've known it was dangerous, but anyway he chanced it—had to give his wife the old stuff about how he didn't kill Adaire. And of course the line was tapped."

"So they've spotted Winston?" Garrett asked.

"Not exactly, not yet. The call came from a pay phone in a dog cart near the South Side Bridge. The D.A. and Russo are both pouring men into that neighborhood. They'll have Winston in plenty of time for our main editions. I'm beating it down there right now, because they're ready for anything—a first class raid—the works!"

"Brent!" Garrett snapped. "Brent, where the hell do you think you're going?"

Brent stopped in the swinging doors, peering back.

"Your copy's late again, Grandma," Garrett said ominously. "I'm warning you, stay in that passion department and keep your hands off the police run, Miss Lorne—strictly off, or else you'll give me a full page six times a week, starting today."

Chin set, Brent pushed out.

ZIGZAGGING THROUGH the narrow streets in the vicinity of the South Side Bridge, Brent found that police sedans were spotted near strategic corners. Prowl cars were touring. Smart-eyed dicks were quietly going in and out of doors. The dragnet was tightening around Timothy Winston.

Brent was relieved to find, however, that the police operations had not yet drawn into focus on Aunt Martha's warehouse. Parking his car two blocks away, he was able to approach it without walking into an ambush.

The building was no more inviting in daylight. The rain had ceased at dawn, but the river was still rising and churning sullenly about its foundations. The garage doors were still barred, as Brent had left them. The cinders on the door-sill were now trampled. Somebody had gone in.

Seeking a telephone, Brent judged that the one in a bar four blocks away was not being watched. His first call was answered by the voice of Richard Kelsie.

"Brent again. I'm still on the subject of marmalade. It's taking a serious turn. I'd like to know if you want Tim Winston to be arrested—for two murders this time."

Young Kelsie blurted: "That's the last thing in the world I want to happen!"

"Is it?" Brent said. "Does Lila feel as strongly about it? Well, Lila can bring you to the warehouse, in case you need direction, which you probably don't. It's only a matter of minutes now—your last chance to see Winston before they grab him."

Brent dialed again, and this time heard the voice of the hunted man's wife.

"This is the payoff, Mrs. Winston. Your husband's about to be taken prisoner. He'll be booked for murder and held incommunicado, unless we get the breaks. If you want to see him one last time before he disappears into the death-house, try to shake off the dicks who are spotting you. Better bring all the moral support you can muster up!"

Brent retraced his steps under a darker sky. Rain was falling again. He scanned the street and turned back into the warehouse yard. The entrance was locked. He knocked and there was no answer.

"Mr. Stone!" he called toward the painted windows on the third floor, not too loudly. "I have a message, Mr. Stone—vitally important!"

Knocking again, he sensed rather than heard footfalls on the stairs inside.

"I've got to see you before the others come," Brent said through the door. "There's not much time, Mr. Stone."

A key squealed in the lock. An apprehensive eye looked out at Brent. Brent thrust inside and bolted the door behind him. A thin-faced, haggard-eyed man backed tensely against the stairs.

"You're Mr. Stone?"

"Y-yes. You have a message?"

"Let's go up to your office."

Hesitating, the lean man climbed. Brent followed him into the murky room on the top floor.

"The message," he said, "is that the cops are almost within reach of you, Mr. Winston."

The gaunt man started. "My name is Stone!"

"Timothy Winston, Thomas Stone, it's pretty much the same," Brent said. "This is a hell of a life you've been driven to. Running a constant risk, living like a recluse in this dump, cut off from your wife and your friends, dreading discovery at any moment—and still you're determined to keep it up, simply because—"

From below came the sound of knocking.

CHAPTER SEVEN
ANVIL CHORUS

SIGNALING WINSTON to remain in the office, Brent hurried down the stairs. When he drew the bolt of the entrance, Lila and Richard Kelsie stared at him. He drew them in, set the bolt again and urged them up the stairs to the dingy office. Timothy Winston stiffened.

"Don't get scared," Brent said. "Lila and Richard already have a pretty good idea of what's been going on. It's high time you told them the truth. Their mother, though, is a different matter. None of you want to disillusion her."

Winston groped into the chair, his face wan and drawn. "I cannot— " he began.

"But I can," Brent said.

He met the strangely fierce light in Lila Kelsie's eyes and the piercing scrutiny of Richard's.

"This business has been a blind from the very beginning," Brent said, "but a blind used with the best of intentions. Winston was forced into it because he wanted to preserve your mother's mistaken faith in your father's innocence. After all these years she still won't admit that your father was actually an embezzler. It would break her heart if she should learn now that her family has really been supported all along by the money Owen Kelsie stole."

Winston sat in despairing silence. Lila's lips were set and Richard's eyes glittered.

"Owen Kelsie never let the world learn what had become of the funds he embezzled. He let rumors run wild while he kept to himself the truth that he'd hidden them. On his death-bed he told his oldest and best friend, Tim Winston, where the money could be found. His last request was that Winston use it for the comfort and welfare of the family he was leaving behind, otherwise unprovided for. Winston secretly recovered it, then set about executing his dead friend's trust—"

Winston leaned forward, speaking to Lila and Richard. "I couldn't return the money to its rightful owners. Simon Harkey was dead. His two sons were irresponsible wastrels. Besides, it would have meant more publicity, which would have shortened your mother's life. I had no choice but to fulfill the promise I'd given Owen when he was dying."

"There were other reasons also," Brent said. "Your career, Lila. Your medical education, Richard. Neither was possible without that money. But Winston had to turn it over to your mother without actually letting her know where it was coming from. A ticklish assignment. Winston managed it by urging your mother to commercialize her knack for making marmalade."

Winston stiffly nodded.

"So he put together this skeleton of a distributing firm. He acted as intermediary between your mother and Thomas Stone, who was really himself. No doubt he tried to make the business prosper, but he hadn't enough time to give it. Though it had practically no income, he kept your mother busy, paying her enough money week after week to keep her family going—you, Lila and Richard. You've suspected this, haven't you?"

Neither Lila nor Richard answered.

"Then Adaire Barclay plunged Winston into an impossible predicament. He was accused of concealing assets in bankruptcy while actually he was concealing the secret fund on which you Kelsies depended so heavily. He knew that if it were discovered it would be mistaken for the assets he was accused of hiding.

"It would mean prison for Winston under charges of which he is innocent. Most of the money would go to Adaire Barclay—and it didn't really belong to her. Martha Kelsie would be deprived of it. Your studies, Lila, would come to an abrupt end. You'd have to abandon your medical career, Richard. I don't need to tell you that all this would add up to a tragedy which Tim Winston, honoring his dead friend's trust, couldn't let happen if he could prevent it. He figured that the only way he could prevent it was to go into hiding."

Lila went quickly to Winston's side. Her hands closed tightly over one of his.

"Now you're exposing all this!" Richard blurted. "In spite of all the terrible things it will mean to everyone!"

Brent wagged his head. "Lord knows I don't want it to go any further. But it will—it will be plastered all over a thousand front pages—if Winston is nailed for murder."

A sharp knock came again from below.

BRENT RAN down the stairs to the entrance. He opened a crack, saw the white face of Ann Winston, then opened the door wide. Her brother, Roy Burrows, was just behind her, again not quite so jaunty as he tried to appear, and not quite sober. Gordon Lane followed.

"Were you tailed?" Brent asked.

"I don't think we shook them off," Gordon Lane said quickly, "but at least we have a little time."

Brent let them hurry ahead into the office. Pausing in the upper storeroom, he gazed thoughtfully out the loading door through which he had almost taken a fatal drop. He returned to the office. The others gazed at him with mixed reactions.

"This will be tough going," Brent said. "It happens that I like all of you. I'd much rather nobody had to crack down on one of you as a two-time murderer. But for Tim Winston's sake it's necessary."

Now there was another knock—this time sharp and commanding.

"We can't waste any time," Brent said, grimly turning back. "Tim Winston has more than a double murder rap to dodge—and I think you all know what I mean. Winston, is the money still in that safe?"

Winston said hoarsely: "There was no other place I could put it."

"Can you trust me with it?"

As Winston hesitated in bewilderment, Roy Burrows said quietly: "You're making a mistake if you don't, Tim."

Ann Winston's nod decided her husband. He opened the safe, emptied the cash box and put the sheaves of bills into Brent's hands. And as Brent stuffed them into his pockets there came from downstairs another imperative knock.

A voice demanded, "Open up!" Returning his eye to the scratch on the pane, Brent saw Captain Russo striding loose-jointedly into the yard, with Valerie Randall hurrying after him.

Brent eyed the others. "Both of our two murders were meant to safeguard Winston and everyone depending on him."

THE KNOCKING had stopped for a moment. Brent heard Captain Russo hollowly issuing orders. Brent knew that the building was being ringed.

The knocking began again.

"One of you," Brent said, moving toward the office door, "wanted desperately to save Winston. You, for example, Mrs. Winston. You're not only aware that your husband is guilty of receiving stolen property, but you've aided and abetted him. If the truth came out, it would mean hardships for the Kelsies, the loss of everything you possess, prison for your husband and for yourself as well."

Ann pressed her fingers to her lips. "Hardships for the Kelsies," Brent repeated. "You would want to prevent that, Richard. And you, Lila. As for you, Gordon Lane, you knew all this, didn't you? You'd sunk all your available capital into Tim Winston's process. The process wasn't destroyed by the fire. All the details are still intact inside Winston's brain. Did you hope that he might get beyond the reach of the law, go back to work and repay you a thousand times?"

Lane was startled silent.

A dull crash below meant that the blade of an axe had cleaved into the door.

"We can't hold out any longer," Brent said, "and I don't think we need to."

He left the office hushed. As he reached the entrance it shook under another blow of the axe. He called.

"Russo! Winston is in here, unarmed. Will you come in alone?"

"Open the door, Brent," Russo said.

Brent opened it with caution. At once Russo squeezed through. He looked unspeakably sorrowful. Brent was pressing the door shut again when it bucked him. A streamlined, silken leg appeared, followed by all of Miss Valerie Randall.

"It's still my story, Bill!" she gasped.

Brent ignored her. "Russo, your killer is waiting for you upstairs."

Russo went up, Val tripping along at his heels. "Which one?" Russo asked.

"That one."

Brent pointed at Lila Kelsie.

Her expression one of dumfounded astonishment, Lila stood still while the startled eyes of the others turned on her.

"Sure of it, Brent?" Russo asked.

"You know that Adaire Barclay's private detective discovered a connection between Winston and the Kelsie family," Brent said. "Well, judge the rest for yourself. Ask Lila for her alibi and she'll tell you she was at home both times, and of course her family will parrot that, since they stick together. As for her motive, Lila knew that Adaire's private dick had found out about her affair with Winston.

"Winston had left home not only to beat the larceny rap, but also to get away from his wife so he and Lila could skip together. She came here last night for a clandestine meeting with him, just when Eastwell showed up. Eastwell was a threat to all her romantic plans, of course, so she—Well, there she is, Russo— Take her down and book her for her two murders."

CHAPTER EIGHT
RIVER OF DEATH

"**Y**OU'RE MISTAKEN about all that."

Roy Burrows was standing near the door, his back to it. He was smiling his oddly sad smile.

"You know as well as I do, Brent, that what you've just said about Lila is hogwash. You accused her because you realized she was the key to the answer. Your idea was that the guilty one, no matter which of us it might be, couldn't stand by and see her put through the wringer. Especially me—and you've suspected me pretty strongly, haven't you? I knew damned well it was a trick, Brent—"

Burrows was moving slowly toward the door while Captain Russo slowly advanced toward him.

"The whole thing's pretty simple," Burrows said to him, still smiling. "I'd have gone to hell long ago but for Ann and Tim, God bless them, so I don't mind explaining. Tim knew I'd stolen the funds from his lab—the money Adaire Barclay was so concerned about. No need for me to say what became of it. I gambled some away and drank up the rest."

The group was still. Brent stood in mute admiration of this killer, knowing that this confession was untrue. Actually Burrows had stolen none of Winston's research funds, for none was missing. By terming himself a thief Burrows was not only protecting the trust Winston had kept for the dead Owen Kelsie, he was also absolving Winston of any blame as a concealer of assets.

"When the D.A. clamped down on Tim," Burrows went on, "well, you wouldn't expect him to defend himself by accusing his own wife's brother, would you? He's not that sort. I was too much of a heel to face the music as long as there was a chance that he'd be acquitted. When Tim's disappearance made it look so black for him, I was willing to try any other way of getting from under—even murder. I wasn't just protecting Tim from Eastwell and Adaire Barclay, but protecting myself too."

Burrows hadn't really killed in self-protection, Brent knew. He was condemning himself with a shrewd and gallant mixture of truth and falsehoods.

"That was the idea," he lied with a smile, "to save my own skin by protecting the man who was shouldering the blame for me. I knew that Tim had come here to hide, of course. I organized this business years ago as a means of helping the girl I love—and it's really done pretty well."

Winston's hand rose in protest, but his wife's closed gently over it.

"Knowing where Tim was hiding, I was able to play a little game of spotting the spotters. That is, by nosing about a bit I learned where the D.A.'s investigators were hunting. It took a lot of time, and that's the real reason I was fired, Lila. Pretending to be Eastwell, I phoned tips to Miss Randall, the *Recorder's* police reporter, who obligingly printed them as news, thereby warning Tim. Then, when Eastwell came too close— Well, Tim didn't even know I'd stopped Eastwell at the door downstairs."

RUSSO WAS shaking his head. "An uncorroborated confession is no good."

"I had to take the body to some other place, of course. Then later, coming home, I overheard Adaire Barclay questioning Ann. Somehow she'd found out where Tim was hiding, and she was going to the D.A. again about it. Of course I had to stop her. I was hiding in the rear of her car when she drove off. I left her dead in front of the D.A.'s office, then came back, most of the way by cab. Talking with you, Brent, I knew you were getting too damned close to the answer. Sorry I had to try, but I'm really rather glad I didn't kill you too."

Captain Russo said again, in his sepulchral tone: "An uncorroborated confession won't stand up."

Burrows was drawing one hand out of the deep pocket of his coat. "You see, knowing I was going to need a weapon,

I got the hammer originally from the first car within reach, which happened to be Ann's. After that I kept it handy. Here—here is your corroboration!"

He hurled the hammer straight at Russo. Its swift flight wrung cries from Lila and Ann. Russo snapped his head aside, it twirled against the far wall. His move gave Burrows the advantage. Spinning about, Burrows broke into a run, vanished.

"Roy!" Lila cried. "Roy!"

Brent went after him. Knowing that capture awaited him below, Burrows sped past the stairs—ran across the top floor storeroom, straight toward the yawning door. Lila, running after him, stifled a scream as he sprang through it.

The rain poured down over the door as Lila stood rigid, her eyes terrified. Ann Winston was hurrying to her side. There were exclamations in the office, men crowding out after Russo. The captain was advancing with reluctant deliberation, and Val Randall was moving breathlessly at his side. They paused near the high door, and Brent looked down with them into the swirling gray of the river.

He turned away, drawing Ann Winston aside. She was trembling and her eyes were big and dark in her pale face.

"Your husband was afraid your brother would do it," he said quietly. "Burrows had sent him a letter—I found it in the wastebasket in there—promising him to keep the cops away. Winston couldn't stop Burrows himself, so he had to appeal to you to try. That's the real meaning of the message he sent to Lora Lorne, isn't it? A concealed warning—Tom meaning himself, Mike meaning Burrows. He knew you'd get it—Burrows being in radio, using a microphone, a mike. But you couldn't have prevented it.

Burrows was determined to protect you all, even if it meant murder—with the best intentions in the world."

Brent removed the orange letter from his pocket and placed it in Ann Winston's hands. Her fingers crushed over it and her eyes glowed with gratitude.

Somewhere in the murk a barge mourned, *Whoo-oo-oo!*

IN THE loneliest corner of the *Recorder's* city room Bill Brent was snipping with his shears and drudging over his paste-pot when the swinging doors parted before Lila and Richard Kelsie. Before he could stop them they were at the sill of his cubbyhole.

"Mr. Brent," Lila said firmly, "I can hardly believe it of Roy, and so many things have happened—I'm so bewildered!"

"Don't be," Brent said in his most reassuring Lorne manner. "Heard the latest? The D.A. will dismiss the indictment against Winston first thing Monday morning. Winston's already receiving offers from new backers and soon he'll be deep in his researches again. As for Roy—well, in spite of everything else, we think a lot of him, don't we?"

Lila's eyes clouded as she nodded. "But there are other things, too, all so sudden. Tim has told Mother that he'd found a very capable manager who's sure he can build up the marmalade business beautifully. And after trying dozens of times to get work at Apex Advertising, they've suddenly called me in to do a series of baby pictures for a new soap campaign. And Richard—he won't have to go through five or six lean years starting his own office, because Doctor Seldon Dockery has asked him to fill a vacancy as house physician at the Heights Hospital. Everybody's getting the best breaks possible now. You're behind all this, Bill Brent, I know you are!"

"Not me," Brent said. "Give the credit to Lora Lorne. I've merely carried out her orders. There's something she asked me to mention. That money Tim Winston turned over to me—he's agreed that it's going to charity. In time you can pay back the part of it you've already used, and then your consciences will be clear. You'd better duck! My city editor's heading this way with fire in his eye."

YOU SLAY ME, BABY

BIG BILL BRENT
THOUGHT HE WAS
SUFFERING FOR HIS SINS
WHEN HE INHERITED
THE MUSHY MANTLE
OF LORA LORNE, THE
RECORDER'S MOTHERLY
MARITAL SMOOTHER-
OUTER. BUT WHEN HE
GOT AN UNWANTED
BABY ADOPTED VIA HIS
COLUMN—ONLY TO HAVE
IT EXPLODE INTO A
FULL-GROWN MURDER—
HE LONGED FOR THE
WHOLESOME SWEETNESS
OF HIS OLD LIFE AS A
POLICE REPORTER.

CHAPTER ONE
THE HAUNTED LETTER

AT THIS unholy hour of the morning, in Bill
Brent's well-considered opinion, the *Recorder* plant
was a dark and dreary hell-hole which no sane man would
willingly enter. Brent, however, was inflicted with an
ingrown sense of obligation. Having fled from the building for a few minutes' respite, he was dutifully trudging
back, bearing a paper bag stuffed with four frosted doughnuts and a quart container of coffee, which he needed,
though he felt an even stronger need for an equal quantity of ice cubes and rye.

Midway along the walk leading to the dim main entrance
he paused. He never liked the looks of the place at high
noon, when the advertising departments busily hummed.
He always felt a definite aversion to it in the evening when
the city room worked at fever pitch getting out the milk
train editions. And he disliked it most heartily of all during
these small hours following midnight when he alone must
stick on the job in the thick of its hushed and deserted
gloom. He paused to regard it warily, not merely because
the entrance seemed as uninviting to him as the iron gate
of a prison, but also because a shadow was now looming
against it.

A man was standing there waiting, his back flat against
the light shining vaguely through the panes, his face a

black patch—and to Brent he seemed, somehow, faintly ominous.

He approached Brent with a long, reaching stride, keeping, Brent thought, his face shadowed. When he halted no more than three feet away Brent could still see nothing of his features except a veiled glint in the whites of his eyes.

"If you're from the post office," he said, speaking in a throaty tone which Brent instinctively felt was disguised, "I've been expecting it."

"Have you?" Brent said.

"The party who sent it phoned ahead." The man's shoulders were peaked up now. "I'll sign for it."

"Sorry. Haven't got it," Brent said. "You might tell me, though, why you're pretending to be somebody on the *Recorder's* staff."

The man stood tightly still and his hand slid back into his pocket—where, Brent hoped, he didn't have a gun. Brent was astonished when the man laughed—a laugh too tense to seem good-natured, as it was intended.

"This is rather embarrassing. I suppose I'd better come clean. I'm trying to get hold of a letter."

"A letter you sent to the *Recorder?*" Brent inquired.

"My—my wife wrote it to Lora Lorne. We had a bit of a disagreement and she asked Lora Lorne for advice." The man was choosing his words almost furtively. "We've patched it up now, though. Everything's lovely again, and it wouldn't do to have the letter made public now. I want to get that letter back—unread."

"Unread?" Brent said. This man, he surmised, was far more anxious about that than he wanted to appear. "I'll mention it to Miss Lorne. How will she recognize it?"

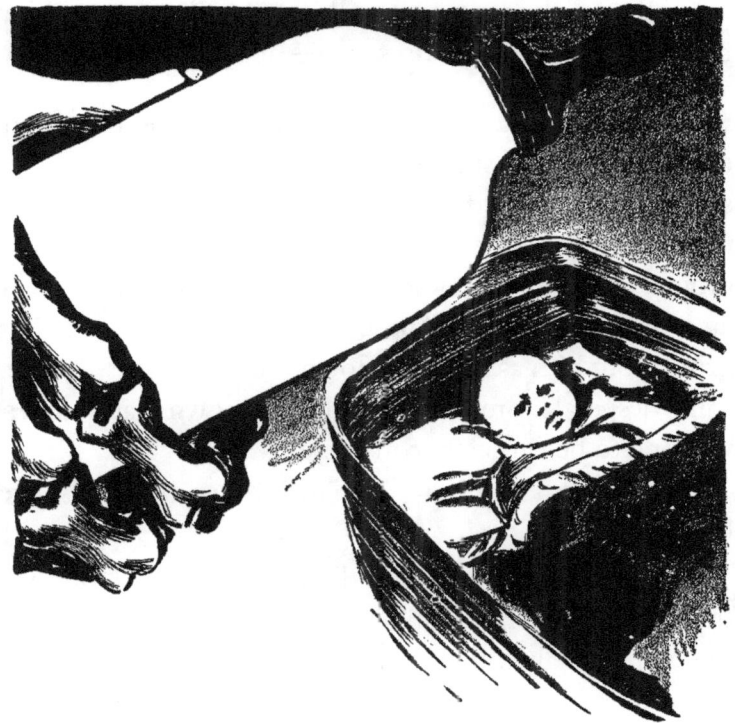

The faceless man hesitated, and Brent sensed the fear in him. "It's a plain white number ten envelope and the address is typed, but it's postmarked early this evening and it was sent special." He bent closer, anxiously intent. "Perhaps it's already been delivered."

"It hasn't been," Brent answered. "I'm sure of that." He had a clear-cut reason for being so certain. "When it comes—"

"Send it right back—unopened," the man urged. "Re-address it to—to the occupant of Room 404 at the Heights Hospital. You'll see that Miss Lorne does that? Returns it unopened?"

"Miss Lorne, as the whole world knows," Brent reminded him evasively, "is an extremely understanding and sympathetic woman."

"Tell her," the man said, still intent, still anxious, "that the contents must remain secret—absolutely must!"

HE PEERED a challenge at Brent with eyes that Brent could not see, and suddenly he stepped past. As he strode swiftly away in the dim light shining from the door, back turned, Brent saw him as a man of ordinary stature and ordinary appearance, but one loaded with much more than an ordinary degree of purposefulness. There was something grim about him as he faded down the dark street—something desperate. Brent decided this unknown man's request was one to be earnestly considered.

"Why, sure, chum, sure," Brent said wryly, aloud. "Just leave it to me."

He pushed his two hundred pounds into the lobby and tramped up the iron stairs, carrying the doughnuts and the coffee. Only a few dim bulbs lighted his weary way. The offices below were empty and the big presses in the basement, their flood of news poured out, were at rest. Another hour or so would pass before the teletypes would resume their clatter, and even the cleaning women had called it a night. In this vast and stilly dungeon Bill Brent alone must remain to toil and mutter blasphemy.

He was parting the swinging doors of the news room when a burst of sound surged up the stairwell. It was a door banging open, followed by the click-click of leather heels crossing the foyer at a terrified pace.

"Cripes!" a frightened voice piped.

Brent started down to meet the noise. He was still en route when it echoed away. Reaching the lobby, he found it as silent as the grave—except for a quick gasping sound issuing from beneath the lowest flight of stairs.

A pair of scared eyes appeared, and then a whole boy. About fourteen, he had a face full of penny-colored freckles, a nondescript uniform and very little breath left.

"A goon chased me!" he blurted. "Out dere!"

He pointed in the general direction of the street. Brent looked through the glass of the entrance and saw nothing but somnolent quietude.

"If I hadn'ta got inside here, he'da grabbed me!" the boy insisted. "I t'ink he had a knife!" Two dirty hands were held up as if to measure a fish that had gotten away. "A knife as big as dat! Bigger!"

"You read too many comics," Brent said. "You should stick to the pulps. Anyway, he's gone now, if he ever was there. Why aren't you home and in bed, getting your growth?"

The boy probed into a small canvas bag suspended from one shoulder by a strap and produced a letter.

"I got a special delivery for Lora Lorne."

"Ah!" Brent sighed. "I'll take it."

"You? Say, you don't look like Lora Lorne to me, mister."

Brent hoped that that was obvious. Lora Lorne was the *Recorder's* love oracle, its own Dorothy Dix or Beatrice Fairfax, who sweetly advised her immense family of readers concerning their philandering husbands, their faithless wives, their broken troths, their unrequited passions and practically anything else that might bother them, including stenographer's spread and the beautification of the bust. Her picture, printed every day above her column of intimately sympathetic expostulations, showed her to be a warm-hearted old soul with wise eyes in a kindly crinkled face, combs in her snowy hair, eyeglasses dangling from a reel pinned to her grandmotherly shoulder. Not in any respect did she resemble William Coleridge Brent, who wore size eleven brogans and a nose permanently flattened by a Princeton goal-post.

Noting this, the boy observed: "You ain't *nothin'* like her!"

"Ain't I!" Brent said sourly. "All the same, I'll take that letter—and shut up."

HE SNATCHED it away, made an indecipherable scrawl on the receipt and pushed the boy out of the lobby, leaving him to wonder what he had done to deserve such harsh treatment. Brent hoped he would never know. It was a closely guarded professional secret that Lora Lorne, as visualized by the thousands who anxiously sought her guidance in their amatory distress, simply did not exist except as a phoney name plus a copyrighted portrait which had graced the *Recorder's* love column day in and day out, unchanged, for the past twenty-two years.

A long succession of female busybodies had masqueraded as the paper's seeress in *affaires de l'amour,* and it galled Brent to think that he was the first Lora Lorne ever to wear his pants long and externally. Rather than have it noised around that saccharine Miss Lorne and burly Bill Brent were one and the same these days, he would gladly have entered a bona fide jail.

Sourer than usual about it tonight, Brent waited to make sure that no monster with a machete was chasing the messenger, then tramped up the stairs again, still carrying the doughnuts and the coffee and now, also, the letter.

He wedged himself into a tiny cubicle in a remote corner of the news room. No bigger than a broom closet, it was crowded by a table heaped with letters, all addressed to Lora Lorne, like the one just received. Most of them ran to type; people as a whole, Brent had found, showed little originality in their tribulations, but seemed to get into the same damned messes over and over again, never learning better. He had come to consider it practically a godsend when someone managed to stumble into a reasonably unusual predicament. Having labored far into the wicked hours over a hundred run-of-the-mill heartbreaks, he hoped he was now about to be rewarded with a problem really worth losing sleep over.

Eyeing the special delivery letter which the unknown man had implored him to return unopened and unread, he shamelessly ripped it open and began to read it.

> Darling Miss Lorne,
>
> Now that my baby girl has come into the World, now that I *have* given her away, I'm heartbroken—and so terribly afraid for her!
>
> You see, dear Miss Lorne, it isn't working out as you and I planned it. We *had* hoped for so wonderfully much, hadn't we? We wanted the baby to have a devoted mother, one who could give so much more time than I can to her care and upbringing, one who could give her every advantage in life that she would never have otherwise. So many women wrote to me after you printed my first letter in your wonderful column, all of them wanting to take the baby, and I was so careful to pick out the one I thought would make the very best mother for her. But I've made a horrible mistake and I'm so afraid—and now I want my baby back.

"Well, for God's sake!" Brent blurted aloud.

Glancing at the end of the letter, he saw a typical signature: "Hopeful." Manifestly it was from a young woman who had first appealed to Lora Lorne's fabulous wisdom a month or so ago. Brent had sweated his brain over Hopeful's plight, writing her fully a dozen long compassionate letters of guidance. Several times, in fact, he had devoted almost his entire column to her case.

SHE WAS young and married but her husband had left her; her health was none too good; she must work for a living. Within the past several days she had borne a child; she had no near relatives to bring up the baby for her and she rebelled at the mere thought of placing it in a charitable institution. While the baby was still unborn, Brent had practically bled himself white helping this girl to find a childless, intelligent, well-to-do woman to adopt it. And now, after all this travail, the dizzy dame wanted to call it off and get her kid back!

"Heaven help me!" Brent moaned. He resorted to the coffee, gnawed off a chunk of doughnut and resumed.

> I'm frantic, Miss Lorne, really frantic. This woman, who had taken my baby, lied to me. She deceived me, Miss Lorne! She even gave me a false name and a false address, so that I can't even get in touch with her. She took my baby under false pretenses—stole her from me, really kidnapped her!
>
> A woman who would do a heartless thing like that can't be trusted at all, Miss Lorne, and now I'm so terribly afraid the baby will be mistreated, cruelly mistreated. Please, won't you help me to get my darling baby girl back? I beseech you—

Suddenly the letter vanished. Everything around Brent was blacked out at the same instant. He stiffened in his chair, hearing the click of the light switch still faintly echoing in a portentous hush.

Peering over his shoulder, he saw a thin vertical flicker at the far side of the room. The lights were still burning at the top of the stairs, and the swinging door in between was just flapping to rest. Brent couldn't see the windowless wall, couldn't see anything against it—but he knew something was there. He heard it coming, rustling toward him.

He sprang up, jouncing the coffee container, hearing it plop wetly to the floor. Instinct urged him to protect the letter he still had in his hand. He groped for the table, intending to thrust it deep into the heap of correspondence and leave it there, buried. He moved fast, but the thing that was coming across the dark room toward him was moving even faster.

It was on him.

An arm hooked under his chin, snapping his head back. Before he could even squirm, he felt a sudden jolt and saw bright flashes like criss-crossing Roman candles. A dim glow swelled and burst like a soap bubble.

"It's a lie!" The words were a snaky hiss in Brent's ears. "You hear? It's false, a malicious lie!"

Then swift footfalls receded down an endless reverberating corridor, echoing long after they were gone.

CHAPTER TWO
MURDER BY MAIL

BRENT SMELLED a nauseatingly sweet odor and gradually decided he was lying on his stomach on the floor. Scores of letters were scattered under and over him and his crooked nose was pressing upon one that reeked of heliotrope. He had acquired a horrible hangover, its pulsing pain concentrated behind his right ear.

He pushed himself dizzily to his knees in a pool of spilled coffee, hung there, then found his feet and propelled himself waveringly across the city room. He listened, heard nothing and thumbed the switch. It went off with a crack like a trench mortar and the blinding force of the light flattened him against the wall. Steadier after a minute, he pushed out.

From the start he felt his belated pursuit of his assailant was futile. The only sound in all the building was the muffled drumming inside his own punished cranium. An air of murky loneliness filled the halls and offices. Brent groped and tottered his way through a sort of vacuum until, abruptly, the sounds of an approach startled him to a standstill. He braced himself against the iron post at the base of the stairs as the street entrance swung open.

The man who strode across the lobby was Garrett, the *Recorder's* hard-bitten city editor. Garrett seemed worried, but not about Brent's evident condition. He gave Brent one stern glance of his flint-gray eyes, jostled past and began climbing urgently toward the city room.

Brent doggedly followed him, blunt chin down. Brent had things to say to Garrett. He wished to point out that he was not an unreasonable man. If it was necessary for him to work twenty-four hours a day at times, he would do it, but he wished to add that when it came to getting his skull cracked into little bits, he drew the line. In a few words, he was quitting.

In advance he knew this speech would accomplish nothing. He couldn't quit, except under heavy penalty. Garrett would remind him of his iron-bound contract, would mention lawsuits and the blacklist. It was hopeless, and anyway Brent found no opportunity even to begin. Garrett had gone straight to the news desk and was impatiently spinning the telephone dial. He was not in a genial mood.

"Grandma," Garrett growled, "when I give you orders I damned well expect you at least to hear them."

"Meaning what?"

"I told you several days ago," Garrett said. "I told you last week. I also told you the week before that. In the clearest and most concise language possible I explained to you that you've got to get more variety into your column. Instead of following editorial instructions, you've been giving most of your space to just one case. For the last time—"

"Hopeful's?" Brent asked quickly.

"Hopeful's!" Garrett agreed with a snap. "Lay off it, Grandma! Kill it."

Brent narrowed one eye. "Why?"

"Because—" Garrett's face took on an angry flush. "Because, goddammit, I'm ordering you to!"

Brent considered this a suspicious evasion. His aching head told him that something strange lay behind this business of Hopeful and tonight it had somehow reached a crisis.

First an unknown man had been lying in wait outside the plant for Hopeful's latest letter, and in a vain attempt to get hold of it he had lied like a trooper. Next the same faceless man, undoubtedly, knife or no knife, had pursued the messenger who had delivered it. Then he had come prowling into the *Recorder* building after it, had peeked into the city room, had seen Brent sitting, back turned, devouring it. He had then forcibly applied a blunt instrument to a spot on Brent's head where it would best serve his purposes. On top of all this, Garrett had come charging into the news-room at a most unaccustomed hour and for certain obscure reasons of his own was summarily demanding that Brent forget the whole affair.

UNDER THE circumstances Brent definitely could not forget it. And besides, any city editor worth his salt ought never to feel so unfriendly toward anybody's new-born baby, because new-born babies were traditionally sure-fire human interest stuff.

"I can't kill it," Brent answered, eyeing Garrett as his suspicions soared. "Everybody's talking about it. Every time I go into a dog cart for a bowl of goulash, I even hear hardboiled truck drivers seriously discussing whether or not Hopeful should have given away her offspring. It's the most appealing case Lora Lorne has handled in years. Instead of ordering me to kill it you ought to be howling for me to play it up even bigger."

Garrett glared at him, continuing to struggle with the telephone, and said: "I don't trust it. I've got a feeling it's a phoney. Hopeful might blow up in our faces and ruin the rapture column for good and all. But never mind my reasons! If you write any more of your sob stuff about that dame and her brat it'll go into the scrap basket, and that's final. Scram, Grandma! I'm busy with a headache."

Intolerantly gesturing him away, Garrett kept spinning the telephone dial. Brent abandoned the issue, unable to understand Garrett's splenetic attitude toward the very young. How, he wondered, could a city editor in his right mind apply the word phoney to a tearful young mother and a brand new baby girl? It was so paradoxical that Brent trudged back to his miserable cubbyhole, grimly intent on discovering for himself, if possible, why Garrett was attempting to deny the validity of one of nature's best-established manifestations.

As a starter he fumbled among the envelopes sent avalanching off the heaped table by his fall. He found the empty special-stamped envelope, but not the letter from Hopeful which it had contained. The letter had been spirited away over his unconscious body and by now, he sensed, it unquestionably had been destroyed. He was certain he would never see it again.

He pulled from his file cabinet a folder containing all the correspondence in Hopeful's pathetic case. In the beginning she had signed no other name to her letters. At first all of Lora Lorne's answers had been broadcast in the passion column for hundreds of thousands of readers to lap up, including Hopeful, for whom they were specifically intended. Later, in order to facilitate matters, Hopeful had identified herself as Mrs. Mira Rainey, 456 Forest Street. Keeping this information confidential, Brent had then written to her directly, though he had, naturally, avoided any personal contact with her.

Also included in the file folder were a variety of letters written by numerous women all eager to help Hopeful in her plight by adopting her baby when ready. Brent had forwarded the most promising appeals to Mrs. Rainey, adding Lora Lorne's own inspired comments, and Mrs. Rainey, in turn, had apparently made a selection and the necessary arrangements. Brent was hunting for a note recently sent to Lora Lorne by a woman who had written that she had been chosen as the foster-mother of Hopeful's then unborn child.

Here it was, a rapturous missive:

> Dear, dear Miss Lorne,
>
> I'm the happiest woman in the world! Thanks to your column, where I first learned of the priceless opportunity, I am to become the new mother of Hopeful's little baby! Rest assured that it will have all my love and every advantage in an ideal home. Of course, the baby is to be known only as my very own. I'm so indebted to you, Miss Lorne!
>
> > Sincerely yours,
> > "Grateful"

The source of this joyous outburst could never have been traced if its sender hadn't supplied Brent with two clear-cut clues. Apparently in an unguarded moment, she had written it on stationery imprinted with the monogram EGF. Moreover, the flap of the envelope she had used bore the name of Bay Terrace House, a swanky apartment building located near the river. The initials plus the address gave Brent hope that a few simple inquiries would identify her as the woman now accused of bad faith and baby stealing. As Lora Lorne, he felt responsible. As Bill Brent, he knew the aroma of news when he smelled it. He got going.

HURRYING DOWN the stairs, he was aware that Garrett had abandoned the telephone and was following him. He ducked into his car and Garrett hustled into another. Starting off riverward, he noticed that Garrett's headlamps were glaring directly behind him. He drove straight away and Garrett tailed him. He turned corners and Garrett stuck close. Annoyed and puzzled, Brent stepped on the gas. When he veered to the curb behind a sedan waiting near the entrance of Bay Terrace House he had gained a block on Garrett, but Garrett was still coming.

"What the hell!" Brent protested.

He swung toward the doors and the breath left his lungs with a quick *whoof!* Suddenly there was hair in his eyes and in his mouth. He couldn't see anything, but in his arms, instinctively closed, he felt the warmth and curvesome softness which could mean nothing on earth other than a young woman's body.

She struggled to free herself of Brent, her breath a fast rushing sound. He had no idea where she had come from so instantaneously, but she was desperate to get herself gone with even greater alacrity. She was afraid, Brent sensed—fleeing from something, terrified.

He was spun half around as she tore away. As if his brain were a camera equipped with a flashgun, it registered an attractive action shot. The girl was diving into the car parked in front of Brent's. She was hatless and both pockets of her loose coat seemed heavily weighted. Her hair was wild in the wind of her own movements. She had legs which won Brent's approval, even though her white stockings and white oxfords did not set them off to their best advantage. Her eyes gave him one glinting glance. Then she disappeared into the gloom inside her car and the picture went out of focus.

She whizzed away without switching on the lights. Her tires squealed at the corner. That was all there was of her, and Brent regretted it.

She was gone, but Garrett had come even closer. He was parking behind Brent's car. Still mystified, Brent strode to him and asked an indignant question.

"Why the hell are you haunting me, Garrett?"

Garrett attempted to brush past without answering, but Brent's hand fastened on his arm. He eyed Brent and countered, "Why are *you* here?"

"In the line of duty," Brent answered. "You don't live in a decent place like this, do you? I always thought you crawled back in a hole during the day."

Too anxious and preoccupied to take offense, Garrett answered: "My sister and my brother-in-law have an apartment here. He's clippering up from Rio and his plane was overdue from New York, but he's due to show up here any second now." Almost to himself Garrett added, "It's a special hurry-up trip because my sister has just had a baby."

Brent winced. "She's just had a what?"

Brent shook him gently. "Who's Abigail?" he asked. "Where is she?"

Garrett scowled at him. "Surely, Miss Lorne," Garrett said with stringent sarcasm, "you know what a baby consists of. You're aware, surely, that a baby is a thing around the middle of which diapers are pinned. You yourself were once a baby, were you not?"

Brent inquired with a grimace, "Boy or girl?"

"Do you mean, which were you?"

Brent flushed angrily. Having to wear Lora Lorne's petticoats was humiliating enough without Garrett's flaunting them in his face. But he controlled his tone and answered, speaking very distinctly: "I mean which did your sister have?"

"A girl." Garrett still eyed him. "Why the hell are you staring at me? What's so startling about that? Women have babies every day, usually at the most inconvenient hours. Approximately half the time they have baby girls. My sister is no exception to the rule. Do you mind?"

"Yes," Brent muttered. "I mind very much. I have lately become allergic to new-born infants."

And new fire was kindled under his suspicions. Garrett's uneasiness had to mean that Brent was not far wrong in smelling a rat. Garrett turned away with guilty quickness, in fact, as a taxi appeared, swerving around the corner. He hurried after it as it stopped at the entrance of Bay Terrace House.

THE MAN who hustled out of the cab was handsome in a gray-templed, sun-browned way despite the gauntness of his face. He was about to pick up two suitcases plastered with hotel labels when Garrett grabbed his hand.

"Mike!" Garrett boomed. "Just in time! Mike, old man, how are you?"

Mike answered the greeting unhappily. "Oh, hullo, hullo. I'm fine, thanks, except I was air-sick all the way up from Rio. Nerves upset. My liver's sluggish again. I've got to get an appointment with Doctor Hartwell first thing. My old indigestion's come back. I don't sleep well any more, either. But otherwise I'm fine."

Urgently he trudged into the foyer as he spoke, with Garrett pacing at his one side and Brent, curiously, at his other.

Garrett said, frowning: "Meet my brother-in-law, Michael Farnam. He's just up from Brazil, where he's been busy these past nine months doing important things about industrial diamonds. This, Mike, is a minor employe of the paper whose name, if I remember rightly, is Brent. You may ignore him."

Farnam did so, after briefly squeezing Brent's hand, but he did it in a natural, charming way. Aside from his physical condition, which was probably not as bad as he imagined, he seemed too good a guy to be related to Garrett even by marriage. After all, too, he was understandably concerned about his wife and new-born daughter. He asked breathlessly of Garrett, "How's Elaine?"

Brent didn't hear Garrett's answer. A realization had pelted him squarely between the eyes. He had come to this building in search of a woman of suspicious character whose initials were E.G.F. and he was immediately connecting. The first initial of Garrett's sister Elaine, plus her maiden name of Garrett, plus her married name of Farnam—it checked! There might easily be another woman in the building whose initials were E.G.F., but certainly not another E.G.F. who had acquired a female infant within the past several days. Suddenly things were tying up with a neatness that had to be more than mere coincidence.

Brent was so struck by it that despite Garrett's forbidding frown he drifted after Mike Farnam into the automatic elevator. Suspecting skulduggery, Brent even trailed Farnam to the door of his apartment. There Garrett turned on Brent with a darker frown. Being a strict disciplinarian who had come out of the first World War a major at twenty-three, Garrett could pull off a scowl of truly formidable aspect.

"What the hell are you after, Brent?" he rasped. "A cigar? If so—"

"Good God!" Farnam blurted.

He had opened his apartment door. He had stopped short, clenching a grip in each hand. He was staring horrified into his living-room.

"Good—God!" he said again.

Brent peered over Farnam's bent back and his whole framework snapped tight.

A man was crawling across the floor—or trying to crawl. Like a mortally wounded animal, he was flopping, writhing himself along. His arms wouldn't work properly and he was dragging his legs. A long streak on the rug showed that he had so far struggled a distance of ten feet from a dark, wet spot in the center of the room. His face was a ghastly smear of blood. The blood was trickling down from his matted hair. Staring at the crown of his head, all broken and pulpy, Brent wondered how he could move at all, how he could live. In a mad effort, blindly sensing that help was near, the terribly beaten man was snaking himself toward the open door.

Abruptly he rolled over, loosely, like an under-inflated inner tube, and an acrid cackling laugh broke from his throat. His smeared lips worked as Brent pushed past Garrett and Farnam and dropped to his knees beside the gasping man. He heard grating words in a mumbled whisper that scarcely reached his straining ears.

"Abigail! Had to come back—must stay with you. Don't do it! Abigail—it's a lie! Don't—Abigail—don't!"

Brent shook him gently. "Who's Abigail?" he asked, his tone low. "Where is she?"

The man's eyes fluttered open and turned unseeingly up at Brent—red-filmed eyes, glazing.

"Heights!" he choked out. "Heights!"

His arms stiffened up as if to ward off more murderous blows and then, with a cry of tortured terror rising thinly out of his lungs, he died.

CHAPTER THREE
WHO IS ABIGAIL?

BRENT HAD not always, God knows, worn the sweet false-face of Lora Lorne. Back in New York, centuries ago, he had been a full-fledged and completely male reporter living only a single life—and a glorious life of newshawking it seemed, now that he looked longingly back on it. It was his aggressive ability, in fact, that had induced Garrett to lure him away with a contract and an inflated salary. Even though Garrett had since condemned him to the passion column as a punitive measure—Brent had merely missed a total of twenty-odd editions, all told, due to having been detained in various bars and boudoirs—he still had a newsman's instincts. They were perked up now, like a fighting cock's hackles, as he frowned down at the broken-headed victim of murder.

Garrett and Farnam had drifted in and were still incredulously staring.

"Who is that man?" Brent asked.

"Never saw him before—never!" Farnam blurted a breathless question of his own. "How did he get in here?"

Neither Brent nor Garrett offered a guess.

"Nobody has keys to this apartment except Elaine and me," Farnam went on quickly, "and of course the maid and the superintendent, but they wouldn't let a stranger in. Elaine's been at the hospital for days, ever since she had the baby, and I've been out of the country!"

It seemed reasonable but unanswerable. Brent, looking quickly about, discovered several red streaks on the back of a yellow leather chair. They were still wet. Fingers had left them there. They evidently meant that the murderer had stepped back, after shattering his victim's skull with repeated blows, and closed a sticky, steadying hand on the chair. Brent saw no ridge patterns. The prints were as smooth as if they'd been made by so many hot dogs, and they were thin. Either a man's slender hand had not pressed hard against the leather, or it had been a woman.

A woman? Brent thought of the girl who had bumped the wind out of him when rushing anxiously from the building. Very likely her precipitate departure had begun in this room. Who was she? Brent recalled her legs with pleasant clarity, but not her face. He hadn't noticed that part of her.

Searching for further indications of her, he went quickly down a short hall. He found a door opening onto the service stairs from a kitchen that had apparently been unused for days. In a bedroom he paused, head lifted, sniffing a flowery fragrance hovering freshly in the air. Turning back, he encountered Mike Farnam. Having followed, Farnam was also noticing the scent.

"Nobody else here," Brent reported. "Whose perfume is that?"

Utterly bewildered, Farnam mumbled, "My wife's!"

"Sure?"

"It—it's her special favorite. She never uses any other. But it—it can't mean—"

"Just when did your wife have her baby?"

"Four days ago," Farnam said, pushing the words out. "She's still at the hospital, of course—will be there probably another week. She couldn't possibly have been here tonight! *No one* could have come in, considering the keys."

"But someone did come in," Brent reminded him. "Two people, in fact. One's scrammed and the other's staying longer than he expected, a little the worse for wear."

The maltreated corpse drew Brent back to the living-room. Garrett was at the telephone—using it to call the Homicide Squad with, Brent thought, reluctance. News was Garrett's business, but he seemed to have little stomach for it when it sprang redly from the midst of his own family. The dead man had been beaten down in this room, certainly, but the weapon, whatever it may have been, Brent made sure, was nowhere in sight.

BRENT TENDERLY fingered the lump behind his right ear. The clout he had received in Lora Lorne's sanctum sanctorum had been the forerunner of the murderous blows struck here. There was one other striking similarity. Having been conked down, Brent had heard his assailant asserting, "It's a lie!" and those very words had been among the last spoken by the man who now lay dead at Brent's feet. But, noting his slight build and short legs, Brent decided the corpse was not the man who had stolen the Lorne letter. The same words had, then, issued from two throats, no doubt for the same reason. And Brent surmised that both he and the murder victim had successively been bashed by the same vicious attacker.

Bending over him again, Brent probed into the corpse's pockets. His hand came up with an envelope. With a frown he saw it was empty. Whatever it contained had been removed. Had *two* letters been stolen tonight, Brent wondered. He couldn't be certain, but the envelope alone was enough to send a shock skipping along his nerves.

It was a plain white number ten. It bore a special delivery stamp. It was postmarked this city, four days ago, and it had been duly delivered to a street address in Chicago. The addressee's name was Victor Rainey.

"Rainey!" Brent blurted under his breath, snapping to his feet.

"Take it easy, Grandma," Garrett growled, and at the sound of that voice Brent's hand dove into his coat pocket with the envelope, unseen. "Remember you're on the rapture column, Grandma, not on news. My police reporter and I will cover this, and you'll confine yourself to Cupid's errant ways."

"Garrett," Brent retorted, "you're too hard-headed for your own good. This happens to be a particularly gory murder involving your brother-in-law and your own sister. Do a little remembering yourself. I came here for a reason."

Garrett asked, his scowl returning, "What was it, Miss Lorne?"

"Don't call me that name!" Brent gritted his teeth but erected his defenses. "I had a good reason and I still smell all sorts of skulduggery cooking behind the scenes. You don't want your own sister to simmer in such a ghastly stew, do you? You don't imagine that Captain Russo and the Homicide Squad will turn off the heat simply because she's related to you!"

"She had nothing to do with this," Garrett said, his stony eyes levelling. "A woman busy with an *accouchement* could have no hand in a killing. Neither could Mike."

"It's her rug that's all bloodied up," Brent pointed out. "It's her special perfume floating in the air here. It's her key that was the only one available. And it's her baby Lora Lorne is wondering about."

"What?" Garrett snapped. "Why?"

"I think you know what I mean, Garrett. Maybe it'll help to remind you that as a highly competent news sniffer-outer I've learned how to tell which facts will force their way into the headlines and which others can be clammed up. Well, I'm on the scent of something more complicated than simple obstetrics, and you can't sidetrack me. This is where I go back on the police trick unless you want to leave yourself wide open to get it where it will sting the worst."

Garrett actually sneered. "This is where you keep right on devoting yourself to the follies of Aphrodite, Grandma," he countered. "I can also issue a few warnings. If you should make this mess any worse than it already is, I'll make it so hot for you at the office that you'll be forced to quit. Then I'll sue the pants off you for breaking your contract and I'll blacklist you besides. Do you doubt that I can do it?"

BRENT BLANCHED. He didn't doubt it for one minute. Prudence demanded that he should not press the issue. Reorganizing his tactics, he retreated to the door. Garrett, however, strode after him, grabbed a handful of his coat with such vehemence that Brent shrank within himself.

"I mean that! This is one time when you'll behave or you'll play hell with yourself. You're asking for headaches compared with which the love column will seem like a bed of roses. Think it over, Miss Lorne. Good night, Miss Lorne."

He pushed Brent out. As the door slammed shut on him Brent said, "I'm scared to death," with an ominously confident smile.

He turned about and his smile waned. The narrow hallway was full of men who had just emerged from the elevator. They were the Homicide Squad and foremost among them was Captain Russo, regarding Brent with sad, lusterless eyes. Seeming to possess the instincts of a buzzard, Russo had appeared at the scene of the killing with his usual uncanny promptness. Even more uncanny was Russo's resemblance to a corpse. He was as gaunt-faced, as clammy-skinned, as imperturbable as any stiff he had ever smelled out.

"You again, Brent?" Russo said in his sepulchral tone. "Are you claiming squatter's rights on another cadaver?"

"By no means," Brent hastened to assure him. "You're more than welcome to it. I'm just an innocent bystander, as usual."

The captain said funereally: "I always wonder just how innocent, Brent."

Brent shuddered and escaped into the elevator. He sent it gliding downward hoping he could escape from Lora Lorne's damnable apron strings—a consummation devoutly to be wished—and doggedly convinced that this time, considering Garrett as an anxious brother rather than a cold-blooded city editor, he had Garrett where the hair grew shortest from a tender area—particularly if he could snag a yarn that Garrett would want to keep unpublished.

Driving through dark streets, he reflected elatedly that he had two leads which Garrett didn't even suspect. One was the empty envelope addressed to Victor Rainey, plus the similar envelope addressed to Lora Lorne. The other was the dying man's words, words too faint to have reached Garrett's ears; an unusual, old-fashioned name—*Abigail*—and a word, *heights*. Taken together, did they mean that Rainey, in extremis, had gasped out an accusation against a woman named Abigail who in some way was connected with the Heights Hospital?

It seemed very likely to Brent, particularly when he recalled the shapely white stockings and the trim white oxfords of the girl who had so anxiously fled the building where Rainey had been brained.

It was a sizzling lead, Brent judged. Detouring in the hope of connecting it with another, he returned to the *Recorder* plant. He ran up the iron stairs, into his cubicle and again tackled his file. In it he found a verification of his growing suspicions—a letter addressed to Lora Lorne by Hopeful last week, in which she had announced the imminence of her baby. "It's all arranged," she wrote, "and at any minute now I'll be rushing off to the hospital—the Heights."

That word again!

BRENT SPED back down to his car and drove rapidly to the Heights Hospital, a small though impressive structure of white stone with an all-glass entrance in modern style—a private concern, he knew, far beyond the means of Mrs. Rainey, alias Hopeful. Pushing in, he heard the muted hustling of the staff setting about its manifold daily duties. Brent took a question straight to a cherub-cheeked woman at the admission desk.

"My friend Mrs. Rainey is a patient here, I understand," he said glibly.

"Oh, yes."

"She's just had a baby, I understand," Brent went on.

"Why, no!"

Brent stared and said, "What?"

"I said, no, Mrs. Rainey hasn't had a baby."

Blankly Brent repeated: "Mrs. Rainey has not had a baby?"

"Not at all," the woman at the desk assured him. "Mrs. Rainey just happens to be in a room on the maternity floor. You seem to have jumped to a conclusion because of that. How amusing! Her trouble is really quite a different sort."

Brent reflected. As Lora Lorne, he was damned certain that Mrs. Rainey had duly given birth. As Bill Brent he was being told authoritatively that she had not done so. It was confusing, but the hospital ought to know. After a numb silence he reverted to his primary lead.

"Is there someone named Abigail on the staff here?"

"Abigail isn't on our staff," the woman said. "Abigail is also a patient."

Taking a breath, Brent asked: "May I see her?"

"I think you may." The apple cheeks bunched, shiningly. "I'll call her special nurse."

When the nurse appeared Brent instantly regretted he was not in immediate need of hospitalization. The nurse was twenty-two or -three and she had natural red hair and sea-green eyes. She had a beautiful mouth. She was, in fact, beautiful all over. Beyond doubt she was one of the most luscious young women Brent had ever seen in or out of a nurse's uniform. She adorned it. She made it seem as svelte and breathtaking as a form-molded evening gown. It was dazzling. Brent goggled, wondering how many men there were in her life. At a moment's notice their number could be increased by one, named William Coleridge Brent.

"I'm Nurse Olive Winslow," she said, and even her voice was beautiful. "You wish to see Abigail? Come with me."

Going with her was one of the easiest things Brent had ever done, but on the way he tried to put his mind back to the business at hand. His immediate purpose was not, regrettably, a delectable nurse, but someone whose name a murder victim had spoken with his last living breath. "Don't—Abigail—don't!" To Brent this had sounded like a frantic, tortured plea. In a delirium of pain, he believed, Victor Rainey had begged for mercy. "Don't do it— Abigail—don't!" What could this indicate, Brent asked himself, except that someone named Abigail had showered those murderous blows on Victor Rainey's head?

"There's Abigail," Nurse Winslow said.

Self-absorbed, Brent had followed her unaware of his surroundings. He had come into the maternity section, he realized, and he was facing a broad window in a partition. Nurse Winslow was pointing through the glass with a beautiful finger. She was indicating a crib in the nursery in which a very small infant was peacefully asleep.

"That's Abigail?" Brent blurted.

"Yes, indeed," Nurse Winslow said. "Isn't she a darling? Only four days old."

Reversing himself, Brent concluded on the spot that Abigail was not a murderess.

"What is Abigail's last name, please?" he asked thickly.

"Why, Farnam, of course."

Farnam! Brent heard it and stared through the pane, shocked and wondering if his tired eyes were tricking him. Was he imagining it, or did Abigail Farnam's baby face actually bear a resemblance to the face of the man named Rainey who had died at Brent's feet?

CHAPTER FOUR

DAMES ARE DANGEROUS

GAZING INTO the immaculate crib in which the four-days-old Abigail innocently slumbered,

Brent muttered: "I realize this isn't the visiting hour. I know I ought to come back later, but I have urgent news for Mrs. Farnam. Could I see her?"

Nurse Olive Winslow gave him a beautiful smile. "Doctor Hartwell and Doctor Marvin are with Mrs. Farnam just now. They just finished an emergency appendectomy on another patient, and dropped in to see how she's doing, and I don't think they'll stay with her long. You might wait here in the hall."

"Thanks," Brent sighed. "I've had a hard night, and that's very nice of you. You're very, very nice. You're so nice you'll tell me, won't you, off the record, whether Mrs. Rainey's husband called here last night?"

"I'm really not supposed to talk." Nurse Winslow's lovely smile faded into a lovely worried expression. "But he was here. He kicked up a frightful row, though I can't say what it was about. Seven or eight months ago he'd left her to shift for herself, and this was the first time she'd seen him since, and then he yelled and ranted at her and made such a fuss we had to put him out of the building. Aren't men terrible sometimes?"

Considering it in the light of Lora Lorne's wisdom, Brent agreed they were indeed. "Is Mrs. Rainey very sick?" he inquired.

"Not very." Observing her professional ethics, Nurse Winslow offered no specific clinical information. "Excuse me."

A door across the hall had opened. A brisk-mannered and darkly attractive woman of thirty-odd stepped out, followed by a younger man whose attitude toward her was markedly deferential. Both were carrying black instrument cases.

The woman spoke to Nurse Winslow in a crisp, low tone.

"Yes, Doctor Hartwell," the pretty girl answered her.

The young man said: "I'll be back later in the morning."

"Yes, Doctor Marvin."

Both physicians—the poised, self-possessed woman and the younger man who was evidently her associate—went down the corridor and Nurse Winslow informed Brent, "You may go in now."

Brent started in but stopped, gazing at the number painted on the door. It brought flashing back to his mind a recollection of a faceless man waiting outside the *Recorder* plant and a disguised voice urging that Lora Lorne must "return the letter to the occupant of Room 404 at the Heights Hospital." This was Room 404.

Stepping in, Brent was further astonished to find it was not a private room, but a semi-private, occupied by not just one woman, but two.

He gazed at them in perplexity as they lay in the two beds gazing back at him with, he thought, a certain wariness.

One of them was rather colorless and ordinary. Her hair was an intermediate shade of lackluster brown and her face was undistinguished except for her large, pleading blue eyes. The other was much more personable. She had finely chiseled features and her sherry-colored hair, neatly brushed, had evidently received the regular attention of an expensive beautician. Obviously she was a young woman of breeding, intelligence and social grace. Seeing a small, ornate bottle of perfume on the table beside her bed, Brent concluded that she was the young woman whom he desired to question.

"You're Mrs. Farnam?"

"Oh, no," she answered quickly. "I'm Mrs. Rainey."

"Mrs. Rainey?" Brent echoed.

"Yes." A neatly manicured hand indicated the other bed where the average- looking girl lay. "*She's* Mrs. Farnam. I'm Mrs. Farnam's maid."

BRENT FROWNED a little at the nondescript girl and asked, "Mrs. Farnam?"

The big blue eyes flickered slightly and the unrouged mouth responded, "Yeh. Whaddaya want?"

Brent gazed from the unattractive one to the attractive one, and back again, and took thought. Something, he assured himself, was screwy here. In the first place, a woman and her maid were rarely hospitalized in the same room at the same time.

As far as he could make out the rest of it now, it added up to this: Mrs. Rainey had given birth to a baby girl, except that Mrs. Rainey had not. In a letter to Lora Lorne she had accused Mrs. Farnam, her employer, of kidnapping the child which she had not borne. And she had written this while lying in the same room with Mrs. Farnam, who was then herself recovering from the pangs of parturition, and even at this moment the anxious, sympathetic glances passing between them indicated they really were on the best of terms. Brent was unable to see, just yet, how anything as wacky as this could ever make sense.

"I've come here," he began, staring blankly at both women and feeling his way through the dark, "at the request of Lora Lorne."

Both women lifted their heads off their pillows and widely gazed at him.

"She received your letter, Mrs. Rainey," Brent added.

The attractive one asked quickly, "What letter?"

"The one you sent her last evening by special delivery."

"But I didn't send Lora Lorne any letter yesterday—or at any other time!"

"No?" Brent turned to the ordinary-looking one. "Did *you* send a special delivery letter to Lora Lorne yesterday, Mrs. Farnam?"

"Unh-uh, I didn't."

Brent was mulling this over when the door opened and Nurse Olive Winslow entered bearing a small florist's box tied with a pink ribbon. She gave Brent a lovely smile and carried the box to the farther bed in which her better-looking patient lay. "For you," she said, placing it on her patient's stomach. "It just came." Still smiling, Nurse Winslow then withdrew, leaving Brent still mulling.

He watched the long, well-enameled fingernails plucking at the pink bow. He saw the lid of the box lifted, the wax paper parted and heard a gasp. He saw rounded violet eyes staring into the box, a slender hand reaching slowly in, then darting back as if from something too vile to touch. Suddenly the cover was replaced and two patrician hands held it down, trembling.

"Something wrong, Mrs. Rainey?" Brent asked.

"No—no, nothing!"

"I'm afraid there is," Brent insisted. "I have shocking news for you. I'll have to put it bluntly. Your husband is dead."

"Dead!" It was a screech. "My husband!"

Brent added gently, "Victor Rainey was murdered early this morning."

A strange series of expressions raced across the delicate face of the woman to whom Brent was speaking. They flickered on and off so rapidly he couldn't identify any of them, except the last one, which stayed—horrified consternation. At the same time the girl in the other bed went through a similar series of chaotic facial reactions and wound up by staring at Brent with tearful incredulity.

To her Brent added: "I also have to report that Mrs. Rainey's husband was found violently dead in your living-room, Mrs. Farnam."

IT WAS the first one, the personable one, who sat bolt upright in bed and gulped out, "Where did you say?" Then, without waiting for an answer, she again snatched the cover off the florist's box. Her hand dove into the waxed paper and came up holding a small envelope such as usually contained the felicitations of the gift's sender. Her eyes sped through the note inscribed on the card, and abruptly she was sent off into a hysterical outburst so vehement that Brent was overwhelmed.

"Who are you? What do you mean by coming here and saying such insane things? You must be crazy! It couldn't happen! It's impossible, do you hear? Go away! Get out, get out!"

Brent decided he had better. Nurse Winslow came running, her green eyes scolding Brent, but beautifully. He dodged along the corridor while other nurses rushed to her assistance. Room 404 was now full of vocal turmoil. Leaving it rapidly behind him, Brent felt that the news he had brought could not entirely be the cause of all that emotional upheaval. The fireworks had really been touched off by the fact that the contents of the florist's box, plus the message on the sender's card, had abruptly conveyed some terrible sort of meaning. Brent wondered what the hell the box contained, if not flowers.

He kept going in his car through still-dark streets. Swinging to the front of Bay Terrace House, he found the Homicide Squad's big limousine still parked. The knob of the Farnam apartment responded to his twist and he sidled in. The corpse was still present. Garrett and Mike Farnam, having not been permitted to leave, were sitting uncomfortably in the foyer. Captain Russo was now supervising the photographing of the blood marks on the yellow leather chair.

"Cat burglar," one of the squad was saying. "A heister, a three-time loser afraid of the Habitual Criminals Act. Otherwise why would he go prowling around with all his finger ridges eaten off with acid?"

It was a fair enough theory, except that it didn't account for Victor Rainey's penetration into an apartment to which he could not have had a key. Brent stood quietly aside, eyed forbiddingly by Garrett, vaguely by Farnam.

"They still don't know who he is." Farnam said.

Evidently, then, Rainey had carried no means of identification except the empty envelope purloined by Brent. Brent began to think about the severe penalty for removing and concealing evidence.

"They think he was beaten with a gun," Farnam added. "They asked to see mine. I used to keep an automatic in the apartment, but I can't find it."

"Never mind," Brent said by way of heartening him. "Your wife's doing fine, and so is Abigail."

Farnam's face lighted up. "Did Elaine name the baby Abigail?" he chuckled. "That was sweet and thoughtful of her! I can't wait to see the kid. Must be a cute little dumpling, ha? I've wanted a baby of our own for years. I'm daffy about 'em!"

He would not continue to be daffy about this one, Brent mused, if he should happen to feel, as Brent did, that it resembled the corpse in the living-room.

A queasy expression passed over Mike Farnam's face. "My stomach's shaking up and down," he said. "My nerves feel like a mass of red-hot spaghetti. I've got to see Doctor Hartwell first thing in the morning."

Garrett gestured unsympathetically. "You're not one-tenth as sick as you think you are, Mike. You can imagine more things wrong with your insides than a quack could. Every time you feel a twinge somewhere you go rushing off to your doctor. You're perfectly healthy but you've been doing it for years. Your bills must be terrific."

Farnam nodded, admitting it, but added in a gone tone: "What can you expect of a constitution as sensitive as mine? It's terrible to need constant medical care, as I do. Perhaps Doctor Hartwell hasn't done everything possible for me. That's it! I'll change. Could you recommend another good doctor?"

"Nuts!" Garrett said. "No!"

CAPTAIN RUSSO was taking his lugubrious time over the cadaver, Brent noted, and nothing new was developing. Having interests elsewhere, Brent turned back to the door. He heard a quick click, the metallic ripple of a key sliding into the lock. The next instant the door opened a scant three inches. Through the crack Brent saw a face—the patrician features and the anxious violet eyes of the woman who was supposed to be confined to a maternity bed at the Heights Hospital!

She stared past his shoulder, then recoiled from him and instantly the door thumped shut.

Dazed by the unexpectedness of her face, Brent fumbled for the knob. Making sure that neither Garrett nor Farnam had noticed the incident, he sidled out and saw the elevator door closing. Gears ground as the car descended. Brent spun about, found the door of the fire stairs and loped out to the street just in time to glimpse a coupe skittering out of sight past the corner.

Brent propelled his own car after it. The streets were thick with pre-dawn darkness and there was no traffic— no car in sight except the one blocks ahead of him. The woman was driving like a female demon. Brent lost sight of her again as she skidded around another corner. Speeding past the front of the Heights Hospital without seeing her, he knew she had run into the alleyway leading to the parking space behind it. He shuttled through, but found the lot completely dark—every car at a standstill, lights out.

A flutter caught his eyes. It was an almost invisible motion against the hospital's rear stone wall. Brent heard the clatter of something falling to the cement pavement and a sound like a woman's wail, muted. He ran closer, his soles making quick sandpaper sounds. There was a basement entrance below the ground level and, directly above it, the rising black zigzag of a fire-escape. The counterbalanced ladder at the base of the fire-escape had been let down. The woman was pulling herself up it with breathless and desperate haste.

Brent slower, knowing now where he could find her when he wanted her, which would be soon. Knowing also that in her hurry she had had no time to pick up the thing she had dropped, he looked for it. It was lying close beside the short flight of outside stairs descending to the basement. In the glow shining down from the windows, Brent saw it was a formidable Colt automatic, a .38. The dark stuff on its butt, crusty now but still slightly sticky too, must be blood—Victor Rainey's blood.

Galvanized by the discovery, Brent scarcely heard the snarl behind him. He removed the clip. While counting the nine cartridges that filled it to capacity he became aware that something like a stormy burst of wind was rushing at him.

A black gleaming shape was looming and advancing on him with a muffled roar. The swift sweep and the swelling sound of it expressed unswerving power. Instinctively Brent leaped backward to escape it. He stumbled into a void. First his upthrown arms, then his head, struck the basement stairs.

Next he was aware that he was on his hands and knees, crawling up them. His throbbing head lifted into darkness that was open and cool and silent. He realized now that he had almost been run down by a powerful car—deliberately. It had spurted out of line in the parking lot and had hurtled upon him, and he had escaped it by a narrow squeak. It was gone now, like Brent's patience.

Brent had an aching hunch that something else was also gone. Lighting paper matches, he speedily confirmed this suspicion. Like the two special delivery letters, the weapon that had killed Victor Rainey had been snatched into limbo.

CHAPTER FIVE

DEATH WITH FATHER

BRENT TRAMPED into the hospital through, appropriately enough, the emergency entrance. He pushed into Room 404 without knocking. He scowled at the two patients. The unlovely one gazed back at him in fright. The better-looking one had the bedclothes tucked closely under her chin and was giving a fairly good imitation of being sound asleep, except that her breathing was much too fast.

Letting her put on her act for the moment, Brent reached into the waste-basket between the beds and brought up the florist's carton and the pink ribbon. The address tag bore the typed name of Mrs. Elaine Farnam. The wax paper inside the box revealed a gun-shaped depression, and there were dark flakes adhering to it—dried blood particles. Brent also retrieved the card. It had been torn to bits. Roughly piecing them together, he made out the typed, unsigned message.

> You carelessly left this in your apartment when you killed Rainey.

Brent gripped the bedcovers and tore them off clear to the foot of the bed. Its uncovered occupant squeaked in terror and sat up. Unlike the usual in-patient, she was wearing a dark suit, apricot-colored stockings and high-heeled suede pumps. She dragged the sheet over her again, Brent grimly allowing her.

"Now," Brent said. "As Lora Lorne's emissary, I'm going to get this thing straight. You're not Mrs. Rainey, as you said you were. Your looks, your perfume, the key you used a few minutes ago to open the door of your apartment—everything proves you're Elaine Farnam."

The blond Elaine Farnam, gulping at Brent, could not summon up a denial.

"And you," Brent added, turning upon the brownette in the next bed, "are actually Mrs. Rainey. Neither of you two entered this hospital under your own name. You entered under each other's. It's cockeyed as hell but it's beginning to jell."

The violet eyes of Elaine Farnam and the childlike blue eyes of Mira Rainey were focussed fearfully on Brent.

"You, Mrs. Rainey, while passing yourself off as Mrs. Farnam, actually had a baby whose birth is now duly certified under the name of Abigail Farnam. As for you, Mrs. Farnam—you're in perfectly normal physical condition, personally concerned much less with giving life than with destroying it. Lora Lorne will be greatly disturbed to hear you're the prime suspect in a murder case."

Elaine Farnam now had a grip on herself. She gazed forthrightly at Brent. "What's Lora Lorne got to do with this?" she asked.

"Why," Brent said, "for at least the past month Mrs. Rainey has been writing frequently to Lora Lorne about her baby, and—"

"I never did!" said the young woman in the other bed, with flat emphasis.

Brent stared at her. "You *haven't* written letters to Lora Lorne about—"

"Not once, I never!"

Blinking, Brent turned back to Mrs. Farnam. "But you did. Miss Lorne received a letter from you a week ago saying how delighted you were to be chosen—"

"Don't be silly!" Elaine Farnam said. "Why should I? Don't forget, the city editor of the *Recorder* happens to be my brother and I happen to be one of the few who knows who Lora Lorne really is, Mr. Brent."

BRENT SWALLOWED hard but, baffled as he was by these denials, he hastily abandoned the subject. Elaine

Farnam, seizing upon his discomfiture, leaned pleadingly toward him.

"You must never mention this to my husband—never! You understand that, don't you?"

"I understand there's one hell of a lot of deceit being practiced here," Brent said.

"You've *got* to understand it," Elaine Farnam insisted, "because you've got to keep quiet about it. I'm sure you won't mention it to anyone once I've told you—"

Suddenly she was telling him in a rush of earnest words.

"You see, more than a year ago, I—I began to lose my husband's love. Miss Lorne would sympathize with me about that, of course! Mike was working in this city then, and somewhere he'd met—a girl. I still don't know where or how, or who she is. I only know she must be something very special, because he—he went off the deep end for her. Not that he wanted to. He fought against the attraction he felt for her, but it was so strong he couldn't control it. Suddenly there was 'another woman' in my life and my marriage was threatened and I was terribly afraid I was going to lose Mike."

Brent observed: "He doesn't exactly look like a heel."

"He's not at all!" Elaine Farnam staunchly rushed to her husband's defense. "Mike is always fair and honest. He told me what was happening. He couldn't help it and he was sincerely trying his best to do the decent thing. Both he and I wanted to be sensible and reasonable about it, to keep our marriage going if we could. When Mike went off to South America on business, I thought that might solve the problem by taking him out of this girl's reach, but it didn't. She wrote him often, and it went right on, becoming more and more dangerous. I desperately wanted to keep my husband—and that's when all this started."

"This baby business?" Brent said.

Elaine Farnam anxiously nodded. "Mike has always been crazy about babies, but somehow I'd never managed to give him one. I thought that if only I could, he'd never leave me then. It began to work out, in a special way. Mira Rainey has been my maid for the past eight months—she came to me shortly after Mike left for Rio, so he'd never seen her. Her husband had abandoned her and she was going to have a baby. Everything Hopeful wrote to Lora Lorne applies to Mira—even though Mira did not write those letters—and she couldn't give the baby a proper home or a proper upbringing, so she and I agreed that I would adopt her child and that Mike must never know the baby wasn't really my own.

"I thought I was all set, and so I wrote to Mike that a baby was coming along at last, He was delighted, never dreaming the truth. He was going to be in Rio for months and months longer, and I thought it would be a simple matter—the adoption arrangements, I mean. But I was wrong! I hadn't realized that legal adoption is a compli-cated, carefully handled, long-drawn-out process. And besides, the adopting husband must sign the various papers along with his wife. Suddenly—after having told Mike month after month that I was about to have a baby—I discovered that my original plan was impossible to carry out, because above everything else Mike *had* to believe that the baby was really biologically his and mine."

BRENT CLUCKED, as Lora Lorne would have done.

"But Mike was so happy about it I had to keep up the pretense. Even to my friends! Whenever anyone dropped in at the apartment I had to sit with a blanket draped around me, so none of them would mention to Mike that I didn't look a bit changed. All the while I was desperately trying to find a way of working it out. And then I did find one—something so simple it seemed foolproof. It was that Mira would have her baby under my name."

Mrs. Rainey, in the other bed, verified this with a vigorous nod.

"So I made these arrangements and named the little girl Abigail because that was Mike's mother's name, and besides, it means 'a father's joy,' and—and the rest is obvious, isn't it?"

"Not quite," Brent said. "You couldn't have pulled it off without inside help."

Elaine Farnam nipped at her nails. "I appealed to our doctor, Doctor Jean Hartwell. Being a woman, she sympathized and fixed it, even though it was unethical. She put us both in this one room, each under the other's name, so that all the records would show it was Mrs. Farnam who had had the baby when it was really the other way around. It solved other problems, too. For example, our special nurse simply shows visitors to this door and they naturally don't know the difference. Mira and I are planning to leave the hospital at the same time, and then I'll simply take Abigail and she'll come back to work for me, and there'll never be any question. Not from Mike, above all! Mike must never know the truth—never!"

"If he should learn the truth," Brent said wisely, "he'd then know that you'd undertaken to hold him with lies and trickery, and it would send him straight into the arms of the other woman."

"You make it sound so awful!" Elaine Farnam protested. "It is deceit, but it's doing nothing but good. It's helping Mira, and the baby too—as long as Mira's my maid, they'll see a great deal of each other—and I'm sure Mike and I will be so happy with little Gail!"

"Your brother—my city editor—has been in on this secret from the very beginning, I suppose?"

"Yes, I had to confide in him. He became very upset when Lora Lorne began publishing those letters from Hopeful, because Hopeful's case so closely paralleled Mira's."

"It's closer than that," Brent answered grimly. "It *is* Mira Rainey's case, in every detail, including the date of the baby's birth and the name of this hospital. Those letters don't refer to anyone *but* Mrs. Rainey. Yet you both say she didn't write them. Yet Lora Lorne received a note decorated with your monogram, Mrs. Farnam, and bearing your return address."

"Neither Mira nor I have ever written a single letter to Lora Lorne!" Elaine Farnam insisted anxiously. "I can't explain it, except by thinking that someone's deliberately trying to make trouble for me."

That suspicion, of course, accounted for Garrett's demand that Brent discontinue printing the letters signed Hopeful. He remembered the urgent whisper of the man who had conked him in the dark—"False—malicious lies!"—and he wondered coldly whether Garrett himself had resorted to a blackjack. As for the other letter monogrammed EGF, anyone could buy stationery so marked, and anyone could scrawl the words, "Bay Terrace House, City," on the back of an envelope. Thinking how he had fretted for weeks over Hopeful's case when all the letters involved were evidently forgeries, Brent muttered.

"Trouble?" he said, echoing Elaine Farnam. "I think so! There's one more troublesome detail worth mentioning— a murdered man. It's pretty clear to me that Victor Rainey was threatening to explode this careful plan of yours. He was going to yell his head off to Mike, which would have wrecked the works—and that's why he was silenced."

ELAINE FARNAM blurted: "You can't think I did that!"

"God knows, not actually being in childbed, you were physically capable of it. Moreover, Rainey came here last night, railed at his wife and promised to make plenty of hot trouble for you, Mrs. Farnam." Brent frowned at Mira Rainey. "Your husband had deserted you and was in Chicago. Had you written him that you were going to give your baby away?"

"I cer'nly did not!" Mira Rainey answered. "I never even told him I was gonna *have* a baby. He'da thought I was askin' him to come back on account of it. I didn' want him comin' back just because he might think it was his duty. He'd left me flat and that was that. I never told him nothin' about any baby."

Mira Rainey's spunk, Brent felt, was of a higher order than her rhetoric. "But what brought him back here from Chicago immediately after you'd had the baby, then?"

"I dunno," Mrs. Rainey admitted. "All to once he come bargin' in here givin' me hell. He wasn't gonna have any kid of his raffled off, he says. He kept saying, 'Don't do it.' He says, 'Abigail—what a name! It stinks,' he says, 'and I'm gonna see you don't do it.'"

This, then, was the real meaning of the dying man's words. Rainey had not been protesting against the blows already struck. Instead, he had babbled his delirious disapproval of these secret maternal machinations.

Mrs. Rainey continued: "Vic says, 'I'm gonna have this out with this guy Farnam right now,' and he kept on sayin' so many things so loud they hadda bounce him. But he never once mentioned how he found out about I had a baby."

"He meant it, Mrs. Farnam," Brent observed. "He did go to confront your husband, and he stayed inside your apartment, dead. Apparently he didn't live long enough to have it out with Mike. He was prevented—beaten down with the gun, the same bloody gun you dropped a few minutes ago at the bottom of the fire escape."

Elaine Farnam blurted: "I don't understand it! The way that gun was sent to me—and the message! I couldn't believe what you'd told us about Victor Rainey's having been killed in my living-room. I was so upset I had to see for myself, as soon as possible. That's why I slipped out of here—and I also had to get rid of that ghastly gun—but you surprised me at the door and chased me back so fast I didn't have a chance." Her violet eyes widened. "Will the police come here? Will they ask questions—questions that will bring all this out? Oh, they mustn't! Mike must never know!"

Brent wagged his head, thinking that the job of concealing Abigail's true parentage seemed almost impossible in the face of the fact that Mrs. Farnam had had the motive, the opportunity and evidently the means of silencing Rainey. Once the circumstances became known, her scheme would not only be revealed to Mike, but she would also stand accused of first degree murder. It seemed hopeless and tragic. Brent was still studying Mrs. Farnam dubiously when a knock sounded and a nurse came in carrying a basin of soapy water. Brent regretted to note that she was not Olive Winslow.

"Your husband and your brother have come, Mrs. Farnam," she said to Mrs. Rainey, and with a significant glance at Brent she added: "They'll be up as soon as I've finished giving you two girls your baths."

Brent rose but paused at the door for another question. "How many bottles of perfume do you own?"

Mrs. Farnam answered: "The one I have here is new. I had another with only a few drops in it, and I left that in my bedroom. Please, you won't mention any of this to Mike?"

"Don't worry about my talking," Brent said glumly. "Worry about getting nailed for murder. Then it will all come out regardless."

HE LEFT both Mrs. Farnam and Mrs. Rainey in a state of agitation. Turning to the elevator, he found Garrett pacing the waiting room, alone. Garrett lifted troubled gray eyes that became fiercely flinty at sight of Brent.

"You again!" and he ominously leveled a forefinger. "I warned you where to keep your nose, Grandma. You quit smelling around here or you'll get it caught in a rat trap."

"I know," Brent murmured. "Captain Russo apparently thinks Mike is in the clear or he wouldn't have let him go. How good is Mike's alibi? I mean, it's possible for a guy to fake his arrival at a certain time, of course."

"Not in this case," Garrett retorted. "Mike's movements can be traced minute by minute all the way back to Rio. Russo's already made sure he landed at the airport here too late to have had a finger in this murder pie. None of which is any of your business, Miss Lorne."

"You'd be surprised," Brent said. "You realize, of course, that you're a prime murder suspect yourself, Garrett?"

"What! Me?"

"Certainly," Brent answered, his spirits lifting with the thought. "You were in on this baby plot from the start.

You've naturally been anxious as hell to protect your sister's secret and to keep it from Mike. She must have told you right away that Vic Rainey had come on the scene and was stirring up a stink. It would be easy for you to get a key to your sister's apartment—easy for you to get to Rainey before he got to Mike." Brent grinned. "I *like* this idea! I find it very pleasant to think of you frying for a killing."

"My God!" Garrett said.

"I must remember to discuss it with Captain Russo," Brent added thoughtfully. "Mike's supposed to be here with you. Where's he gone?"

Garrett sat again, making a vague gesture. "He wandered off somewhere, probably in search of Abigail. You can't expect a man who's just had a baby for the first time to act like a normal human being. But *you* haven't had a baby, Miss Lorne. I expect you to make yourself prudently and permanently scarce."

Brent turned about regardless and trudged in search of Mike Farnam. No one else was in the hall. A few rooms were unoccupied and Brent glanced through their doors as he passed. Abruptly he was standing stock still, staring into the gloom inside one of them.

Mike Farnam was in there and he was not alone. His arms were pressing around a luscious white-clad body. A fluff of copper-red hair was brushing his face. A pair of red lips were crushing his. It was as passionate a clinch as had ever wound up a two-hour movie. Suddenly aware of Brent, Farnam and the girl broke apart. He was struck with consternation, but Nurse Olive Winslow returned Brent's gaze with beautiful coolness.

"A fine thing!" Brent blurted. "Your wife lying in child-bed practically in the next room! Your sweet little baby blissfully asleep in the nursery! And here you are, making love to this wench behind their backs! I must say this is one hell of a fine situation, Farnam!"

The sentiment Brent expressed was Lora Lorne's, but inside him there was a thoroughly masculine envy, strictly his own. He turned about, hot with jealous indignation, and went away from there.

CHAPTER SIX
ALL'S FAIR—

LEAVING THE hospital, Brent saw the Homicide Squad car stopping. Captain Russo was tracing a routine lead. As to what the captain might think when he discovered the dead man's wife reposing side by side with the woman in whose home the corpse was found, Brent hesitated to guess. He hurried on his way.

He strode into the *Recorder* building to find the business departments functioning and the teletypes clattering, but the news staff not yet on the job. The pile of mail on Lora Lorne's table had grown with the day and the sight of it made him faintly ill. He remained in his cubicle no longer than necessary to dig up the number ten envelope that had been delivered to him during the night.

Comparing it with the other envelope which he had stolen off the corpse, he found the letter *n*, occurring in both Lora Lorne's names and Rainey's, to be nicked, indicating that both envelopes had been addressed on the same typewriter.

In the *Recorder's* morgue, Brent delved into a folder tabbed with Michael Farnam's name. It contained only two clippings. One concerned Farnam's departure for South America last year. The other was headlined, *Burglars*

Surprised in Act. Farnam had captured one of the burglarous pair after a disrupting tussle, during which he was slightly injured, and the crook had been so incensed by these unfair tactics as to vow that his pal would return to hurt Farnam even worse. As a precaution, the item concluded, Farnam had promptly applied for and been granted a license to own a gun.

Brent was certain that Captain Russo, checking the records, would identify Farnam's missing gun as a .38 Colt automatic. Very shortly thereafter the captain would busily cook Elaine Farnam's goose to a brown turn, and Garrett would inevitably blame Brent for it.

Full of uneasy premonitions, Brent next made use of the telephone directory. He drove six blocks to the Medical Arts Building. On the tenth floor he opened a door bearing the names of Doctor Jean Hartwell and Doctor John Marvin. Behind the reception desk he was astonished to find Nurse Olive Winslow busily billing a list of patients for the month's services.

"You can't be twins," Brent observed. "There couldn't be two women like you. The nation's social structure couldn't stand the strain."

"I'm Doctor Hartwell's office nurse." Having taken a dislike to him, Miss Winslow did not give Brent one of her beautiful smiles. "I'm not usually at the hospital, but Mrs. Farnam's is an exceptional case. If you're here to see Doctor Hartwell, you're outside her office hours."

"I, too, am an exceptional case," Brent said.

He stepped into a corridor before Nurse Winslow could stop him, then into an office where Doctor Jean Hartwell sat at her desk. Jean Hartwell eyed him with brisk disapproval, but he sat down nevertheless.

"It's a felony, isn't it?" Brent inquired.

"What?"

"I mean conspiring to circumvent the child-adoption laws and to falsify the public records. As I further understand the law, a physician convicted of a felony in this state is ever afterward forbidden to practice medicine. Surely you considered that when you connived with Mrs. Farnam?"

Doctor Hartwell paled and her dark eyes grew more intense. She had a fine, strong face. She was, Brent felt, considerable of a woman. Though a bit older, she could, in her own way, stand right up alongside Elaine Farnam and even Olive Winslow. Brent could never bring himself to accuse her outright of illegal acts. His purpose was simply to verify the story Mrs. Farnam had told at the hospital.

"I have nothing to say."

THAT, BRENT thought, was straight, honest talk. She was neither denying it nor confessing. There was none of this overly feminine why-I-really-haven't-the-faintest-idea-what-you're-talking-about stuff. Fact was, Brent didn't need to hear any answer from Jean Hartwell. Judging her, he knew she had weighed the problem of Mrs. Farnam's false motherhood and then, with sympathetic courage, despite the risks, had gone ahead and arranged it.

But she was shaken. Brent's knowledge was too fraught with catastrophic consequences. Potentially it was enough to wreck her practice, ruin her reputation, rob her of her profession and even pack her off to prison.

"What do you want?"

"A man has been murdered," Brent said. "The murder is being investigated. The investigation is turning up facts. The facts in this case are threatening to play hell all around. The evidence says that while Mrs. Farnam was supposedly in confinement she actually was on the loose, doing a bit of murdering."

"Incredible!"

"But once the cops learn her true situation," Brent pointed out, "this whole thing is going to blow up in a lot of faces. You and Mrs. Rainey and Mrs. Farnam are confederates, which perhaps makes you technically a first-rank accomplice to the crime of homicide."

Doctor Hartwell was even paler now, but her fine strong face was set. "I have nothing to say to you or to anyone else."

"Well," Brent observed, "that rules out any further discussion of the matter."

He rose with wagging head. Whenever he talked with any woman in this case, it seemed, he must leave her steeped in anxiety. Regretting it, but seeing no help for it, he trudged out of Doctor Hartwell's office and, six steps later, found himself confronting young Doctor Marvin.

Having just stepped from another room, and apparently having overheard Brent's remarks, John Marvin's face was livid with anger. He grasped Brent's shoulder, pushed Brent through a doorway and shoved him hard against a wall.

"Whoever the hell you are," Doctor Marvin asserted hotly, "you're going to keep your damned mouth shut!"

"I feel—"

"Jean Hartwell's too swell a woman. Her work is too important to her and to me. She wouldn't want me to say this, but I can't let it ride, not by a long shot. I'm in this with her. Nobody's going to make trouble for us if I can help it."

The guy was plainly in love with Jean Hartwell and Brent couldn't blame him for that.

"I was only going to say—"

"Don't!" Doctor John Marvin's eyes were two fierce blazes. "You're the only outsider who's messed into this thing and if any trouble comes of it I'll be damned sure it's your doing. If you want to keep your skin whole you'll clam up and fade. This is the last time I'll mention it. After this I won't waste time talking—I'll act."

He swung Brent back into the hallway, gave him a push, then shut the connecting door, no doubt as a measure of self-control, in order to keep himself from doing violence to Brent then and there. Brent felt it would be unwise to attempt to explain that Doctor Marvin had misinterpreted his purposes. He kept going until he came to the little office where Olive Winslow was still making out the month's bills.

BRENT WENT to her, leaned over her shoulder and punched the letter *n* on the typewriter she was using. The character impressed on the paper, he saw, was familiarly nicked. Stepping back, he took a good look at Olive Winslow's legs. He recognized them easily as the very nice legs he had seen fleeing from Bay Terrace House. As a final test he brought Miss Winslow to her feet and snugly wrapped his arms around her. That settled it. She also had the same soft and curvesome feel.

Olive Winslow briskly slapped Brent's face.

"I don't fool!" she said furiously.

"You certainly don't," Brent agreed, rubbing his smarting cheek. "You play for blood."

He turned to the hat-tree in the corner. Miss Winslow's loose gray coat was hanging there. He quickly turned both its pockets inside out. The lining of the left pocket, he found, sniffing it, smelled faintly of Elaine Farnam's perfume. The lining of the right one was stained in several brown, crusty spots.

"The bottle and the gun," Brent said. "Proof that you were in the Farnam apartment when Rainey was murdered. Headquarters will be glad to hear they've found the guilty woman. It's too bad, but that closes the case."

Olive Winslow was struck breathless. She could make no move as Brent hurried out the door. An elevator carried him down to the lobby. Remembering one of Hopeful's letters that had informed Lora Lorne her name was Mira Rainey and her address 456 Forest Street, he turned to a phone booth, consulted the directory and looked up the address listed as that of Olive Winslow's home. He smiled wryly when he discovered that Miss Winslow lived at 456 Forest Street.

Going out to his car, he sat watching the entrance of the building. After a short moment Olive Winslow appeared, her lovely legs flashing in a run. She halted uncertainly, lips parted, red hair blowing, and Brent opened the door.

"Get right in," he said. "I've been expecting you."

Miss Winslow slipped onto the seat beside him. She was more indignant than frightened. "Are you out of your mind?" she snapped. "I won't let you prattle all that nonsense to the police. It doesn't make sense!"

"You can't deny you've been trying to frame Elaine Farnam," Brent answered. "Who but a guilty woman would ever want to frame an innocent one?"

"An innocent one would want to frame a guilty one when the guilty one stands a good chance of getting away with it!" Olive Winslow blurted.

Brent frowned over this and decided to go back to fundamentals.

"You're the 'other woman' who's been such a worry to Elaine Farnam," he said. "She might have guessed. You're the type who makes any man's mouth water. The first second I laid eyes on you, my glands felt it right down to their toes. That same thing must have happened to Mike Farnam. Being a harmless sort of hypochondriac, he had a way of rushing to Doctor Hartwell's office every time he thought he felt bad somewhere, which was pretty often, and each time he went he was exposed to your attraction. Stronger men than Mike would have succumbed. Probably every one of Doctor Hartwell's male patients carries a torch for you, longs to be greeted by you in that office and runs up extravagant bills. Mike is the one you chose. He's a very good guy; he makes big money; his many little ailments aroused the possessive, maternal instincts in you, a nurse. Now that I've found out about you two, it seems inevitable."

"Who's denying it?" Olive Winslow said.

BRENT EYED her skeptically. "Everything else logically follows. Your idea has been to get Elaine Farnam into the worst possible jam by framing her for a killing. Whether or not she actually gets nailed for it, you've meant to do your damndest to expose her false motherhood, you witch—to win Mike away from his wife, the lucky dog."

"I didn't have to kill a man to manage that!" Miss Winslow retorted disgustedly.

"The evidence says you did," Brent answered. "As Mrs. Farnam's nurse at the hospital you could easily get hold of her keys—take them from her purse when she wasn't looking. That's how Rainey got into that apartment where his death would prove most embarrassing to her. Rainey wasn't fully dead when you began falsifying the evidence against her. You sprinkled a few drops of her perfume from the bottle she'd left on her dresser, making it seem she'd just been there, and later you chucked the bottle into a trash basket somewhere. You carried the weapon of murder away with you, then delivered it to Mrs. Farnam in that flower box, hoping she'd get caught with it in her possession. You couldn't have managed all that if you hadn't pulled off the killing yourself."

"Get it straight, get it straight!" Olive Winslow almost screeched. "Don't you see I'm the one who wanted Rainey to live—wanted it more than anybody else concerned? He was much more useful to me alive than he is now. The one who wanted most of all to shut him up was Elaine Farnam!"

This, Brent realized, was love and war and anything went. Olive Winslow considered herself Elaine Farnam's deadly enemy, and Mike was the prize of conquest. She was not one to pull her punches, and she couldn't feel ashamed of having punched her hardest, even below the belt. To be merciless and unscrupulous was all part of the emotional feminine game she was playing, a game never governed by any rules of sportsmanship.

"Look," she said earnestly. "I'll spell it out for you. I'm as nuts about Mike as any woman can be. From the very beginning I've meant to get the exclusive rights to him. When Elaine Farnam began playing right into my hands with this scheme of hers about the baby, I decided to make the most of it, damn her."

Brent let Olive Winslow talk.

"Mike had written me from Rio that his wife was going to have a baby, and so, he said, he'd have to do the honorable thing—call it off between us. I doubted it, though I didn't tell him so. Weeks and months went by, and I kept wondering why Elaine Farnam didn't come to see Doctor Hartwell about her condition. Finally Doctor Hartwell was called to see *her*. Something funny was up. I began to suspect Mike's wife was trying to put over a fast one and I was damned if I'd let her.

"Wanting to find out what was cooking, I just sat outside Bay Terrace House in my car and watched. Once Elaine Farnam came out wearing a big loose coat, but her profile didn't look right, especially when the wind blew. Then another girl showed herself, and there wasn't any doubt about *her* expectations. I followed her into a shop while she did some marketing and overheard remarks that told me she was Mrs. Farnam's maid. Then I *knew* what the scheme was."

"So then, in your ruthless female way," Brent said, "you set about wrecking the works."

"You bet I did!" Miss Winslow admitted without batting an eye. "I posed as a welfare worker—easy for a nurse—and asked questions in that neighborhood and found out all about Mira Rainey's situation. Then I began—"

"Writing letters to Lora Lorne, signing yourself Hopeful and pretending to be Mira Rainey," Brent went on. "You wanted to publicize the thing guardedly, without appearing to have any connection with it. You wanted people to talk about it, including Mike's friends. You even planned to call the printed letters to Mike's attention, subtly, after he got back from Rio, and let suspicion grow in his mind. Then, with that last forged letter—the special delivery, the one howling about kidnapping—you even hoped to bring the cops into it and expose the whole thing on the front pages of the entire country. You weren't giving Elaine Farnam a chance!"

"**NOT A GHOST** of a chance—and that's not all of it," Olive Winslow said with shameless candor. "I also got

Victor Rainey's address out of Doctor Hartwell's file and told him the whole story in an anonymous letter. I thought it would bring him running, and it did. He barged into Room 404 at the Heights, raising all the hell I'd hoped he'd raise. I grabbed him on the way out. Having heard from Mike that he was due in town right away, I told Rainey how to connect with him. I even drove Rainey over to Bay Terrace House and waited in my car while he went up to have it out with Mike."

"A slight miscalculation there," Brent said. "Mike hadn't yet arrived. His connecting plane from New York was late."

"I didn't know that then," Olive Winslow continued. "I waited so long for Rainey to come back down that I got worried. I went up, which was taking a chance, because I didn't want Mike to know I was having anything to do with this blow-up. It would turn him against me too, if he knew I was engineering it, so I had to stay behind the scenes and be ready to comfort him when he came to me broken-hearted. I just went up on the chance that I might hear through the apartment door what was being said between Mike and Rainey. There wasn't a sound. The door wasn't locked, so I looked in, and there was Rainey with his head bashed in. He looked dead to me."

"He wasn't, very," Brent put in.

"Holy cats!" said Olive Winslow. "What could be plainer? In 404 Rainey had sounded off about having it out with Mike. What was more natural than to think it had thrown Elaine Farnam into a fancy panic? The way I figured it, Elaine had slipped out, had managed to reach the apartment first—using her own car, which she'd left in the parking space ever since entering the hospital—and she'd been waiting for him. She'd slammed Rainey down, to keep him from blabbing to Mike, then she'd beat it out by way of the service stairs. Well, it wasn't long dawning on me that the murder could be used as the best means of all for exposing Elaine Farnam's scheme about the baby."

"So you sprinkled her perfume about," Brent said, "and confiscated the gun."

"It was lying right there beside Rainey's body," Miss Winslow admitted, "and I had good use for it. The hotter I could make this mess for Elaine Farnam, the sooner she'd be shown up as a fake mother. It wasn't as good as if Rainey had given Mike the straight dope about the baby, but it would do. You see that, don't you? It should be perfectly clear now that I was the last person in the world who wanted Rainey to get killed."

Brent reflected that this dame was all woman, and as such was a dangerous character. According to her book, any tactics that promised to get her man, no matter how extreme, were thoroughly justified. She was emotionally incapable of feeling that anything she had done was wrong. Did she, then, also feel it unnecessary to lie about her actions? Brent wondered, peering at her.

"See here. Do you actually believe Elaine Farnam really killed that man?"

"Believe it?" By this question, strangely enough, Olive Winslow was shocked. "Certainly I believe it! Everything points to her. Who else could possibly have done it? How can any sensible person believe anything else? I'm absolutely certain Elaine Farnam is guilty as hell!"

"And when she's nailed for it," Brent mused, "it'll no doubt make you very happy."

"She'll be getting what she deserves—and I'll be getting Mike." Miss Winslow turned to slip out of the car. "That little scene you interrupted between Mike and me at the hospital this morning was just for old times' sake—or so Mike thinks. Now that he's assumed the responsibilities of fatherhood, it was all over between us, he said. That was farewell and good-bye—one last kiss. Little does he know! Will he be surprised—and pleasantly, I think!"

With the deep confidence and self-possession which only a triumphant woman can feel, Olive Winslow ran back into the building, leaving Brent shuddering and chilled.

CHAPTER SEVEN

WHILE ABIGAIL SLEPT

BRENT TRUDGED dejectedly into the news room, avoiding Garrett's glare from the city desk in the far corner. Eight news men were now busily punching their typewriters. Among them Valerie Randall, the only girl police reporter in the fourth estate, who worked Brent's old trick these days under Garrett's fond tutelage, was fumbling with second-hand details about the corpse that by rights belonged to Brent. He took his woes into Lora Lorne's overcrowded cubbyhole and groaned with dismay when Garrett squeezed in, shoving the door shut.

"Don't try to blame me for this mess, Garrett," Brent said quickly. "*I* didn't kill Rainey. *I* didn't leave his dead body cluttering up your sister's parlor. My own personal relations with Abigail are above reproach."

"Like hell they are, Grandma," Garrett grated. "Russo is no dope. He's wondering how you happened to walk in on that cadaver and why you've been chasing in and out of hospitals ever since. When he found Elaine and Mrs. Rainey both in the same room, he just made a few remarks about strange coincidences and went thoughtfully on his way—but he'll be back. What it all adds up to is enough to freeze my blood."

"Is Mike suspicious?"

"Mike is curious about that wifely tie-up. He knows there's more to it than meets the eye. You're responsible for plenty of these complications, my dear Miss Lorne—the way you've been throwing your weight around. If Mike should find out the truth about Elaine—if their marriage should go on the rocks, they'll have you to thank. You, Lora Lorne, who's supposed to safeguard our happy homes, not wreck 'em!"

Having some degree of truth in it, the denunciation touched Brent's quick. "So far, anyway," he pointed out, "nobody in an official position has found out anything from me. If I can work it, they never will. But the problem's much bigger than that. If we can't manage to keep it under wraps, somehow, it'll splash out in such nationwide proportions that even you won't be able to keep it off the *Recorder's* front page. What's more, Garrett, your sister may very likely get fitted for the chair."

"You're telling me?" Garrett growled. "You think Russo's not working around to that? Once he snags onto the facts Elaine will be minus a husband and a baby too, and she won't stand a chance against the homicide charges. All right, Grandma. You're the heart-throb specialist. Just how will you go about solving this little predicament? Just how, for God's sake?"

Brent came to his feet. "I've got ideas," he retorted. "But I want you to understand one thing. This isn't Lora Lorne on the job. It's Bill Brent, police reporter, successor to Val Randall. Is that clear?"

Garrett's jaw pointed a threat at Brent. "This is no time for horse-trading. I just had a call from Mike. Russo's got him cornered right now. Russo's next move will be a show-down with Elaine and that'll be the payoff. Don't try to dicker with me until you've done something helpful—assuming you can think of something helpful to do."

Brent could. He caught up the telephone and the directory, urgently demanded the number of Doctor Hartwell's office and heard Nurse Olive Winslow answer.

"Please inform Jean Hartwell that all hell's due to pop," he said, "and she'd be wise to keep out of Room 404 for the duration. It's now the objective of hostile forces. The chief of the Homicide Squad may even bring along a police surgeon to examine those patients on his own hook. If you've any means of preventing that, you'd better grab it."

HE DISCONNECTED and caught up his hat. Abandoning the comparatively minor items of international news piling up on his desk, Garrett went after him. Garrett was ominously quiet while Brent drove, and Brent devoted himself to thought. They strode together into the Heights Hospital and saw that Olive Winslow and Doctor John Marvin were just entering the doorway of Room 404.

Brent closed the door behind Garrett. Elaine Farnam and Mira Rainey watched him tensely, sensing that crucial developments were at hand. Doctor Marvin placed himself as if to balk any unfriendly approach to his patients, and Nurse Winslow looked beautifully, grimly pleased. This, Brent realized, was what she'd been hoping for. When all the loud noises had echoed away and the pieces were being picked up, she expected, Elaine Farnam would find her home and her marriage wrecked, at the very least, and Olive Winslow would go wandering happily down lover's lane, hand in hand with Mike.

"Mrs. Farnam," Brent said. "After Victor Rainey was bounced out of this room last night, did you warn Doctor Hartwell he was about to wreck the works?"

Elaine Farnam answered quickly: "I couldn't reach her on the phone, but when Doctor Marvin came in a few minutes later I told him. It worried him, but he said he couldn't see how any of us could do anything about it."

Brent's gaze turned sharply and John Marvin flushed with indignation.

"You're looking at me," Marvin said in a brittle tone, "as if you suspect me of every crime on the calendar. Well, it's too late for that sort of bungling. I'm going to talk and talk straight. If we've all got to get hurt, I'll see to it that the right one gets hurt the worst." Deliberately he pointed at Olive Winslow. "There's your killer."

Miss Winslow stiffened. "Don't be silly!" she retorted. "I've already explained myself, and I'm in the clear."

"She has," Brent admitted, "but is she?"

John Marvin's lips curved in an acrid smile. "She most certainly is not. She's a conscienceless little schemer, an expert liar and completely treacherous to Doctor Hartwell and everyone else concerned, except herself. I can tell you exactly how she maneuvered the whole thing."

Brent silenced Olive Winslow with a gesture and urged, "O.K., tell us."

"She's the one who brought Victor Rainey here, of course, and she promptly took him to the Farnam apartment," John Marvin continued, his eyes fiery upon her. "But after his first explosion Rainey began to cool off. I saw her leaving the hospital with him and heard him saying, 'Oh, the hell with it, let it go, let it go.'"

"John Marvin," Olive Winslow said, her fists clenched, "that's an outright lie! He said nothing of the sort!"

"But he did," Marvin insisted, "and his change of heart was knocking the props from under your slick little scheme to expose Mrs. Farnam to her husband. You weren't aware that I followed you, were you? I saw you and Rainey go into Bay Terrace House together, bound for the Farnam apartment."

"Another lie!" Olive Winslow asserted furiously. "He went in alone!"

"You went up together," Marvin insisted, "and it's very easy to picture what happened next. Rainey didn't want to see Mike Farnam. He wanted to call the whole deal off, wash his hands of it. Without Rainey's help you'd be left out on a limb, so you tried to force him to wait and talk to Mike."

"Force him?" Olive Winslow answered scathingly. "How could I do that!"

"With a gun," John Marvin said. "Last year, after Mike got hurt capturing that burglar, he came to Doctor Hartwell for treatment and he said he was buying a gun—and besides, it was in the papers. You knew the gun was somewhere in that apartment, so you got it and tried to hold Rainey there. Rainey'd had a bellyfull by then. He tried to take the gun away from you. You lost your wits and hit him over the head with it and kept on hitting him. There's your answer, gentlemen. Little Olive overplayed her hand. No matter how the rest of us may come out of this, she's not going to wind up owning Mike after all."

OLIVE WINSLOW was now too furious to speak. Elaine Farnam was gazing at her open-mouthed and Garrett was scowling his darkest. Brent weighed Marvin's charges and nodded.

"That's good," he said. "But it's not quite good enough. It's a bad fit in places, and it leaves things out."

"Nevertheless," John Marvin asserted tersely, "I imagine the police will be satisfied with it."

"But I'm not," Brent said, "and I happen to be in a better position to judge. For example, that letter Olive wrote to Rainey, which he brought back from Chicago with him, the one stolen off his dying body. Olive had no reason in the world for removing it. Quite the contrary. The letter told the inside story about Mrs. Farnam's little Abigail. If found on Rainey's corpse, Olive would have loved it. The letter was taken away in order to keep all this baby business dark. That lets Olive out. At the same time it lets in Jean Hartwell, Elaine Farnam, my pal Garrett—and you, Doctor Marvin."

Marvin's face went white. "You can be damned sure Jean Hartwell didn't do it!" he snapped. "As for Elaine Farnam, you've only to look at her—"

"You've only to look at the evidence," Brent corrected him, "to see that no woman could have committed that murder. A woman facing Rainey in that apartment, with so tremendously much at stake, would have been overwhelmed with emotion. With a fully loaded gun in her hand, would she have stopped to think she mustn't make too much noise? Certainly not. Without thinking at all, but feeling to the utmost of her capacity to feel, she'd have pulled the trigger—pulled it again and again. But that didn't happen. The careful way was taken. The loaded gun was used silently, as a club, and the letter was remembered. Behind the murder of Rainey there was a thoughtful mind—a mind thinking all the while of protecting its interests—a man's mind."

John Marvin's lips were curling scornfully.

"That's only the beginning of the evidence," Brent went on. "You've admitted you knew Olive Winslow's purpose was to wreck Elaine Farnam's scheme. You probably saw her typing the special delivery letter to Lora Lorne, but you couldn't stop her from mailing it, so you tried to get it back before anyone could read it. Being Doctor Hartwell's associate, you also knew there was a gun in the Farnam apartment. Coming here to this room several times a day, you were able to get Mrs. Farnam's keys out of her purse when you needed them, without being seen. You clubbed me with the gun, in order to get Lora Lorne's letter back, and later you beat Vic Rainey to death with it."

Doctor Marvin pressed back against Elaine Farnam's bed and his teeth shone between drawn lips.

"Mrs. Farnam had told you Rainey was bound for her apartment to spill the works to Mike. To you that meant disaster. It would plunge Jean Hartwell, the woman you're crazy about, into the worst possible trouble. Not only that, but you as her accomplice in this baby business, would go through the same wringer. You saw that both of you were in grave danger of disgrace, of losing your careers and your profession. So you got into the Farnam apartment first, and then Rainey appeared at the door. If you tried to reason with him, it didn't work. Thoughtfully and carefully, in a way allowing you to get away without raising an alarm, you killed him."

"I'm very much afraid you've no way of proving any of this hogwash," John Marvin said.

"You forget those finger-streaks you left on the yellow leather chair," Brent said. "They show no ridge patterns. Thinking you had to be careful not to leave any fingerprints on the doorknobs or on the gun, you'd put on rubber gloves—a surgeon's gloves."

Doctor Marvin's whole body snapped tight. The door was opening. Mike Farnam appeared first, and Captain Russo followed him.

Sight of Russo's cadaverous face wrung a groan from Brent. He had the whole story now, and he couldn't tell it. To use the facts to pin Rainey's murder on John Marvin would mean that he must also expose the truth about Abigail, not only to the cops but also to Mike. Garrett was glowering at him, warning him, and Brent felt keenly the sharp points of his dilemma. He threw his brain into high and hoped desperately it would reach a safe solution.

"Well?" Captain Russo said in a tone that seemed to float out of a grave. "All this meddling of yours must add up to something by now, Brent. Surely you've solved my case for me by this time. Well?"

BRENT'S MIND groped. Gazing at John Marvin's drawn face, he realized that Marvin was also fearful that the truth would flood out now—fearful not for himself, but for Jean Hartwell. Marvin had committed a murder largely for Jean Hartwell's sake, and the facts would condemn her—undo all his desperate work. Everyone's purposes were at stake—even Olive Winslow's, now that her part in it might be revealed to Mike Farnam.

"It's clear enough," Brent began, his words racing with his mental gyrations. "There'll be denials, of course, but it's such old stuff you won't be able to question it, Russo. The old stuff about two men being nuts about the same woman. There she stands. Who can blame them?"

His fingers indicated Olive Winslow, and astonishment held everybody silent.

"Working with Nurse Winslow day in and day out, Doctor Marvin couldn't help going tail over tincup for her. Miss Winslow, though, preferred a guy named Rainey. When Rainey came back to town last night, incidentally to see his sick wife but chiefly to renew relations with Miss Winslow, Doctor Marvin's jealousy drove him berserk. He found out that Miss Winslow had snitched Mrs. Farnam's keys, and that she and Rainey were going to hold an amorous rendezvous in that conveniently empty apartment. The rest is just the same as it's happened thousands of times in the past. Man kills rival over woman in love nest. Consult your local newspaper files."

Mike Farnam was staring scandalized at Olive Winslow. Brent saw that, thank God, he was impressed. "Is that true?" he blurted at her. "In Heaven's name, is it?"

Miss Winslow was stunned. "It's a filthy lie!" she screeched. "Me and Vic Rainey? It's crazy!"

She was right about that, Brent reflected; but the false crime picture he'd painted was so familiar it was carrying conviction. Doctor John Marvin was smiling tightly.

"That's the setup, Captain Russo," he said. "I don't see any hope of denying it, so I must admit it's exactly right. I killed Rainey in the Farnam apartment last night while he was waiting there for Olive to join him. A sordid mess, isn't it? Unfortunately that's the way life goes—and death too."

Nurse Winslow blurted out more high-pitched denials, but nobody heard them distinctly. Mike Farnam was staring at her, too revolted to speak when Doctor Marvin, with a sudden snap of his body, vaulted Elaine Farnam's bed. He landed at the window. In another instant he was scrambling out on the fire escape. Wild eyes turned back, he clambered down.

"Why doesn't somebody stop him?" Russo complained hollowly.

The captain scurried after Marvin, seeming to creak in every joint, like a skeleton. He squirmed onto the fire escape platform, his service gun gripped in a bony hand. Brent dove for the door. It was the longer way around, but he gambled on reaching the alley leading to the parking space before Marvin could dodge into the street. When he reached the mouth of it, he saw nothing of Marvin. There was a single muffled, blasting report.

Heels pounding, Brent came into the parking lot to find Captain Russo standing morosely at the head of the short flight of cement stairs leading to the basement door. John Marvin was lying at the base of them, loose as a bundle of old clothes, blood trickling from his open mouth, the back of his head blown out, Farnam's automatic lying beside his lax hand.

"He made it easy for you, Russo," Brent said, knowing that Marvin had really made it easy, instead, for Jean Hartwell and Elaine Farnam. "You'll never have to try him. But understand one thing. Those two patients upstairs are completely outside the case, both of them—and Mrs. Farnam's little Abigail, too."

The captain looked sadly at Brent. "Who am I to go prowling around a nursery?" Russo said. "Healthy babies aren't nearly dead enough to interest me."

BRENT WAS breathless when he hurried into the *Recorder* news room. With typewriters clattering and teletypes clicking, the busy night was at its height. Leaning over the city desk, Brent talked while Garrett's blue pencil skipped over pages of copy.

"Everybody's happy," Brent reported, grinning, "except our Olive, who's up a tall tree. She's denying that extemporaneous explanation I cooked up, but it's not doing her any good because she can't defend herself with the truth. She can't because it would turn Mike against her even more. Being the woman she is, she still thinks she might snag him sometime, so she's clamming—but she really hasn't got a chance. Doctor Hartwell's protected, Mike and Elaine are talking about a second honeymoon and their little Abigail still slumbers peacefully. O.K., Garrett. Tell Val Randall to vacate my desk. I'm back on the police trick, of course."

Garrett's pencil poised. "Just a minute, Grandma," he said evenly. "We're all grateful as hell, personally, but the real story you dug up is one that can never see print. I can't value a reporter highly because he produces stuff I can't publish. On the contrary, you've proved your skill as a solver of marital problems. As Lora Lorne nobody could ever replace you. Back on the job, Grandma."

Brent was aghast. "What! After getting myself bashed on the head, after being practically ironed out by a murderer in a high-powered car— Good lord, Garrett, where's your appreciation? You can't mean it!"

"But Miss Lorne," Garrett said implacably. "What would the paper do without you now? Besides, I've got a gigantic idea! A contest based on this case! A prize for the best letter on the subject, 'What Would *You* Do About the Other Man?' Swell stuff and exactly your dish!"

The enormity of it stunned Brent. He trudged morosely back into his cubbyhole and slumped in his chair. Automatically he plucked a letter from the mound on the table. His dulled eyes swam over words written in passionate red ink on lingerie-pink paper.

> Dear Miss Lorne,
> You've been so wonderfully sympathetic with Hopeful, I must turn to you for guidance in my own trouble. My husband

has left me, and I'm in terrible circumstances, and very soon now I too am going to have a baby—

"Sometimes I wish to God women were salmon!" Bill Brent moaned. "God forbid!"